THE FAMILY THAT PREYS TOGETHER ...

I opened the door and entered a room that was all things pink and frilly, with spindly-legged chairs and a preponderance of mother-of-pearl gilding any available surface. Madeline sat in the middle of it, a tiny woman with a Barbara Bush hairstyle, pink fluffy slippers and matching bathrobe over a standard little old lady dress, cornflower blue eyes, and a face so wrinkled that she makes the Dalai Lama look like a third grader. It was a perfect illusion of innocence until she set down her Sevres teacup and gave me a smile that showed off a perfect mouth of teeth and a set of fangs that a tiger would be jealous of.

"Darling," Madeline said, taking off the large grandma-glasses that she doesn't need, but likes to wear for effect. "What an unexpected pleasure." Her voice is another giveaway. It's low and sweet, with some age showing in her pauses, but it sets every instinct in you on edge. I've known Madeline my entire life, yet listening to her still makes all the hair on the back of my neck stand up, and I hate turning my back on her.

"It's not a surprise if you send people to get me, Mother," I said. Sometimes I wonder what a psychiatrist would make of my relationship with my mother. If I could go to a psychiatrist, of course, and tell them everything about my life without them immediately throwing me into an insane asylum. Or, worse, believing me.

She just gave me a grandmother̶͟͞ ̶͟͞ ̶͟͞ ̶͟͞ ̶͟͞y ruined by the fangs th ̶͟͞ ̶͟͞ ̶͟͞ ̶͟͞ ̶͟͞ ̶͟͞l lipstick. "But it is still ̶͟͞ ̶͟͞ ̶͟͞ ̶͟͞ ̶͟͞ refused to visit. And y ̶͟͞ ̶͟͞ ̶͟͞ ̶͟͞ Youngest of my little s ̶͟͞ ̶͟͞ ̶͟͞ nest. Isn't that lovely?"

I hate coming home.

GENERATION V

M. L. BRENNAN

A ROC BOOK

ROC
Published by the Penguin Group
Penguin Group (USA) Inc., 375 Hudson Street,
New York, New York 10014, USA

USA | Canada | UK | Ireland | Australia | New Zealand | India | South Africa | China

Penguin Books Ltd., Registered Offices: 80 Strand, London WC2R 0RL, England
For more information about the Penguin Group visit penguin.com.

First published by Roc, an imprint of New American Library,
a division of Penguin Group (USA) Inc.

First Printing, May 2013

 REGISTERED TRADEMARK — MARCA REGISTRADA

ISBN 978-0-451-41840-1

Printed in the United States of America
10 9 8 7 6 5 4 3 2 1

PUBLISHER'S NOTE
This is a work of fiction. Names, characters, places, and incidents either are the
product of the author's imagination or are used fictitiously, and any resemblance
to actual persons, living or dead, business establishments, events, or locales is
entirely coincidental.

The publisher does not have any control over and does not assume any
responsibility for author or third-party Web sites or their content.

ALWAYS LEARNING   PEARSON

For my husband.

ACKNOWLEDGMENTS

With deepest thanks to my agent, Colleen Mohyde. I also am exceedingly grateful for my amazing editor, Anne Sowards, for not only deciding to roll the dice on me, but for making every part of the editing process a delight. Everywhere you touched the manuscript, it got better. Thanks also go to my copy editor, Dan Larsen.

Enormous thanks go to Sarah Riley and Karen Pelaez, great friends and incredible readers. I am deeply indebted to the many writing instructors I've had over the years, most particularly Chuck, who was able to show me my mistakes and make me laugh at the same time. To my family—thank you for rooting for me, despite all available evidence. Finally, again, this book could not have been written without the support of my husband, Adam, who sees up close what my writing process looks like, yet still believes in me.

I am indebted to the following books, which I relied on heavily while I was constructing the kitsune: *Fox* by Martin Wallen, *The Fox's Craft in Japanese Religion and Folklore* by Michael Bathgate, *The Moon Maiden and Other Japanese Fairy Tales* by Grace James, and *Kwaidan: Ghost Stories and Strange Tales of Old Japan* by Lafcadio Hearn.

Chapter 1

I knew the moment that my brother, Chivalry, walked into the coffee shop. I always know whenever a member of my family is around. I'm not sure whether it's because we're family or because we're vampires, because I've never met a vampire I'm not related to.

But even if I hadn't been able to sense Chivalry with a bone-deep certainty, I would've known by the way that Tamara at the register and my boss, Jeanine, suddenly snapped to attention. Two of the buttons on Jeanine's blouse came undone with a speed that I've never seen her demonstrate in any of her administrative duties. Tamara's top was already pretty low, but she leaned down over the counter in a way that now had her very ample breasts spilling out in a manner that I was certain the Health Department would find concerning. I was able to observe all of this from my crouched position behind the counter, where I'd been retrieving more stacks of paper cups. I occupy the low end of the totem pole of power at the unfortunately named Busy Beans coffee shop, which managed to remain marginally profitable despite grimy floors, hard scones, and truly terrible coffee owing entirely to the free wireless connection and the high level of chain-store-eschewing college dissidents in Providence. It was the latest in the series of crappy jobs I'd held since graduating from college with a degree in the shockingly unemployable field of film theory.

I stood up, paper cups in hand, and watched my brother move through the crowd of ironic cardigans, horn-rimmed glasses, and vintage dresses. Heads were turning, and the hum of conversations dimmed as everyone looked him over. Even with all eyes on him, though, Chivalry seemed completely unaffected, letting the adulation of women and envy of men roll off him with complete aplomb. Just over six feet tall, with perfectly tousled chestnut hair and chiseled good looks that would've made a casting agent weep, Chivalry wore black slacks, a white collared shirt, and a perfectly tailored dark car-length jacket, all designer. He had just enough of a tan to suggest a life lived outdoors, but not so much that he looked like he spent all day lazing on the beach. He looked expensive, restrained, and capable of seducing every woman in the coffee shop.

I, on the other hand, was cringingly aware of my ratty jeans from Walmart, the tomato sauce stain on my T-shirt, and the duct tape that I'd used to reattach the sole of my left sneaker this morning, all topped off with a green Busy Beans apron that did not do wonders for my ego. My hair is a bit darker than Chivalry's, and prone to sticking up in weird little tufts no matter how much hair gel I use in the mornings. Height that is imposing and impressive on Chivalry is gawky and awkward on me, and my face is forgettable at best. I'd once been with my girlfriend, Beth, when we were looking for some friends of hers we were supposed to meet up with, and had reached the level of cell phone calls along the lines of "Do you see the blue sign? We're standing right under it," and Beth had finally said, "Look for the tall, average-looking guy." That had been about a month before she'd suggested that it would be good for our relationship if she had sex with other people.

If Chivalry looked like someone who could put on pancake makeup and play a vampire in a movie, I looked like the guy who'd be fetching that guy coffee. Of course, Chivalry actually *is* a vampire—I'm still just *mostly* a vampire. As my family is always reminding me, I have a lot of human left.

By now Chivalry was at the counter and placing an order for a hazelnut cappuccino. He was smiling politely at Tamara and looking completely unaffected by her borderline toplessness, much to her apparent frustration as she managed to lean over even farther, with the result that two men seated at tables behind Chivalry but with good eye-lines to the counter choked on their drinks, and one unlucky guy spilled coffee all over himself. Chivalry didn't so much as glance below her collarbone. I felt a little bad for Tamara, despite her tendency to leave me stuck with all the cleanup work. The elegant but extremely expensive wedding ring on Chivalry's left hand meant that Tamara could strip down right in front of him, beg him to take her, and Chivalry probably wouldn't even blink as he strolled away.

Now Chivalry was smiling at Jeanine and politely greeting her. "What a great little coffee place," he said, prompting preening. "I just stopped by to say hello to my younger brother."

Now everyone was staring at me—my coworkers with

shock that I could be related to this god among men, and my brother with that calm steadiness that made me squirm inside at the memory of the sixteen calls of Chivalry's that I'd dodged over the last month and a half. Nothing in Chivalry's face suggested that he was pissed off at having to trot his thousand-dollar shoes into one of the mangier areas of Providence and over what was certainly one of its most disgusting floors to track down a brother who was avoiding him. I felt that very familiar sensation of gut-wrenching guilt and embarrassment that was my almost constant companion when I was with my brother.

"Hi, Chiv," I said lamely.

"Hello, Fortitude," Chivalry said, his voice grave and calm. "Would it be possible to have a word with you before you return to your" — and just the slightest flick of a glance to the collection of coffee bags, filters, and paper cups that lined the soiled workstation — "endeavors?"

I felt color creeping up my neck. The madder Chivalry was, the more he tended to show his age. Chivalry might look like he was in his early thirties, but he'd been born just as the Civil War was winding down. When he forgot himself, Chivalry sounded like a soldier's letter home read in a Ken Burns special. At twenty-six, I'm not an infant compared to him — I'm a fetus.

"Fort, you bad boy," Jeanine cooed, giving me a swat that might've looked playful but still packed some punch. "Why haven't you ever mentioned that you have an older brother?" The unspoken *stud muffin* part of her statement hung in the air. "And" — here she turned to Chivalry, giving him a full-on eyelash batting — "of *course* Fort can take a break and talk to you. The little darling has been on his feet all day."

That was laying it on a bit thick, I thought, but I wasn't going to turn down a break, especially since Jeanine was usually of the thankless-taskmaster school of management. While I walked around the counter, ignoring Tamara's glare of death, I watched while Jeanine leaned even farther toward Chivalry on the pretext of giving him a little pat on the chest. She failed to notice when Chivalry's expression went from glacially polite to frigidly homicidal. Of course, she wasn't the one who was going to have to deal with it—I was.

I picked a table as far away from the register as possible, and even as I waited for the ass-ripping to follow as Chivalry settled himself in front of me, I couldn't resist giving a little grunt of pleasure at the sensation of sitting. Jeanine didn't allow stools behind the counter, even during slow days, and my sneakers were so worn down that I could actually feel the curling edges of linoleum through my soles.

Chivalry glowered. Sometimes I wondered if that was his default expression or if I just brought it out in him. "That woman," he pronounced, "is a whore." He dropped a crumpled piece of paper onto the table and gave it a glare that should've ignited it.

"That's harsh," I said. "You're acting like no one ever slipped you their phone number before." He chose to ignore that, giving only a very regal sniff of distaste, and cautiously sipped the sludge in his paper cup. Nothing in his face gave any outward indication about his feelings, but then again, he came from a more mannered time. Anyone born in this century would've given a spit-take. Rinsing out the machines between batches was Tamara's job, and it hadn't been done since she was hired.

Chivalry set his cup down with exquisite care, another reminder that the places he preferred to eat at would've served it to him in a nice mug rather than a partially recycled paper cup. A small part of me felt hurt at how disgusted he was by where I was working. Not that I didn't spend half of my own time being disgusted by it, but that wasn't exactly the point.

"I am concerned," Chivalry said.

"Don't be," I snapped.

"Mother is also concerned," Chivalry continued as if I hadn't said anything. To him I probably hadn't. "You haven't come home to feed in over five months."

"I don't need to. Not yet."

"At your age, you should be feeding every month, if not more often."

"I'm fine," I insisted. I hated visiting my mother's house to feed, and I always put it off as long as possible. I hated what it involved, and what it meant to me. I hated the way it made me feel. The longer I could go between feedings, the weaker I became, but I preferred it that way. It made me feel human. If I tried very hard, I could even pretend that vampires were all make-believe, and that I wasn't turning into one.

Chivalry made a low grumbling sound and pushed his cup away from him. "If you wait too long, your instincts will take over. Even as young as you are, you will become a risk to all around you."

"You don't care about the people around me. You wouldn't care if I snapped and went on a murder spree."

Chivalry's mouth thinned. "A murder spree would be most inconvenient. Our mother has better things to spend money on than covering up your foibles."

"But that's all you care about, isn't it? People's lives don't matter at all to you."

One second Chivalry was tapping the table in irritation, and the next second his hand was around my jaw. He'd moved too fast for my eyes, or any of the humans around us, to follow. The palm of his hand was against my chin, and his fingers were wrapped almost gently around my face. I waited, not moving—one squeeze and I'd be sucking Ensure out of a straw for the next twelve weeks.

Not that he'd do it. My sister, Prudence, fantasized about breaking all of my bones to kindling (as detailed to me last year at Christmas), but Chivalry wouldn't. He was just giving me a reminder of what I wasn't. He was a full vampire, and could break a person's neck before the person even realized he was moving. I was still mostly human, and sucked at sports.

"You wouldn't even care if I killed everyone in this building. Lives don't matter, just your convenience." Talking was difficult, but I managed. Another reason to avoid my family was that I almost routinely manage to piss them off. He didn't move his hand, just looked at me. "Chiv," I nudged, "this is getting weird and you have an audience." Already people from other tables were sneaking glances.

Chivalry didn't bother to look around, but released my jaw slowly, leaving me with a pat on the cheek that managed to convey both fondness and a warning.

"You're right, baby brother," he said softly, his voice cold enough to put my freezer to shame. "I wouldn't care. Not really, or at least not for long. But you would."

He stood up, and made a show of smoothing the

wrinkles out of his jacket. His dark eyes gleamed like ocean water under a full moon, and the cold part of me that is entirely vampire seemed to sit up in response. I could hear the heartbeats of all the humans around me, smell the blood running through their veins. I pushed that part of me back down hard, until the people were only people again, and I could fool myself that I was one of them. Not feeding does sometimes have its drawbacks, especially when I pushed it to the edge.

Chivalry gave a soft snort, unimpressed. "Mother has asked me to invite you to dinner tomorrow. It's not a command . . . yet." He turned and walked out the door, not having to push through the crowd, since everyone took a few steps back when they saw him coming, unintentionally creating a path. They probably didn't realize they were doing it, or if they did, they thought it was because he was good looking. They didn't realize that it was because he was a predator, and that lizard part of their brain that was in charge of keeping them alive knew enough to get out of his way.

I finished the rest of my shift, ignoring Jeanine's not-so-subtle questions about my older brother and refusing to let it rile me when Tamara left ten minutes early, making me stay twenty minutes late to do both of our cleanup work. The sun was just starting to set when I finally left Busy Beans, and I gratefully inhaled a few breaths of air that weren't permeated with the smell of coffee grounds. As I waited at the bus stop, I looked over the tops of the buildings and enjoyed the last few sunbeams.

True vampires prefer overcast days, but I can lounge on the beach all day and the only price I'll pay might be a slightly worse sunburn than the human next to me. Time leeches away at our more human traits. At his age, Chivalry will avoid the afternoon sun, and he spends a lot of time complaining about how hats have gone out of style. My sister, Prudence, was a little girl when the British blockaded American ports during the Revolution. She sticks to the shade as much as possible, and carries both an old-fashioned parasol and a ready set of excuses about a family history of skin cancer.

Our mother lives behind blackout curtains and can't go outside until hours after the sun sets.

The bus arrived, and I climbed up. I found a seat in the back and tried to keep my mind on good, human things. The vegetarian wrap that I'd pick up at the deli a block from my apartment for dinner. The Humphrey Bogart marathon that started tonight. The twelve hours between now and the next time I had to put on my green apron. But seeing Chivalry was tugging my mind back to all the things I spent so much of my time trying to avoid.

Unlike with Prudence and Chivalry, Madeline had decided that I would be raised among humans. Why she'd changed her parenting approach after two successful runs already remained a mystery that she'd flatly refused to explain to me, despite the many times I'd asked. My foster parents were named Jill and Brian Mason. Jill was a dental hygienist, and Brian was a cop. They were nice, normal people. Not much money, but a lot of love, and despite years of trying, no baby. They'd tried looking into adoption, but a misspent youth with a militant wing of the Sierra Club and a stack of arrests from chaining herself to redwood trees in the Pacific Northwest had left Jill with a record that Brian's decorated public service just couldn't offset. No one cared that Jill had never hurt a single person—forty-three arrests were enough to make sure that no adoption agency, public or private, was going to touch them. Then one day Brian and Jill got a call from a lawyer asking if they'd be interested in a special kind of foster care.

I don't think they listened to anything past the part where they'd be given a healthy infant. I was three months old, and the family that was giving me up wanted to retain a connection with me that required one dinner a month, unsupervised. But this was their only chance to be parents, and they thought that anything was worth getting me.

It was a long time before they learned how wrong they were.

But they took me into their little house in Cranston, and I had the kind of childhood everyone should have. Cub Scouts, Little League, dog in the backyard, and cookies in the oven—we were a Norman Rockwell painting. And when a black Mercedes pulled up in front of the house once a month and I was taken away from them, I was always back four hours later, no worse for wear.

Maybe if Brian hadn't been a cop, everything would've been okay. Maybe it would've ended in blood no matter what. But as I got older, I started whining about going to my relatives' house for dinner. For a while they were able to dismiss it, but when I was nine, my whining was getting worse, and one day I made a mistake. I told Brian that I didn't like the way my blood mother touched me. That it made me uncomfortable. He asked for details, which at first I was smart enough not to give. But he reassured me, told me that he could protect me, and I was dumb enough to believe him, so I told him what I had to do at those monthly dinners.

Brian was on the phone with my mother's lawyer within half an hour. The lawyer was expensive, and the first thing he started doing was threatening to take me away from them. Brian and Jill didn't have much money—that's why they'd been chosen to take care of me, just in case this happened. They didn't have enough money to fight for me, and maybe another couple would've backed down, would've believed what the lawyer was saying—that nine was a difficult age, I was an imaginative child, and that everything was just fine. Don't rock the boat.

Brian went to work and started looking into my mysterious relatives. He hadn't done that before—maybe he knew on some level that he wouldn't like what he'd find. He'd made a total of three phone calls before he got one of his own, from the chief of police. The message was simple—if you want to keep your job, stop looking into Madeline Scott.

At home, Jill got a call as well, from Prudence. She wanted to come over, to talk to them, to clear up any confusion that might've arisen because of my "story."

Maybe if she hadn't said it that way, it would've been fine and she could've smoothed things over. Maybe if Madeline had told Chivalry to handle it, everyone would've been okay. But maybe Madeline already knew what direction this was heading, because she gave it to Prudence.

Jill called Brian. He pulled all the money they had out of the bank, and Jill started packing.

I didn't really understand what we were back then. Maybe if Madeline and Chivalry hadn't shielded me so much, I would've known enough to try to talk Jill and Brian out of it, to calm them down, to lie. To save their lives.

Prudence arrived before Brian came home. I knew she was at the door and I begged Jill not to open it. She loved me enough to believe me, and she didn't open it, but it didn't matter. It's only in stories that vampires need an invitation.

Jill was dead when Brian came home. He saw her body before Prudence killed him.

Prudence made sure that I watched it all.

Then she brought me back to Madeline.

The bus jerked to a stop, and I realized that I'd missed my stop. I got off and walked an extra four blocks, trying to push the past away.

My apartment was the third floor of an old Victorian that had probably been stately and grand when it was built. It was still pretty nice on the ground floor, which was a women's lingerie boutique, but the upper two floors were showing the wear and tear of about two decades of renters. I paid more than I could really afford for the apartment, but I liked the old woodwork, the big windows, and the hardwood floors. I had an only moderately overpriced parking space in the back where I kept my aging Ford Fiesta, which I'd bought at a police auction. I'd later learned that its suspiciously reasonable price was not because it was the older (and far homelier) model of Fiesta, but because at one point it had been Exhibit A for the state of Massachusetts. During my ownership it had shown no further murderous tendencies, however, and now seemed content to simply rust and drip oil. Because the bus lines were within walking distance, I even had the hope that I could baby the Fiesta into lasting another few years for me. I was close to Brown University, where I'd gone to college, and my expired ID card got me access to all sorts of college facilities.

The apartment had two bedrooms with a kitchen that had been updated in the 'seventies, and a bathroom whose peppermint pink amenities were authentic to the 'sixties. The wallpaper said *visually impaired old lady*, but my daring decorating mix of IKEA and roadkill furniture, plus the piles of DVDs, said *cheap student*.

I stepped inside, wishing that the memories would stay away. They waited in the back of my mind, and I knew that tonight I'd dream of blood.

There was nothing I could do about that, so I focused on the now. Specifically, my roommate, Larry, whose clothing was scattered all over the living room. If I could've afforded to live alone, I would've, but living here meant sharing space. And Larry was a philosophy grad student at Brown who had liked the apartment for all the same reasons I did, and who even seemed like he'd be an okay guy to live with. I'd gone through five roommates in four years, but I always thought that the next one would be different.

Larry had been different—he'd been the worst one yet. Since signing the lease he'd shown a noticeable tendency to avoid cleaning any of the common spaces, clog the toilet (and leave it for me to fix), have obnoxiously noisy sex with a series of women (culminating recently with my girlfriend, Beth, after which they both found it useful to quote Sartre at me to explain how unreasonable it

was of me to object), and lately a propensity of not paying his half of the rent. As of last count, he was four
months behind, a weight that I was now having to pull
double shifts down at Busy Beans to offset.

But worst of all was the meat.

I'd gone vegetarian when I started dating Beth, who
was militantly vegan. At first it had just been a pacifying
measure to sustain my likelihood of having sex, but after
two weeks I noticed that it helped me keep that vampire
part of me pushed down, and I stuck with it. I wasn't a
particularly great vegetarian—I don't think I could give
up cheese or eggs if I tried—and periodically I'd back-
slide and eat chicken. But I avoided red meat.

And tonight, just as on many other occasions, Larry
had left his leftovers in the fridge.

Not paying his part of the rent seemed to give Larry
a lot more spare change, and he ate out a lot. For an un-
apologetic carnivore, that meant a lot of steak, ribs, rack
of lamb, and burgers came home in doggie bags. Whenever his date didn't finish her meal, Larry brought the
rest of it home so that he could still get his money's
worth. That would've been hard enough, except Larry
would take the food *out* of the nice foam containers,
stick it on a plate, and put that in the fridge without a
cover. He said it made it easier to eat at two in the morning when he got hungry.

I looked in the fridge. It was steak this time, still with
a few leaves of parsley clinging to it. And even old and
half-eaten, it was rich and red. Rare. There was some
juice on the plate, making little red droplets.

Jill's blood had made pools. Brian's blood had made
patterns on the walls.

I realized that I was licking my fingers, and that I'd dipped them in the steak juice. A minute ago I'd felt the warmth of a stuffy and un-air-conditioned apartment on a June evening, but now everything felt cool and comfortable.

I'm mostly human. But that leaves me a little vampire.

I pushed it down, all the way down, washing my hand off at the sink and wishing that it wasn't so hard to watch the last of the juice run down the drain.

Tonight I'd eat my vegetarian wrap and try to convince myself that it was everything that a nice *human* guy could want for dinner. I'd watch Bogey movies until I fell asleep. I'd nag Larry again about the rent, even if he had a girl with him when he came home. Even if it was Beth again.

Tomorrow I'd accept my mother's invitation.

Chapter 2

Trying to outrun dreams and outflank Larry, I'd watched the movie marathon on the futon until my body finally gave out at the end of *The Maltese Falcon*. I failed on both counts—my subconscious subjected me to a walk down my worst memory lane, and Larry managed to come in and leave again without waking me up. My own alarm clock was muffled enough by the dividing wall that I didn't even get up on time, and ended up at work late, groggy, and with a really frightening case of bed head. Even by the standards of a job that at its best always carried the strong whiff of despair, failure, and burned coffee beans, the day was horrible. Jeanine was fuming over Chivalry's failure to make the expected bootie call, and the few morning customers who were old enough to still buy a coffee and a newspaper were irate over the delay in their schedule, since I'm the one who always sets out the papers and Jeanine hadn't bothered. After several lectures from octogenarians about the lack of work ethic inherent in my generation of whippersnappers, Tamara showed up even later than me and took increasingly longer cigarette breaks that finally culminated in her just never coming back, and the combination of insufficient sleep and dread over the evening's plans caused me to screw up almost every order I took, plus spill coffee on myself a grand total of three times. By the time my shift was finally grinding to a halt, Jeanine subjected me to a screaming fit that several loyal customers captured on their iPhones, and was being uploaded to YouTube before I even managed to head out the door.

I missed my usual bus, which left me with the unappealing choice of waiting twenty-eight minutes for the next one or spending roughly the same amount of time walking home. I'm normally a huge fan of sitting still for long periods of time. My degree, after all, is really just a glorified justification of my love of spending all day watching TV. But today I walked, and was subjected to the dubious distinction of seeing my bus beat me to my stop by about thirty seconds.

Larry was home when I entered the apartment, as evidenced by the sounds of thumping bass and squeaking mattress coils emanating through his bedroom door. After spending the last few days trying to corner him long enough to make my latest plea for rent money, it was frustrating, but also nothing less than I expected. I'm not much for believing in a higher power, but sometimes it's tempting to believe that a strange and mysterious force likes to fuck around with my life. Besides my family, that is.

Dinners at my mother's are typically formal dress events. When I was younger this meant a full three-piece suit, as if I were a prepubescent ring bearer at a wedding, but as I got older I started pushing against that line a bit, and had slowly worn my way down to business casual. I was fairly sure that it burned Chivalry's retinas every time he saw me show up dressed in the Gap's end-of-season sale stuff, but it was the small things that made my visits there livable. Besides, it wasn't as if I actually could afford anything fancier.

After a quick shower and enough hair gel that I looked like I was on my way to a high school prom in New Jersey, I hauled on a pair of relatively clean khakis and a collared green dress shirt. I was still buttoning up my shirt as I put the key in the ignition of my car.

"Good car, nice car, pretty car," I said to it, patting the dashboard with my left hand while I turned the key with my right. The engine gave a sulky little grumble as it tried and failed to turn over. I turned the key a second time, and this time the engine caught. This had been my car since high school, bought with the money I'd saved up by busing tables at a neighborhood Greek restaurant, and while its engine was getting progressively crankier, and its body was now so eaten away by rust that the best I could do was periodically slap on some extra body putty and hope for the best, it had yet to let me down. Of course, every time I said that to someone who had seen the car, their inevitable response was "Yet."

It was almost seven in the evening, and most of the commuting traffic had cleared out when I hit the road. The humidity of the day was dropping, and with the windows rolled down I was getting a nice breeze to clear the remaining day's heat out of the Fiesta's interior. The highway took me quickly out of Providence, and as I turned onto Route 4 southbound, the thick suburb of ticky-tacky small houses melted away into quiet little New England towns separated by dense maple trees.

The drive from my apartment to my mother's house takes just around fifty minutes, and takes me across almost the entire length of the great state of Rhode Island. The sun was just dropping in the sky, with the shadows lengthening, when I went from Route 4, which is a smallish highway, onto 138 East, which is a simple two-lane road and is always the place where my fifty-minute estimate is either made or broken. There are almost no places at all to pass on that road, so if I get stuck behind Grandma on a Sunday outing, I'll have no other option than to creep behind her and add twenty to thirty minutes to my arrival time as we weave in and out of little towns and past the kinds of stores that exist primarily to sell overpriced antique furniture to summer tourists.

Madeline's house is in the town of Newport, which even for New England is excessively picturesque. It's on an island on the southern tip of the state, accessible by two very long and beautiful suspension bridges, the Jamestown and the Claiborne Pell. Driving over the bridges is probably the best part of a visit to my mother—on a clear day all you see is the beautiful expanse of the Atlantic Ocean, dotted with little yachts and skiffs, with seagulls drifting on the wind overhead. When I was little, being driven by a silent chauffeur in the black Mercedes, I would press my face against the window when we passed over the bridges—now I have to restrain myself to quick glances as I do my best to stay in my lane. The Claiborne Pell is the longer of the two bridges, with small white lights built into it, so that when you see it at night it looks like someone wrapped it in Christmas twinkle-lights. On very dark nights, when the moon isn't out, with just the right amount of fog to cover the stars and mist, the top of the water, it is eerily beautiful.

The town itself was one of America's most thriving port cities before the British blockade during the Revolution broke the economy, and it didn't quite recover until the wealthy industrial families of the Gilded Age realized that a gorgeous little island with soft breezes and sandy beaches would be the perfect place to build a summer home. That passed Newport into its current incarnation as a historic town with a reliance on summer tourism and wealthy recluses, all within reasonable driving distance of Boston and New York. The main streets are still paved in cobblestones, the Historical Society rules with an iron fist over anyone who happens to buy any of the older houses, and most of the houses that crowd together with year-round views of the harbor were built before the transcontinental railroad was completed. The docks where whaling ships used to unload their cargo are still there, but are now lined with seafood restaurants and signs for sportfishing tours. There's a small Catholic college that set up shop in many of the old mansions when scions of the old industrial families realized that a tax-deductible gift made more sense than maintaining a forty-room house with only two flush toilets and no modern heating. There's a coast guard academy as well, along with a strong naval presence, and a few jazz and folk festivals to keep the bar scene hopping. Little boutique stores line the cobblestone streets to entice roaming pedestrians in the summer, and make it through the winter by renting out their upper floors as apartments. Chain stores have made very slow inroads, and you have to drive out of Newport and to the other side of the island to find a McDonald's.

As I drove in I could smell buttered lobster from the many restaurants that had opened all their doors and windows. Families walked in and out of the fudge shop that still made all of its product on huge marble slabs that you could look at through the windows, while a few shops over, girls in short skirts flirted with men in navy whites at the sidewalk tables of a bar. I loved this town, but the farther I drove into it, the more I could feel my hands sweat and a metallic taste enter my mouth. Worse among all my Pavlovian symptoms, though, was the hunger in my stomach that had nothing to do with a need for a vegetarian pizza down at the firehouse pizza restaurant.

Well, almost nothing. I'd skipped lunch, and pizza sounded really good. If I hadn't been running late, I would've stopped and committed the cardinal dinner party sin of prearrival snacking.

I drove past the tennis hall of fame and the Belleview Supermarket, then turned onto Thames Street, where claustrophobically cluttered Victorians interspersed with boutique shops suddenly gave way to the huge and manicured lawns, Grecian statuary, and Gilded Age splendor of the mansions. It was late enough that most people were done for the day, but some tourists were still strolling along the wide sidewalks and taking photos. I drove past The Breakers, the two-hundred-room summer cottage that the Rockefellers used to rough it in, and hung a left onto the long white gravel driveway that led to my mother's house.

For the mansions that remain in private hands, keeping the tourists from roaming up to your front door because they bought one of the all-access passes and have now mistaken your home for the Marble House is a summer-long headache. Most privately owned mansions, therefore, are distinguishable by their massive front fences, controlled-access gates, and incredibly groomed ten-foot privet hedges. When a celebrated romance novelist moved into town, she impressed the neighbors by erecting an eight-foot solid granite wall around her entire property, and was only prevented from putting barbed wire on the top when one of the grand old dames of the Historical Society happened to stop by the day they were being installed, and through great persuasive effort convinced her that black ironwork spikes would be more visually restrained but have the same effect.

Given that Madeline is a vampire, and presumably has more unsavory peccadilloes to cover up than a romance writer, most people would probably assume that her home would have more security than Fort Knox. But for the neighborhood, her security is extremely restrained. She has the same black and gold ironwork fence between the end of her lawn and the sidewalk as the public mansions do, with batches of hydrangea planted alongside to soften the look with heavy batches of luxuriant blue flowers that curl around and through the base of the fence. There's the obligatory tall privet hedge along the boundaries between her property and the neighbors', but the driveway doesn't have a gate at all. What it has is a small and comfortable little guardhouse, where an old and genial man named Wilson is employed year-round to sit and cheerfully give directions to all of the confused tourists who end up in the driveway, or drivers who have gone just too far and need a convenient place to turn around in. He keeps stacks of maps and brochures to give out, and when I was little he never failed to greet me with a butterscotch candy.

I waved a little to Wilson, who sat at his window and gave me a cheery little two-fingered salute. Madeline's driveway is very long, and winds a bit. She had the benefit of buying property back when she essentially had her pick of the entire island, and now she has a huge parklike estate with unimpeded views of Narragansett Bay, dotted here and there with topiary that her crack team of gardeners sculpt into horses, dogs, and, when one of them is feeling feisty, the occasional llama.

The sun was just dipping down to touch the bay when I pulled the Fiesta into the parking area beside Madeline's Mercedes, Chivalry's Bentley, and an unfamiliar Rolls-Royce. While Chivalry would be annoyed with me for arriving late, at least he wouldn't have to see my car, which made it look like the gardener had pulled up to dispute his last paycheck. Little things tend to get Chivalry worked up.

Madeline has company a lot, so strange and expensive cars like the Rolls-Royce aren't unusual, but I was grateful that Prudence's car was nowhere in sight. As I got out I hoped briefly that the Fiesta would restrain itself from leaving an oil stain on the immaculate white gravel beneath it.

The house itself is two stories tall and made of white marble that was shipped in from Italy. While Madeline has owned the property so long that her deed has "God Save the King" written across the top, she likes to keep the house fairly modern. When I once asked her if she wouldn't be more comfortable living like she did when she was growing up, she said that my question showed a fundamental ignorance of fourteenth-century English plumbing. She has leveled and completely rebuilt the house at least twice, the last time to incorporate dual advances in toiletry and electricity. The only reason that the outside of the house has remained Italian marble (which, I'm told, is a real hassle to patch after winter storms) is that she doesn't like getting into fights with the Historical Society, and so now the outside of the house remains the same while whole wings inside are periodically gutted and redone. There are local contractors whose families have worked for my mother for six generations, and they sing hymns whenever they hear that Madeline Scott would like to bring her wiring up to code. Oddly, none of those contractors (or anyone else, for that matter) ever seem to register that they are being cut a check from the same individual who hired their grandfather, and great-grandfather. I asked Chivalry about it once, but he'd been very cagey, telling me that convenient ignorance was at least ninety percent due to the wonderful influence of excessive wealth and checks that never bounced. When I'd asked about that remaining ten percent, he'd just smiled and said that I'd understand when I had finished my transition. The front door was unlocked, like it always is, and I let myself in. The main foyer is a bit of an homage to the expectations of her guests, with a mosaic-tiled floor depicting ocean waves, marble statues of Nereids cavorting along the walls, and a huge ceiling mural that depicts Neptune in all his tridenty glory. The chandelier is festooned with handblown fish from Newport's own Thames Glass-blowers Company—a nice touch, showing that Madeline believes strongly in shopping local.

The main staircase sweeps extravagantly upward in this room. It's made out of solid marble, carved with porpoises and scantily clad mermaids that fascinated me as a child and deeply embarrassed me from puberty all the way to the present day. While the mermaids at the bottom of the staircase would be perfectly at home in a Disney film, the mermaids toward the middle steps are topless, and the ones at the top of the staircase have located some human men and are engaged in decidedly X-rated activities. When I was little Chivalry used to conceal those with newspapers and masking tape.

There was a middle-aged man standing at the top of the stairs, closely examining one of the frolicking mermaids. He was deeply involved with his study, and hadn't noticed me yet, so I had a chance to look him over and recognize him from the last gubernatorial election. He was dressed in a nice suit, just like when I'd seen him on TV, but his shirt collar was unbuttoned, his tie was at half-mast, and there was a deep flush along his cheeks as he stared glassily at the mermaid. Even from the base of the stairs, I could see that there was a small red stain on his shirt collar.

Madeline's interest lay in politics and power. I'd met senators, congressmen, CEOs, and three future presidents, all over her dinner table. During the downfall of Enron I'd watched C-SPAN as a whole parade of my mother's former visitors testified before Congress. Having no desire to talk with yet another politician, I quietly walked out of the main hallway and through opulent yet steadily more restrained rooms until I reached the family living room. It's still expensive as all hell, but it is the difference between a Fabergé egg and a Rolex watch. With parquet floors, oriental rugs, a granite fireplace, and small clusters of comfortable armchairs and sofas, it's a welcome retreat from the showboating that goes on in the rooms where Madeline conducts her entertainment. Tall, narrow windows give the viewer breathtaking views of the back rose garden. You have to know where to look to see the tall wooden shutters that can be easily drawn over the windows and locked in place. As a family area, it has a balance between Madeline's comfort and her children's desire for daytime views. In Madeline's suite of rooms on the second floor, where many of her visitors end up, it takes a careful eye to see around the sumptuousness and notice that there isn't a single window.

Ensconced in the chair closest to the windows was a thin woman with loose black hair that curled its way down her back, and rich brown skin that perfectly offset her bright red dress. There was a white knitted blanket draped over her lap, and someone had turned on a small lamp for her, forming a small nimbus of cheerful light in the increasing twilight. She was deeply involved in a paperback book, the turning of pages the only sound besides the distant rhythm of the ocean that drifted in through the open window.

I didn't think I made a sound, but something alerted her, and she glanced up. Her large dark eyes widened, and she smiled.

"Fortitude!" she said, stretching out one hand to me. I crossed the room quickly to take it. I squeezed it carefully, aware of how delicate her hand felt. There was an overall air of fragility that hadn't been present the last time I'd seen her.

"Bhumika. It's good to see you," I lied. Seeing her always hurt. "Are you staying downstairs for dinner?" Over the past year, Bhumika had steadily fallen more and more into the habit of having dinner upstairs in the suite she shared with Chivalry. And to call it dinner tended to push it—most nights, she was asleep before six.

"Of course, sweetheart. It's been so long since I saw you that I insisted. I want to hear all about what you're doing up in Providence and how much fun you're having."

Bhumika was Chivalry's wife. She was his third spouse that I'd known. When my foster parents were killed, Madeline decided that it would be too risky to put me with another set of humans, so I lived in the mansion until I finished high school. After the shock of Jill's and Brian's deaths, I spent weeks refusing to talk with anyone. My family tried to force me to talk again, either subtly or directly, but it was Chivalry's then-wife Carmela who brought me out of it. She just inserted me into her everyday routine, taking me along grocery shopping, her daily walks on the beach, her soap operas, talking almost constantly the entire time, a steady monologue of her thoughts and impressions that made no demands at all on me. She didn't try to justify the deaths to me, or tell me to forget them. She just let me grieve for them, acting as a buffer between me and the world as long as I needed it. She could never replace Jill and Brian, but I did love her. I was fifteen when she died, and it hurt like hell. I was never really able to forgive her replacement, Linda, even though she was very nice and showed tremendous grace through the worst of my teenage angst. I was already away at college when Linda died, and I was introduced to Bhumika on my next trip home after the funeral.

"Are you sure you want to stay?" I asked. I could feel the little shaking and tremoring in Bhumika's hand, and how cool it was in a room that was just on the uncomfortable side of warm.

"Bhumika has made her decision," Chivalry said from the doorway. I'd felt him in the house when I walked into the foyer, but I've never been very good about tracking either of my siblings' specific locations unless I'm concentrating very hard, and I jumped a little. He was dressed for dinner in an elegant black suit, with a black shirt and a silk black tie. All that unrelieved black should've made him look like a lounge lizard's undertaker, but instead he looked like he'd just come from a red carpet. He walked over to us and smoothly took Bhumika's hand from me, bringing it up to his mouth to drop a small kiss on her palm. I shuddered at the way her face lit up at the sight of him, for a moment almost erasing the marks of illness and wear, returning her for just a second to the beautiful and lively woman she used to be.

"If she's tired, then she should go rest," I said stubbornly. "What does her doctor say?"

Chivalry's face stayed immobile, even as his eyes started to gleam with temper. His pupils expanded slowly and the hazel of his irises disappeared. When a true vampire is really pissed off, his eyes can't pass for human anymore. Chivalry wasn't near that point, but he was getting there. "Bhumika has made her decision," he repeated, his lips barely moving. His eyes never left mine, and eventually I had to drop my gaze.

Bhumika lifted her other hand to pat my shoulder. "It's okay, Fort," she said, her tone urgent. "I'm doing just fine."

"Okay," I said. "It's all okay." I pasted on a fake smile for her. I wanted to scream in her face that it wasn't okay, and that it was obvious that she was dying, but I had no desire to either rub it in her face or get my own punched by Chivalry. Besides, she'd been dying since I met her.

Popular fiction suggests that vampires seek out innocent victims every night, accost them in the dark, and with one easy tap of an artery can drink them down in mere seconds, with just a few artistically placed drops of blood at the corner of their mouths to look sexy and dangerous. That's fairly far from the reality. After the final transition into adulthood, vampires require human blood on a regular basis to stay healthy, but nowhere near enough to kill a person. Chivalry and Prudence only fed on humans once a week or so, and never took more than a pint or two at a sitting. But while I wasn't entirely certain who Prudence chose to drink from, knowing only that she rarely repeated donors, Chivalry preferred monogamy. A few feedings here and there were no more damaging than a trip down to the Red Cross, but all of Chivalry's wives invariably suffered from anemia, and despite iron supplements and regular transfusions, at our heart vampires aren't as benign as a surgical needle. Something happens during a feeding that's more than just losing a pint of blood, and apparently that something is corrosive and cumulative. There were two, maybe three, years of good, almost enhanced, health and vitality, and then a long and steady decline that always ended in death.

If he'd simply fed off his wives, it would've been easy to dismiss Chivalry as a fashionable modern Bluebeard, but he didn't. For Carmela, Linda, and now Bhumika, Chivalry was the model spouse: devoted, supportive, and loyal. Of course, I think in the ideal marriage your husband shouldn't suck your blood. Or remarry the day after you die.

But I'm still mostly human, and apparently a bit of an idealist. Watching Bhumika cling to the hand of her killer, seeing Chivalry lean down and tenderly adjust her lap blanket and retrieve her book from where it had fallen, I felt that sharp fear that I always experience when I'm around my family: would I still find this horrible when I'd fully transitioned? Or would my fully vampire brain look at this and decide that I'd spent years overreacting?

My face must've given me away. Chivalry glared at me and Bhumika made a show of flipping through her book to find her place.

"Dinner is in twenty minutes." Chivalry's voice was tightly controlled. "Perhaps it would be felicitous to pay your respects to Grace and Henry before we dine."

Despite the two centuries that Chivalry waited to become an older brother, his instincts are unmistakably well honed. There were few things I hated doing more than sitting and making pleasant chitchat with Bhumika when she was looking this fragile, but making a visit to my host parents was definitely high up on that list.

"Gosh, Chiv, what a great idea," I said, making sure that my voice was as chirpy as possible.

"Hurry back," Bhumika said. "I want to hear all about what you've been up to." Her honest interest and the unappealing prospect of trying to find upbeat anecdotes to tell about my current living situation were even worse than anything Chivalry could've thought up to punish me, and I hurried out of the room with a mumbled reply.

Grace and Henry are the nasty secrets of the house, and they are very fittingly kept down in the basement. Madeline might keep kindly Wilson in the driveway to divert the curious, and visitors are encouraged to roam around the house to their hearts' content, since she knows that there's nothing on the main two floors that is going to scream *vampire* to them, given the modern person's willingness to rationalize anything before reverting to superstition, but the door to the basement is kept secure. Madeline had a butler's pantry built around it, where a member of her staff is located at all times, day and night, ostensibly polishing up the silver. In reality, they are there to unlock the door for anyone who needs to go down there. Well, the first door. After that there's a short staircase, then a very high-tech door that requires an authorized thumbprint to open, then an even longer staircase.

It isn't a dank basement with drips and weird rock outcroppings. It used to be, but Madeline brought in contractors about ten years ago, and now it just looks like you're in Area 51. Discreetly placed surveillance cameras lend it that homey feel as you head down.

I reached Mr. Albert's room. He's the caretaker. I

probably should be comfortable just calling him Albert, but I've never been able to get that out of my mouth. At six and a half feet tall, he's a former wrestler, with his graying hair trimmed ruthlessly into a jarhead's buzz, a nose that has been broken on more than one occasion, three long, curving scars that rake down his forehead, and the precise manner of the butler in a British period film. Simply put—he's intimidating. I knocked, heard his "come in," and went inside.

It's a small sitting area, just some tables and chairs, with stuffed bookshelves from floor to ceiling along every wall except the one between his room and the holding area, which is made of one-way glass so that he can keep an eye on Henry and Grace at all times. Mr. Albert's Taser hangs next to the door, easy to grab if he has to run into the enclosures suddenly.

Mr. Albert stood up when I walked in. I wished he wouldn't do that. Having him tower over me makes me feel like a child again. "Good morning, Mr. Scott," he said.

"Hi, Mr. Albert. How are they doing today?"

"Just fine. They've been looking forward to your visit."

Guilt trip. What a bliss.

Mr. Albert unlocked the door for me and took a seat in front of the glass. He has observed every interaction I've ever had with my host parents.

I walked slowly into the room, closing the door behind me. The walls and floor are laboratory white, and the overhead fluorescent lights never go out, so I always spend the first few minutes of my visit squinting. Henry and Grace live in side-by-side plastic cubes, ten feet by ten feet. There's a slot for each of them, like at a bank or a prison, that their food trays pass through, along with the door that Mr. Albert uses when he needs to interact with them—I've never been through it. In each cubicle is a chair, a single bed, a table, and a toilet. Everything is metal, and everything is bolted to the floor. They're allowed one book at a time each. If they want to watch television, they can ask Mr. Albert and he'll turn one on that is mounted across the room from them. There's a bright red line painted five feet in front of their enclosures, and a small chair placed just behind the line. That's as close as I'm allowed to go.

It's very Hannibal Lector chic. The only thing breaking the monotony of the white walls are a few framed pictures. There's one rainbow, two birds, a beach, and a turkey. They are all terrible, since I made them with finger paints when I was five. Each one is dedicated to Henry and Grace, even though I remember how Mr. Albert had to guide my hand through the letters.

Henry and Grace sat in their respective cubes. Both in their fifties, with graying hair and increasing crow's-feet around their eyes, and dressed in white hospital scrubs, they should've look harmless. They were trying very hard to look harmless, in fact, each seated with folded hands and crossed feet, attentively looking toward me as if it was parent-teacher night in the Arkham Asylum.

They couldn't manage it. Their eyes never stopped darting over me. Even as we exchanged pleasantries and started a completely banal conversation about the weather (they hadn't been outside in over thirty years, and their skin was albino pale, but they did like to watch the Weather Channel), Henry's fingers started tapping frantically, and Grace got out of her chair to come closer to the edge of her cage. She wasn't touching it yet, but I knew that she would soon. They always tried their best to show interest in my life, but it was an uphill battle, always doomed to fail.

We managed a full ten minutes before they were both out of their chairs and pacing. It was like seeing tigers at the zoo as they walked back and forth. Having both of them so focused on me was always nerve-racking, and even though I tried my best to stay calm, my body started showing the physiological signs of stress. My breath began coming a little bit faster, my heart sped up, and I could feel the start of sweat at my temples and under my arms. The more my body reacted, the faster they paced, the more stressed I got, and soon enough Grace snapped and started slamming her fists against the wall between us. It would've been easier if she was screaming, but she wasn't. Instead she had dropped all pretence of our earlier conversation, and was now whispering to me, very softly and sweetly.

"Come to your mommy, darling, come here. Let me hold you, sweetheart. Come to Mommy."

Then Henry started. "Come here, son. Come to your father. I've missed you so much."

Suddenly Mr. Albert was at my shoulder. The Taser was in his hands, and he'd hung the cattle prod on his belt. Henry and Grace lost all restraint at the sight of him—they began throwing themselves at the walls and started screaming obscenities. They were both foaming at the mouth, and Henry's hands were already bleeding.

I hurried out of the room, not looking back as their voices rose and there was the brief whiff of burned flesh and urine. The walls of their cages could be electrified. Then I was back in Mr. Albert's sitting room, and I didn't slow down. My visits were always enough to ensure that his hands would be too full to say good-bye.

Between them, Grace and Henry have killed five people. For hosts, I'm told, that is a very low number. Famous hosts have included Jack the Ripper, whose career total was much higher than historians assume. One of the last people Grace killed was right after she gave birth to me. Not that she actually went through labor. A week before her due date she was put under and I was delivered via caesarian and whisked upstairs by Madeline. Not a moment too soon either, because as Grace was being stitched up, she came out of the anesthesia, grabbed a scalpel, and things ended very badly for one member of the surgical team. The rest got away with moderate scarring.

Vampires don't fall in love with other vampires, throw on a little mood music, and have babies. Both genders of adults have functioning sex organs, but that's not how they procreate. Adult vampires usually don't live together— most branch off, claim territory, and then begin the task of nesting. If they are successful in procreating, then they live with their offspring until they also begin to feel the ticking of that biological clock, and the system continues.

But to get that little future vampiric bun in the oven going, they need humans to do the dirty work for them. Hosts are created when a vampire drains a human right down to the point where the fuel meter is pointing to empty, then fills her back up with the vampire's own blood. I'm told that this process used to be messier before IV drips.

Small blood exchanges are no big deal for adult vampires. After snacking on her politicians, Madeline always has them take a sip from her. Chivalry does the same with his wife. Prudence doesn't even like sharing an order of Chinese food, so I doubt that she does this. But both Madeline and Chivalry claim that there are no negative long-term effects to humans drinking small amounts of their blood, just a slightly increased feeling of loyalty and devotion from the human. I'd call that a sizable negative side effect, but neither of them listens to me. Whatever the arguable emotional impact, though, a human can walk away with a bit of vampire blood and be physiologically unchanged.

It's when the blood exchange gets a lot bigger that other things start happening. A little psychosis here, increased strength there, and at two pints and up humans tend to start dying on the spot. Whole blood transfer survival rates are extremely low, and those hosts then get to undergo a few months of prolonged changes as the vampire blood starts tinkering around with their fundamental makeup. It starts with big things, like bone density and organ resilience, but then it goes small. By the time Henry and Grace were at the end of the process, their reproductive systems had been altered on critical levels, so that any child created with Henry's semen or Grace's eggs was going to be a vampire. From what Chivalry has told me, on the basic DNA level, I actually have more in common with Madeline than either of my host parents.

Vampires gain in strength as they get older, and reach the point where they might be able to create a host around the two-century mark. There's an emphasis on the "might" there—Chivalry had told me that there were vampires who spent their entire lives trying to create a host and were never able to achieve it. When we celebrated Madeline's birthday, the cake had six candles on it—one for each full century she'd lived, but even for her it was apparently a very arduous undertaking to make a single host. With the fun addition of homicidal psychosis, actually keeping hosts intact long enough to breed is also a challenge for any vampire in the mood for a baby shower. The vampire blood running around in their systems isn't natural, so whenever Henry or Grace get a cut, no matter how minor, their bodies can't produce more blood. It's up to Madeline to come replenish it from her own supply, another process that I'm told is (ha-ha) draining.

So vampires have a bit of built-in population control.

In vampire parlance, Madeline is my blood mother, the real parent. Henry and Grace are the host parents. All I know about them are their first names. I don't know who they were, where they came from, or even why Madeline chose them. If they had any idea at all what was going to happen to them, or if they'd been completely misled. If somewhere in that madness they were fond of each other. If they were actually fond of me, as they suggested, or if it was just another attempt to escape.

Visits home are always full of these kinds of wonderful experiences. As I came out of the basement, the pantry maid stepped aside from her pile of already gleaming silver spoons.

"Mrs. Scott would like to see you before dinner," she said. There wasn't any curiosity in her limpid blue eyes.

Madeline liked her staff friendly, pretty, and dim. There were benefits to falling into those categories. Literally. Madeline provided full health and dental packages, plus the promise of almost lifetime employment. The only other place that could offer that kind of provision was Disney World. I thanked the maid, who turned back to her Sisyphean polishing.

Madeline has a suite of rooms on the second floor. There are also suites for all of her children, even though Chivalry is the only one who lives in the mansion. Prudence has a very modern town house one town over, and I've lived on my own ever since I left for college. Madeline's rule is very simple—if we live with her, she'll cover all our bills. If we live elsewhere, we have to support ourselves. Whether that is an attempt to keep us close, or to push us out of the nest, I have no idea. Whatever her intention, it would suggest that she has had mixed results.

I tapped lightly on Madeline's door, heard her response, and walked in.

Madeline was the first vampire to arrive in the New World, and so she had her pick of territory. Hemmed in by Puritan-run Massachusetts and Connecticut, Rhode Island was the most inclusive of the new colonies. The oldest Jewish cemetery in America is located in Newport, and periodically people accused of witchcraft in other states would pack up their belongings and run to Rhode Island, which had a strong tradition of choosing *not* to burn people at the stake. People were a bit more alert to differences in their neighbors back then, and most vampires preferred to hunker down in Europe, where money and ancient family prestige could cover up all sorts of eccentricities and atrocities.

Her territory is all of New England, plus New York state, a sizable chunk of Canada, and northern New Jersey. I learned this when I was applying to colleges and Chivalry handed me a map of what areas I was allowed to go into. When I protested this, still entertaining the dream of leaving all of them in my dust and going out to UC Berkeley, I was told that I was still too young to go unescorted out of our home territory. So if I planned to attend Berkeley, Chivalry would be going with me. The thought of living with my brother was enough to kill all desire to go to Berkeley. I asked at the time what I was supposed to do if I met up with a vampire I didn't know in *our* territory. Chivalry just smiled and said that that wouldn't happen, because no vampire would dare come into Madeline's territory without an invitation.

Vampires aren't the only things that stay hidden from humans, and the other kinds of supernatural creatures usually have to negotiate with Madeline before they can settle anywhere within her borders. Sometimes that's just a courtesy call, and other times there's a full exchange of emissaries and forging of alliances. Not that I know much about it—the closest I want to come to the supernatural is summer blockbuster movies. When I was still living with Brian and Jill, the only people other than my family who I saw during my visits were a few politicians. After their deaths, when I'd lost the last of my illusions that all those things that my friends and I dressed up as on Halloween were just make-believe, I made a very conscious decision that I didn't want to know anything about it. There wasn't any hiding from vampires, of course, but I managed to give the rest a very wide berth.

But for the woman herself who wields so much power, it's easy to underestimate her. At first.

I opened the door and entered a room that was all things pink and frilly, with spindly-legged chairs and a preponderance of mother-of-pearl gilding any available surface. Madeline sat in the middle of it, a tiny woman with a Barbara Bush hairstyle, pink fluffy slippers and matching bathrobe over a standard little old lady dress, cornflower blue eyes, and a face so wrinkled that she made the Dalai Lama look like a third grader. It was a perfect illusion of innocence until she set down her Sèvres teacup and gave me a smile that showed off a perfect mouth of teeth—and a set of fangs that a tiger would be jealous of.

Madeline's fangs are another sign of age. Chivalry and Prudence have fangs, but they retract so that both of them pass through the human world normally enough that they could probably sit in a dentist's chair and just get a lecture on flossing. When they do emerge, their fangs are thin and sharp, designed to make surgically precise punctures on their victim to get the blood flowing, but not leave large marks behind. I don't even have fangs at all, just the human incisors that are basically vampire baby teeth. But Madeline's fangs are fixed in place like a cat's, and are the size and sharpness for ripping and tearing.

"Darling," Madeline said, taking off the large grandma glasses that she doesn't need, but likes to wear for effect. "What an unexpected pleasure." Her voice is another giveaway. It's low and sweet, with some age showing in her pauses, but it sets every instinct in you on edge. I've known Madeline my entire life, yet listening to her still makes all the hair on the back of my neck stand up, and I hate turning my back on her.

The knowledge that at some point I'll start the transition that will make me a full vampire like my siblings and Mother makes me dread every birthday and routinely check my teeth in the mirror. Because popular vampire lore is wrong in another key aspect: vampires do age, and we aren't immortal. Each of us will eventually succumb and die of old age, a thought that is not as comforting as it should be, given that every person in my graduating high school class as well as their great-grandchildren will be dust in the ground before I'm even ready for vampire AARP, but even for us, Madeline is very old.

"It's not a surprise if you send people to get me, Mother," I said. Sometimes I wonder what a psychiatrist would make of my relationship with my mother. If I could go to a psychiatrist, of course, and tell him everything about my life without his immediately throwing me into an insane asylum. Or, worse, believing me.

She just gave me a grandmotherly smile, completely ruined by the fangs that rested against her bright coral lipstick. "But it is still a surprise. After all, you could've refused to visit. And yet here you are, my darling baby. Youngest of my little sparrows, hopping home into the nest. Isn't that lovely?"

I hate coming home.

Before I could come up with a suitably smart-ass response, Madeline had breezed the conversation forward. There's a great French expression that I learned during a foreign film class called *l'esprit de l'escalier*, which basically means "staircase wit." It refers to when you think of a great comeback line, but it's too late to deliver it. I experience that a lot around my mother.

Madeline's sweet smile of fang never wavered. "We have exciting things to speak of, darling. But first, let's get this out of the way." And she rolled back her sleeve, exposing her pale wrist. Her wrist isn't smooth—there are liver spots, and the skin has lost elasticity as she's aged, leaving it to hang droopily, bumping here and there with the long veins that have darkened from the blue you'll see in very fair-skinned people to almost a lavender. Against the sticklike skinniness of her arm, her wrist bone is a disproportionately huge bulge. In a movement too fast for me to see, she slashed her wrist with one of her nails, creating a small cut that sluggishly oozed blood. Her blood was thicker than a human's, and darker. It didn't move correctly either. There was no dribbling, because it was coagulating too fast.

I was so hungry.

I was crawling toward her wrist, even though I didn't even remember dropping to my knees. There was no control anymore, no holding back, and I locked my mouth around her wrist and sucked as hard as I could. It was like trying to drink a thick milkshake, and I struggled to get the blood in my mouth. It was like fire on my tongue, and I could feel each individual drop as it went down my throat and into me. Then it was finally flowing faster, and I could hear myself making small whimpers, like a young animal nursing. I could feel her skeletal fingers running through my hair as she petted me with her free hand, encouraging me to drink more. My eyes weren't closed, but the room seemed dark, with nothing existing except my mouth and the blood that I needed more of. I wasn't aware of my knees against the carpet, or my hands clutching at her arm, but somewhere in the distance I could hear heartbeats that I know didn't belong to my family—these were human heartbeats, too delicate to be ours, and I wanted to be closer to them, to feel them speed up when I got closer, and then to make them stop—

And then I was aware of myself again, of how desperately I was drinking, of how I'd pressed myself up against Madeline's legs. Of how I must've looked. All I wanted was more and more of her blood, but I forced myself to swallow what was left in my mouth and pull back. The slice on her wrist began to close even as I watched, and the remaining blood didn't stain the surface like mine would, but instead pulled back inside the closing wound, leaving her skin unmarked. I turned away from it, awkwardly pulling back from her and standing up. I caught a glimpse of myself in a large antique mirror. My hair looked like I had gotten caught in a cyclone, my hazel eyes were lost in the size of my pupils, and there was still one drop of blood left on my lip. It took every piece of control I had not to lick it up. Instead I grabbed a napkin from Madeline's table and wiped it off. I mourned its loss even as I dropped the napkin down onto Madeline's tea tray.

Madeline laughed at me, a dry cackle that sounded like the rustling of autumn leaves.

"Foolish little darling," she said. "What do you gain by drinking less than your fill? If you imagine that by drinking one less drop you can put off your transition, I assure you that you cannot. As for why you would want to, I cannot even imagine."

"What's wrong with wanting to stay the way I am? To stay human?" I was still bent over, my hands resting on the back of one of her Louis XIV chairs. I was breathing deeply, and I could feel every vein in my body shivering. I was like a parched daisy that had just been drenched in water, and I hated how happy my body was.

Madeline scoffed in disgust. "I cannot even fathom the state of your mind sufficiently to begin debating such a ridiculous concept. Besides." And here she picked up a cream envelope from beside her tea set and shook it. "There are more important things to discuss than your infantile existential crisis."

"Your mail is more important than my crisis?"

"Infinitely." Her blue eyes glowed like stained glass windows on a sunny day. "I will require your presence tomorrow night."

"No."

"Yes."

"I have a date," I lied.

"Really, dear, this is childish."

"I have to wash my hair."

"You'll be interested in this." She wiggled the envelope invitingly.

I eyed the envelope. It was expensive, and there was a wax seal on it. I wished that I could just storm out of the house, but now I was curious. "Why would I be interested?"

"Because we are to have company. A scion of the Naples nest has requested visitation into my territory. Here is your opportunity, darling, to have that question that you have always asked yourself answered."

"What question?"

Madeline leaned forward and her ever-present smile

became unfriendly. "Whether other vampires are like us. Whether I am better or worse than the others of our kind. Whether your destiny is truly tied in blood, or whether others walk different paths."

A long moment passed, and I knew that I was caught. Madeline knew me too well, and knew all the things that haunted me at night.

"Naples in Florida?" I asked, goading her a little.

"Italy," she said blandly, not rising to the bait. "He is a descendent of a nest mate of one of my blood siblings. The vampires of the Old World are forced to cast their eyes to the New, and they have dispatched an emissary that hospitality dictates I must welcome."

"Why are they interested in you?"

"Because, darling, their numbers have dwindled. Few of our young are born, and fewer still survive infancy. Some old ones die with no heir to claim their territories, leaving them in dispute between their neighbors. More perish in those conflicts who cannot be replaced. And yet I sit in a young land with many healthy offspring." Her smile widened. "Their emissary wishes to learn my secret."

"Do you have a secret?"

"Of course, my darling."

"Will you tell it to him?"

"Perhaps." She laughed. "Though it is unlikely to do him any good. So tomorrow you will return and meet someone who is so distantly related to you that he cannot in any honesty claim a kin tie. I hope that this will be an illuminating experience for you and that"—here she swept a sharp eye over my clothing—"you will endeavor to launder your clothing before you come. There is a stain on your trousers."

My cheeks heated even as I automatically stepped in to help her get out of her chair. I'm never sure how many of these moments of fragility are acts and how many are the actual weaknesses of her age. I once tried to test that theory and she fell over, leading to a horrible lecture from Chivalry, and the headache of wondering whether she fell over to trick me or fell over because she fell over.

"Now help me downstairs," she said as I handed her her cane, which was silver with a top knob inlaid with mother-of-pearl. "The cook has made beef bourguignonne."

My vegetarianism has been a hard sell in this house.

Chapter 3

Madeline's blood left a certain spring in my step on the drive home, despite my best efforts to ignore it. The enhanced sense of hearing and the rush of predatory instincts had faded almost as soon as I stopped drinking, thankfully, but I was still nervous that it might return. I wouldn't need to drink human blood until I fully transitioned into a vampire, an event that no one seemed interested in giving me a general estimate on. Prudence rarely deigned to talk to me at all, and Chivalry would only admit that he'd been a lot younger than me when it happened for him. Madeline would just give a very unhelpful cackle. But if I could put it off forever, I would.

Back at home, I staked out space on the sofa and waited for Larry to get home. This wasn't an aftereffect of the blood—this was an aftereffect of my last credit card bill's minimum payment nearly clearing out my checking account. I needed this month's rent payment, and preferably all the money he owed me on top of it. Unlike with a lot of down-and-out postgraduate film students, the option of selling plasma and semen was cruelly withheld from me. The latter was sterile and useless, and the former was not exactly a substance that I could offer the Red

Cross with any ethical comfort. After all, a pint of Fort-positive would probably kill anyone who needed a transfusion. I have enough self-loathing in my headspace without asking for extra helpings.

I did manage to confront Larry, but I didn't even get a satisfactory fight out of it. He was accompanied by an extremely drunk college undergrad, which gave Larry the frustrating high ground of accusing me of being a poor host to our visitor. I didn't get a dime out of him, and even his empty promises were beginning to sound halfhearted. All I did get was the opportunity to prove my exemplary hosting abilities by cleaning his date's vomit off the sofa before I went to bed. By that time it was clear that she was feeling well enough to engage in amorous activities with Larry, and I took the precaution of hiding my toothbrush and locking the door to my bedroom. The last time Larry had romanced a drunken eighteen-year-old, she had gone to the bathroom, gotten confused, and tucked herself into my bed. Having just pulled a double shift, I was dead to the world and didn't wake up, leading the extremely awkward morning-after discussion where I explained to the confused maiden that while she and I *had* technically just slept together, I wasn't the person she had had sex with. I did my best to turn it into a teachable moment.

At work the next day, I wasn't even able to muster the illusion of being a productive employee, much to Jeanine's frustration. But even when she was yelling directly in my ear, all I could think about was that tonight I was going to meet a new vampire, and maybe even get the opportunity to get real answers to my most pressing questions. I went onto autopilot, pouring coffee and taking money while my brain was miles away.

It wasn't until I heard a familiar voice that had been sanded down by cheap booze and two decades of unfiltered cigarettes that I blinked and came out of my fog. The grinning man in his midforties with salt-and-pepper hair who I'd just made change for was Matt McMahon. I apologized, and he laughed, but I felt like absolute shit. Not that that is an unusual state of existence for me.

Matt was my foster father's old partner. When Brian and Jill were murdered, Matt devoted himself to finding the killer. Given Madeline's influence in Providence politics, Matt almost immediately found himself stonewalled in the investigation. The police did eventually pin the crime on a homeless man, but Matt never believed it. He was a good enough cop to see all the holes in the story, and be suspicious when the homeless man died of a massive heart attack the same night he delivered his confession. For everyone else the case was closed, but Matt refused to let it rest. He was finally told that he had to either abandon the case or find a new line of work. He turned in his badge and became a private detective.

The one thing Matt had never questioned was my story. Under strict orders from Madeline, I told everyone that I'd been in my room when Jill was attacked, and had hidden under my bed while everything happened. I had only come out when all the noises stopped, and that's when I found them. I hated lying to Matt, but I did it because now I knew the consequences for telling the truth. Seeing him run down every false lead that he rustled up was better than going to his funeral.

"Late night, buddy?" Matt asked. "You're working a thousand-yard stare."

"No, I'm sorry," I apologized. "I'm just zoning out here. What's up?"

"I've been staking out a real estate developer, ended up in the neighborhood, wondered if you were free for lunch."

"Sure, that's great." My stomach gave me a fast reminder that I was overdue for a break. "Just give me a second."

One of Jeanine's less delightful managerial quirks was her apparent feeling that the federal regulation that employees on an eight-hour shift are required to be given a food break is designed solely to ruin her business. She had an annoying habit of never reminding us to take our breaks, hoping that we'd get so busy that we'd forget entirely. By the time I'd reminded her about how I was owed one and got out the door, Matt was waiting by his car and, from the expression on his face, had just taken a big swig of his coffee.

"I won't feel bad if you dump it," I said, shoving papers and files over so that I could get into the passenger seat. Matt drove an old Buick that was about the size of a boat, with beat-up leather seats and probably twelve different types of fungus brewing in the fast food graveyard that built up in the floor space of the backseat. Matt had an actual office that he shared with two Realtors and a home decorator, but no one would ever guess it from his car, which was loaded down with almost all his files and paperwork, making it basically his office on wheels.

"I miss your job at the bakery," Matt said. "The scones were fantastic."

"All the leftover Danishes weren't enough of a trade-off for getting up at three a.m." Two months on that schedule had left me feeling more like a vampire than usual, and despite the perks, I'd quit. Regular exposure to sunshine was now one of my few job requirements.

"God, and the cannoli," Matt reminisced as he pulled into traffic. "I gained like ten pounds from that alone."

"Dude, where? Your arms?" Matt's suits might look like he pulled them from Goodwill boxes, but he does serious lifting and cardio. I asked him about that once, and he said that sneaking around trailing people resulted in a lot of backyard encounters with dogs and irate boyfriends. "Anyway, what's up with the developer? Cheating?"

"The wife thinks so, and I've got about six more days on payroll just to be sure, but check this out." Matt rooted around in a stack of file folders balanced precariously on his dash, and handed me one. Years of being handed innocuous folders just like this, however, had left me cautious.

"What's in here? I'm about to eat, you know."

"Nothing bad, just open it."

"There's no sex-swing bullshit, is there? Because that's what it was the last time you said 'not bad.'"

"No, no."

"No furries either. I had nightmares for a week."

"Jeez, you have no trust, Fort. Just open it."

I eased it open, ready to slam the folder shut again if it was something awful, then just stared.

"That's . . . um . . ."

"Live-action role play, yeah. I got those photos two nights ago in the park."

"And your guy is . . ."

"The one dressed up like the wizard."

I peered closer. Not really what middle-aged accountant-looking guys usually were up to in one of Matt's folders. "What's up with the tennis balls?"

"He was yelling 'lightning bolt, lightning bolt' every time he threw one. It was frickin' awesome."

"The wife has no idea he does this?"

"Apparently not. She was sure he was doing his secretary. Guess cheating comes in many forms, and not just drunk sorority girls or people dressed up like teddy bears."

I gagged a little. "Please don't mention the furries."

Matt just chuckled, then flipped on his turn signal. We pulled into the lot of one of those great corner greasy spoon diners where the parking spots are still sized for finned Chevys from the 'sixties and the waitresses all look like they miss the days where they could work with a cigarette hanging out of the corner of their mouths. I raised my eyebrows when Matt snagged another file from the dash pile.

"Is this a working lunch, Matt?" I asked. I've posed as Matt's son, nephew, employee, coworker, and, on one never-to-be-discussed-again occasion, boyfriend. I guess that one of the drawbacks of knowing a private detective is that he's almost never fully off the clock, and a lot of what he does involves subterfuge. Matt's dating life was pretty much a wasteland, so whenever he needed a second person on a job, I tended to be tapped.

"No, the owner is a client. I just have to drop off some updates. Grab a booth. This won't take long."

The whole place had that kind of look that could've passed for deliberately retro, but it hadn't been cleaned in so long that it was obviously original. I'm not sure why, but these kinds of health-code-flaunting places always seem to make the best burgers. I had to engage in a brief tussle with my principles when the kitchen door flipped open and I got a full whiff of the sizzling, grease-soaked meat. My stomach gave a very audible rumble.

While Matt went straight into a back room that said EMPLOYEES ONLY, I sat down in a booth that was probably bright aqua once but that a thousand shifting butts had worn down to a mix of dull aqua and powder blue. It was one of those squeaky vinyl ones, repaired in a few points with duct tape.

I flipped through the menu, looking for something vegetarian that could be a worthy trade-off for the burger that my saliva glands were craving. Since this place probably hadn't changed its menu since Eisenhower was president, that was a tough task.

Matt's definition of "won't take long" is pretty elastic, so I was surprised when he dropped into the booth before I'd even gotten through the list of hot dog combinations.

"That really was quick," I said.

Matt grunted and pulled out a menu. "Not much to say."

I glanced over at him again. His mood looked a lot gloomier than it had in the car, and he was tapping one hand against the table as he paged through the menu.

"What's this case about?" I asked.

Matt's mouth thinned, and for a minute I thought he wouldn't tell me, but then he shrugged and pushed the folder across the table.

"Owner's daughter. Senior in high school. Told her parents she was going out to a party one night. Never arrived there, never came home. Cops thought it looked like she ran off with her boyfriend, but the family always maintained that she must've been kidnapped." Matt's voice was clipped and professional, very Joe Friday. Just the facts, ma'am.

"How long ago?" I flipped open the file and my jaw dropped when I saw the photo, which featured some extreme Farrah Fawcett hair.

"'Seventy-seven," Matt said blandly.

The waitress chose that moment to come over, plopping glasses down and filling them with water. With her frizzy, overdyed hair, wide hips, and tendency to call both of us "honey," she matched the diner. I liked having waitresses like her—her smile was forced, and she was probably as tired as she looked, but she had the menu completely memorized, and she didn't even have to bother to write our orders down.

Matt ordered a bacon burger with all the fixings, while I settled on a grilled cheese sandwich with extra fries on the side.

"You're still sticking with the no-meat thing, huh?" Matt shook his head. "Once a girl cheats on you, I'd say you should feel free to get some sausage of your own. No pun intended on that one." Matt wasn't a fan of Beth. He thought about it for a second, then amended, "No implications either. What's the female equivalent of sausage? Skirt steak? Hamburger patty?"

"It's not for her anymore," I said, brushing the topic off. "But this missing girl. Nineteen seventy-seven? So she'd be . . . ?"

"Fifty-three this year, yeah." Matt took a swig of his water.

I blinked, feeling blank and uncertain. "They've been looking for her the whole time?"

"Since the day she didn't come home. Police poked

around for about two months because the parents kept calling, but that was it."

"How long have you been on it?"

"The parents hired me on about ten years ago."

I stared at Matt for a long second, surprised. I'd thought I knew what his job was like, with a lot of time spent in public offices tracking down people's paper histories, and even more time spent sitting in his car trying to see if someone was cheating, but he'd never told me about this or anything like it. The only lost thing he'd ever mentioned was pets or the occasional piece of artwork that he'd been hired to hunt down.

"Have you found anything?" I asked cautiously.

Matt shook his head. "I told the parents when they hired me that we'd probably never know anything. The trail has been cold too long, and if she was still out there she would've found a way to contact them by now, if that's what she wanted. In all likelihood, she died years ago."

"So why are you looking?" I asked. "Is it the money?" I knew that there'd been a few times when Matt had ended up living out of his office because he couldn't afford an apartment.

"Nah, I stopped charging them years ago. Told them they were wasting their money. We ended up agreeing that they'd comp me meals in exchange for me keeping up with it. It's not that much, really. I keep an eye on morgues, halfway houses. Sometimes if I'm talking with working girls or druggies, I'll flash her photo, see if anyone recognizes it. Run Web searches for her name every now and then. Whenever I'm out of town I'll stop by the local police station, ask around."

That didn't sound like not much to me, but the waitress

came by and set a huge plate of food in front of each of us. Matt took a big bite out of his burger, and I gnawed away at some fries for a second, thinking about everything.

We ate in silence for a few minutes before I finally asked my question. "So, why keep looking?"

Matt lifted his eyebrows. "She's their kid, Fort. They're never going to stop until they have an answer."

"Not them, you. She's not your kid, and you don't know her. You're not getting paid for this." Matt looked annoyed, and I rushed to explain. "I'm not trying to be a jerk and say you shouldn't. I just really want to understand."

Matt chewed for a long second, considering. "It's like this," he said finally, speaking in a low, tight voice. "When I was a cop, I saw a lot of really bad stuff. People whose kids or parents just disappeared one day, never to be seen again. Or someone was murdered, and we never really found out why." We very carefully didn't look at each other for that, because I knew he was talking about Jill and Brian. "And you could see how it just tore people's lives apart. We'd look for a while, but eventually the brass would sit you down and say that it wasn't going anywhere, and that you had to move on to something else. Now, though, I don't have anyone saying that I can't keep looking, and I always think to myself, what if I stopped and I could've actually found something if I just kept on it? Give someone answers, give some closure, or maybe even bring someone home who might not get there if I wasn't there to help. And once I think that, I feel responsible, like I have to keep going." Matt gave a small shrug, then an uncomfortable smile. We usually didn't get this deep. "I'm starting to feel like I'm in a chick flick, all this feelings shit, Fort. We're going to have to start talking about baseball."

We both laughed for a minute, and then I glanced over at him again. I remembered that when I was little, Matt always seemed to be laughing, and that he had a revolving series of girlfriends, but now there were a lot of frown lines around his perpetually tight-lipped mouth, and I knew that his relationships usually couldn't outlast green bananas. I felt like I wanted to ask him more about it, but he was clearly uncomfortable, so I let it go while he started a long monologue about the Red Sox that lasted through the rest of the meal.

When we were heading out, the waitress waved us off, pocketing the check, and I knew that she must know about the owners, and who Matt was. My stomach was full, but for a second I thought about the owner, still looking for a daughter who he must know was dead, and I actually felt guilty for the free meal.

My guilt lasted through Matt dropping me back off and the rest of my shift. I managed to miss my bus again, and I counted all the things that I had to do on the long walk home. It was a warm afternoon, and I'd worked up a sweat by the time I got to my apartment. The door was unlocked, an unfortunate but not entirely unusual by-product of living with Larry, who on more than one occasion had lost his keys and just left the door itself unlocked when he went out.

I opened the door slowly and cautiously, just in case a thief had finally taken Larry up on this repeated offer to steal all of our stuff. But instead of some crackhead bent on financing a drug addiction, I found something far more unexpected in our kitchen.

Beth, my girlfriend—if I could even call her that any-more.

I hadn't seen her in almost three weeks, after a shared trip down to a film festival on the Brown University campus. It had been a great date, with lots of clandestine groping and making out intermixed with whispered comments about directorial decisions. Later, Beth got us into a festival after-party organized and hosted by the film studies department, and I'd finally begun hoping that we were getting over the whole sex-with-my-roommate business. She'd excused herself to go to the bathroom, and I was going for a second pass at the buf-fet table when a casual glance over my shoulder re-vealed what she was actually doing: giving her phone number to a doctoral candidate in his thirties who, judg-ing by his bright red slacks, was clearly a tool. The eve-ning had ended in one of those crappy party situations where you're having a fight in a hallway, and everyone you know ends up walking past you. The result of the fight had not been positive—Beth had accused me of having repressively traditionalistic gender and sexual beliefs and told me to read Judith Butler. I'd ended up so much on the defensive that I actually apologized to her when I dropped her off at her apartment. Two days later she'd sent me a sixteen-page e-mail that outlined her view of what a modern and liberated relationship was supposed to look like, which boiled down to her be-ing able to have sex with as many people as she liked.

To give credit where it was due, it was really well ar-gued, and the footnotes were flawless. I'd told her that I'd need some time to think about our relationship's "new direction," and we hadn't seen each other since then.

Mostly I'd been trying to come up with a better response to her e-mail than "You shouldn't because it makes me unhappy (plus I really don't want to catch venereal diseases)." Try as I might, I hadn't been able to stretch that longer than three pages, and I had the distinct impression that word count mattered in this situation.

Now Beth was unexpectedly standing in my kitchen, having apparently made use of the emergency key I'd given her. She was dressed in her usual mix of vintage finds and hippie chic, with her long black hair with its ebullient bouncing curls tied up with a pristine white scarf. I'd noticed that she almost always wore white clothing—she was obviously aware of just how good it looked against her flawless olive skin, courtesy of her Greek heritage. She was putting a used glass into the dishwasher (not one that I'd used—she'd obviously helped herself to a drink in my absence) when she spotted me. I was still standing in the doorway, finally understanding what deer experience when they see bright lights.

Beth gave me a big, bright smile, the one that changed her face from an average level of cute to drop-dead gorgeous, and immediately rushed over to throw her arms around me and drop a very affectionate kiss on my mouth, reacquainting me with her tongue in the process.

"Hey, sweetie!" she burbled when she came up for air.

I was panting a little after the exuberance of her greeting. "Uh, hi," I managed, trying to remind my sex-starved body that I wasn't sure where the relationship was going. "This is kind of a surprise." She was reaching Spanish Inquisition levels of unexpected, after all.

"I know, I'm absolutely swamped with work lately.

I'm really glad you're here. I wasn't going to be able to wait up for you." Beth had eyelashes so long and full that it looked like she'd mugged a Disney character for them, and now she batted them at me.

"Oh yeah, well, I understand," I said, struggling to remain unmoved in the face of such eyelash action.

Beth gave me another long kiss. One of the many things I liked about her was that she was only a few inches shorter than I was, which meant that neither of us got stiff necks trying to kiss, but she was clearly abusing her easy access. "That's why I love you, Fort," she said, making my heart flip around in my chest. "You understand that my thesis has to be my priority right now."

I could feel my face flush as I said, "Sure," though I honestly would've preferred that her list of my lovable qualities be somewhat longer and more eloquent. Then I belatedly remembered those pesky relationship problems, and added, as seriously as I could given that she was completely wrapped around me, "But we probably should find some time to have a real talk." I glanced around, trying to distract myself from how close she was and how long it had been since we did anything in this relationship *other* than talk, and suddenly realized that her visit had clearly brought some changes to my apartment.

"Um," I asked hesitantly, "why is my living room filled with drums?"

"That's what I was here for," Beth said, letting me go and pacing around my kitchen, overcome with excitement and moral outrage as she unfolded her tale of woe. "The drumming circle is having incredible problems right now. We usually store the drums on campus, but Kyle accidentally left some of his weed in the storage room. I mean, the campus police are being complete fascists and accusing him of being a dealer or something, which is so typical of them to jump to conclusions about, just because of how much there was and a few crybaby narcs who reported him. Then someone was a complete snitch and called those Gestapo goons to say that the entire circle was getting high on campus property during our scheduled practices, which only happened *twice* at most. So we got kicked off campus, and everyone was completely bummed, but I told them not to worry, because I knew exactly where we could store the drums until we got reinstated."

There was a long pause while she caught her breath and I tried to take all of that in. Choosing my words carefully, I addressed the most pressing issue: "Beth, when did you join a drum circle?"

"You are so funny, babe," Beth said, kissing me again. "This will only be for two days, tops."

My brain had fizzled again when she kissed me, but after she pulled back it started working again and I asked, "You were smoking up on the campus? Really?" I'd never done any kind of drugs, acutely aware of the possible ramifications of what would happen if I lost the ability to self-censor my conversation, but Beth was something of a pot aficionado, and owned a number of shirts that clearly expressed her desire for its legalization.

Beth ignored the question. "I mean, maybe a week at the most." Another synapse-fogging kiss, but this one was quick and almost distracted. "I've got to run. This is the last thing I needed right now, but we're organizing a protest for tomorrow and they need me to help make the costumes."

I shuddered at the thought of a protest. Beth had roped me into more than a few, and I was torn between being glad and concerned that for once she wasn't asking me to participate in the fight against the establishment. Then she turned to leave and I saw the fresh hickey on the back of her neck.

Suspicion flared. "Beth, who the hell is Kyle?"

But she was already halfway out the door in a whirl of burlap purse, jingling ankle-length skirt, and cruelty-free sandals. "It's in the college bylaws that we have to be given a hearing within three months!" she called over her shoulder as she left.

Then she was gone, and I was left with that familiar feeling of having just been caught in a hurricane. I tried calling her phone, but I went straight to voice mail three times. Finally I glanced at my watch, swore when I saw the time, and had to focus on getting myself to Madeline's on time and presentable.

I barely had enough time to run a load of laundry to get the stain out of my khakis and take one rushed shower before I dodged through the obstacle course of drums currently gathered in the living room and ran out the door. I tried calling Beth twice more on the road, again getting sent to voice mail, and ended up stewing in irritation for most of the drive down to Newport, until nervous anticipation slowly pushed its way to the foreground. Chivalry had been very specific about when I was supposed to arrive, because apparently vampire shindigs begin precisely at ten at night. Probably for the ambiance. I was secretly hoping that our visitor would have a Dracula fetish and would show up in a cape.

Thanks to an elderly driver on Route 138, I pulled

into Madeline's driveway at a quarter of ten. I tucked my Fiesta next to Chivalry's Bentley and hurried inside.

Madeline and Chivalry were standing in the foyer. Madeline stood on the fifth step of the staircase wearing a long golden gown and an ermine overrobe, lacking only a crown to look like Helen Mirren in the opening shot of *The Queen*—assuming that Helen Mirren decided to revisit the role in about thirty years. Chivalry stood two steps below her and slightly off to the side, wearing a black silk three-piece suit complete with an ebony dandy's cane and an actual top hat that brought to mind all manner of Oscar Wilde jokes.

At that moment, I was extremely grateful that I'd splurged on the OxiClean and had gotten the stain out of my khakis. I was also very conscious that when it came to my shirt I'd been relying on bounce sheets and quick hanging to substitute for ironing. Chivalry had been very specific that this was a formal event, but given the way he was glaring at my tie, apparently I'd missed the mark a bit. Maybe it wasn't Brooks Brothers, but it had looked pretty good in the thrift store. It didn't exactly match the color of my shirt, true, but neon orange could be an accent color to green, right?

As I stepped farther into the lobby, I felt a chill at the back of my neck and that innate lizard/vampire-brain knowledge. I turned and saw without surprise that Prudence was standing behind me.

The fine tracings of early wrinkles around her eyes are what make Prudence look like she's in her early forties. She works out a lot, and her extremely impressive body was on display in a floor-length gold satin dress that was cut to offer everyone a generous view of her overflowing décolletage. Her hair is cut in a severe bob, and I happen to know that its brilliant red color is the work of chemicals, not nature. It's been dyed the same color since the late 'fifties, but Madeline has a turn-of-the-century oil painting of Prudence hanging in her sitting room that shows that her real hair color is a mousy brown. I try to focus on small personal hypocrisies like that whenever I'm around Prudence. I've learned that screaming and throwing myself at her might be personally satisfying, but ultimately comes to nothing more than a cracked rib.

"Hello, sister." I forced myself to speak normally. I can never look at her and not remember the way that Jill's and Brian's blood dripped off her shoes. Unfortunately, interacting with her is a fact of life.

"This greeting is a sign of our strength and power," Prudence said, her high voice cutting. She's never been much for pleasantries. Her bright blue eyes were slitted in temper, and she looked over at Chivalry. "Didn't you tell him how to dress?"

"I believe that by the standards of his generation, Fortitude has dressed appropriately," Chivalry said mildly. He was probably already planning the ways that he would corner me later and disparage my sartorial decisions, but Chivalry has always stood up to Prudence for me, and has often suffered the fallout.

"I work with stockbrokers younger than him every day," Prudence said. "He is dressed worse than the intern whose entire job revolves around bringing back lunch."

Apparently the tie had been a poor choice. Prudence and Chivalry both looked to Madeline, whose eyes had been fixed on the door the entire time.

"What Fortitude wears is unfortunate but ultimately uncorrectable at this point," she said. "Our visitor has just arrived. A show of unity is in order, my children."

There was a brief pause, and in the silence I could hear the sound of a car crunching up the gravel driveway. Apparently deciding that no tie was better than this tie, Prudence had it loosened and over my head before I even knew what was happening, and dropped it into the mouth of a convenient urn.

I let out a less-than-impressive squawk of irritation. "That's mine, Prudence!"

"Yes, and now you are no longer wearing it and I have less desire to claw out my own eyes. Everyone wins."

I glanced up, but Madeline wasn't paying any attention to us, and Chivalry gave me a very pointed shake of his head, letting me know that on this one he wasn't going to get involved. Given that I had as much chance of winning a fight with Prudence as I did with slapping a jaguar in the face and not getting mauled, I gave my tie up for lost. I did give Prudence my best glare. She returned it with interest.

Prudence positioned herself on the step just below Madeline, and the process of elimination left me trying to situate myself impressively on the lowest step, just to the side of Chivalry. I was uncomfortably reminded of posing for photos for my senior prom. On that occasion as well, I'd been a disappointment.

There was the sound of footsteps now. At least an academic question had been answered—I didn't feel the new vampire the way I felt my mother or siblings. With them there was a complete certainty about identity and location. With this one, there was just an odd little buzzing in the back of my head, as if I were standing too close to high-voltage wires.

Three loud knocks on the door, then a pause. Madeline called, "You are granted hospitality. Abide by its rules and be welcome."

I elbowed Chivalry for the CliffsNotes translation. "It means that our visitor behaves himself or we kill him," Chivalry muttered just loudly enough for me to hear.

I risked one more question: "Where's Bhumika?"

"Already in bed. Now please shut up."

The vampire entered first. He was tall and lean, with a pouty lower lip, slicked-back black hair, and an almost feathery thin mustache. He had black pants, glossy black wingtips, and a dark purple shirt with a few too many buttons undone that exposed a few curls of dark chest hair. Even though it was a dark night with no moon, he was wearing designer sunglasses. I felt distinctly disappointed—the first nonrelated vampire I'd ever met, and he was a Euro-trash tool.

Two more people stepped through the doorway to flank him, and my disappointment melted away to be replaced by nervous discomfort. On the vampire's left was a cadaverously thin man, whose olive skin was pocked and scabbed on almost every surface. Nothing had scarred, and some of the marks sullenly oozed pus and fluid. Even as I watched, the man was digging his long nails at a gouge on his chin, yanking and scratching with frantic motions. He giggled quietly, and his eyes were scanning over everyone in the room yet not seeming to absorb anything. His teeth looked sharp, and he didn't have a lower lip anymore, just a line of gnawed and sullenly bleeding skin that made me cringe. He was dressed identically to the vampire, but his shirt and pants were covered with dark, stiff patches where his dripping fluids had clearly already seeped.

On the vampire's right was a young girl with long dark hair that hung in two braids, looking like a high school freshman dressed up to play Juliet. Her neck and arms were covered with old and half-healing bite marks. Her eyes were dull and uncaring, already half-dead, and she never even glanced at us, looking only at the floor.

"I thank you for your hospitality, Madeline," the vampire said. His Italian accent was thick, and there was something in his voice that made me grateful that Chivalry was beside me. He took off his sunglasses and smiled widely. His fangs were extended, long and needle-like. "I am Luca, blood son of Dominic, who was nestmate to your brother Edmund. I carry greetings and affection, and a desire for knowledge."

"Welcome, Luca," Madeline said. There was a formality to this exchange that was weirdly offset by the incessant giggling of the skinny, and I was guessing crazy, man. "I am pleased by your greeting, and introduce you to my blood children: Prudence, Chivalry, and Fortitude. I hope that your visit here is fruitful." She paused, and I risked a glance back at her. She looked completely at ease, despite all her formal trappings and phrasing. Prudence looked bored, while Chivalry's face was deeply disapproving. Madeline continued. "I see that you have created a host. My compliments to you on your accomplishment."

Luca's smile became even broader. "Yes, I am the first in Dominic's nest to craft a functioning Renfield.

This is Phillip, who I wished to speak to you about, and this"—his hand dropped onto the shoulder of the girl, who didn't seem to even notice it, her gaze never deviating from the floor—"is my dear little Maria."

"You are all welcome in my territory," Madeline said. "And now I believe that dinner has been served."

Luca walked forward and offered his arm to Madeline, who leaned on him and led the way to the dining room. Phillip and Maria followed Luca, trailed closely by Prudence, whose long skirt swished loudly on the floor. At the end, I grabbed Chivalry's arm.

"What's with the entourage?" I asked, tipping my head toward the oddly matched pair.

Chivalry's voice was so soft that I had to strain to hear him. "A Renfield is a less polite term for a host, though still an improvement from those who prefer to call them thralls. Phillip is the same as Grace and Henry."

"But why is he walking around? Grace and Henry don't ever get to leave their cells."

"Clearly Luca has less reverence for life than our mother."

I let that horrifying thought roll over me, then asked, "And what about Maria? She looks really young."

"She *is* very young, Fort. Not more than fourteen if I'm any judge."

I hadn't really wanted to believe that my impression had been correct. I'd been telling myself that she was probably one of those eighteen-year-olds who looks really young.

"But—"

"Don't say anything," Chivalry hissed in my ear, and I could feel his hand gripping my wrist tightly enough to make the bones ache. "Mother has already welcomed them to the territory."

"But that girl—"

"Be silent. Mother will handle it."

I bit my tongue and followed them into the dining room.

Dinner was a long and difficult affair. Vampires slowly lose the ability to digest food as they get older, deriving more and more of their primary sustenance from blood. Madeline's cook had prepared three versions of a meal—for me, another jab at my vegetarianism with a filet mignon, which meant that I had to spend the entire meal eating around the beautifully prepared steak and filling up on potatoes and veggies. For Chivalry it was a thick stew with chunks of meat, and for Prudence a potato soup with finely diced shavings of steak. Madeline sipped at a glass of wine.

Luca had dished himself out some of the stew, but I noticed that he avoided most of the meat, and eventually he set it all aside and ladled a small bowl of the thinner soup. Noticing my attention, he gave me an oily smile.

"I have found lately that dishes that used to entice me are more difficult to eat. But such is our lot as we get older. For the gifts we gain in power, small sacrifices must be made in comfort."

"How very true," Prudence said. Luca gave her an even oilier smile, along with some significant eyebrow action, not realizing that he was barking up the wrong tree. I was seated next to Prudence, and I knew that she'd been checking stocks on her BlackBerry underneath the table for the last twenty minutes and tossing in the occasional conversational sop to make it look like she was paying attention. Apparently she felt that having dressed up, she'd completed her contributions.

"Won't Phillip and Maria be joining us?" I asked. They had been standing against the wall since we walked in, and while I was very happy to have Phillip and his pus as far away from my meal as possible, it was hard to eat while Maria just stood there.

Luca's eyebrows shooting up his forehead alerted me to my faux pas, as did Chivalry's quick kick under the table. After an elaborate mouth dab with his napkin, Luca smiled expansively and waved a finger at me. "How droll you are, Fortitude. I would certainly never insult your family by having my servants eat from your table."

"Yes, Fort's wit is our constant companion," Chivalry said, straight-faced. His second kick was even harder, and I shut my mouth on what I would've said next.

"On a serious note," Madeline said, leaning forward. Everyone sat up straighter, and I saw Prudence slide her BlackBerry back into her evening bag. Apparently now we were getting down to business. "Given that you have already created Phillip, Luca, I wonder that you have come to me for advice. Surely with this accomplishment there is little that I could tell you that your own father has not already."

"You cut right to the heart of me, great lady," Luca said, making a little flourish with his spoon. But there was a more calculating aspect to him that wasn't quite covered up by his compliments. "My esteemed sire, Dominic, is most eager for me to successfully brood offspring, and of course Phillip is but the first step in this process. I have attempted to breed him with my little Maria, but as of yet with no success." I looked over at the scabrous, mangy Phillip and at Maria, who might as well have been carved out of stone as Luca talked about her. My stomach tightened and I fought to keep down my dinner. "Dominic has cautioned me that some Renfields can be bred a lifetime with no success, yet you are known the world over for your easy fecundity, so I felt that I should naturally seek out your expertise in this area."

"Perhaps you should restrict your Phillip's efforts to mature women," Chivalry growled. He was giving Luca extremely unfriendly looks, and I felt a rush of pride in my brother.

"Oh, but I do assure you, my Maria reached maturity almost two years ago." There was a malicious gleam in Luca's eyes as he looked at Chivalry. "It was of course most distressing to me when it happened, but at least she can continue to serve me in her own small way, despite her current shortcomings."

"Maria's youth is rather separate from your problems," Madeline said, smoothly cutting in. "You could attempt Phillip with a dozen young women of proven ability and likely come to the same result. Our blood changes much about a host, enough that he is no longer truly human. To breed a host to a human is therefore often an exercise in frustrated hope, for the odds of a successful pregnancy are low, and the resultant offspring are exceptionally difficult to coax beyond infancy. If you truly wish quick success, I would recommend crafting a true mate for your Phillip. A matched set, if you will."

Luca stared at Madeline, who sipped at her wine.

"You say that I must maintain *two* Renfields?"

"I certainly do. Of course, as it is almost certain that you required Dominic's assistance to even create Phillip, I do not expect that you will achieve this. Not at your age, Luca, or at your abilities. But perhaps in another fifty years or so you can give it another try. Do give my best to Dominic, however."

"But Dominic—"

"Yes, Luca, I knew from the moment you walked in that you are the offspring of a host and human pairing. I imagine that Dominic spent the better part of a century in dreary repetition before he was rewarded with you, and that your lack of siblings is due in no small part to his inability to create and maintain two concurrent hosts. Heaven only knows just how many women he had to breed his own host to until you caught. Dominic probably also buys lottery tickets. Heed or dismiss my words, it matters nothing to me, but they are the truth behind my success."

There was a long silence, and Luca managed to force another sickly smile across his face. "I will certainly pass your observations along, madame. And now I have obviously taken up enough of your charming company."

Luca made a show of getting up. Phillip and Maria immediately returned to their positions at his side. I started to stand, but another kick under the table kept me seated with the rest of my family.

Chivalry cleared his throat, drawing Luca's attention. "And how long do you intend to remain in my mother's territory?" he asked.

"Not more than a week," Luca said, inclining his head by a few very precise degrees, then raising it again. "I do desire to see the sights before I return home, and I have found sufficient lodging in Providence."

"Be welcome, then, Luca," Madeline said. This time Luca did a full-on head dip, then turned and started for the door. Phillip fell in behind him, like a twisted funhouse mirror image of his master, and Maria walked last.

I was seated closest to the door, and they all had to pass close by me. I stared at Maria, looking at that shuttered, empty expression on her face, and the bite marks that ranged from purpling scars to cuts so fresh that they'd barely even scabbed over. I glanced back to my family—Prudence was on her BlackBerry again, while Madeline was fussing with a napkin. Only Chivalry met my eyes, and whatever look I gave him had him shaking his head frantically. I pushed my chair back from the table abruptly, feeling a whooshing sensation under the table as Chivalry's behavior-enforcing kick failed to land. He was on his feet in a second, moving to stop me, but it was too late. I leaned out and grabbed Maria's wrist with my right hand.

Her skin was cold and dry under my hand, and her arm was so thin that I could feel the bones practically flex under my grip. My hand not only completely circled her wrist, but there was enough room to spare that my fingers pressed against the back of my thumb. Maria didn't jump or say anything, which was how I would've reacted if someone suddenly grabbed me. She just froze in place, not reacting or looking anywhere except Luca's back. It was like stopping a robot. Even her pulse, which I could feel against my palm, failed to deviate from its steady beat. Whatever she'd seen in her life, my action wasn't enough to make any impression.

I could hear movement and rustling behind me, but I didn't glance back at my family. I kept my eyes fixed on Maria's face, which I saw only in profile. A second later I was also looking at Luca, whose expression was less than thrilled.

"Leave her here," I blurted out. That brought a reaction from Maria, a full-bodied twitch, as if she'd just been startled awake. Her eyes shifted off Luca for the first time, and she looked down at me with those dead, despairing eyes.

"Fortitude," Luca said, and there was the tight control and forced jocularity in his voice that people have when their bosses' dogs pee on their shoes. "Perhaps you are too young to know this, but this is hardly a good example of manners." He forced a smile that showed too much tooth in it for humor.

"She can't do what you want her to," I said. Having so much of Luca's attention on me was making me sweat, and I tightened my hold on Maria's arm. "You can't use her. Leave her here." I didn't know what any of my family behind me were doing, but I didn't even dare to glance over my shoulder and find out. I kept my eyes on Maria and Luca. I had no idea how this could end, had no idea if grabbing Maria was a little offense or a vampire super insult, but I could feel Maria turning her wrist, that cold, dry skin sliding along my sweaty palm, and then I felt her fingers brush against my sleeve, so light and tentatively that if I hadn't glanced down to confirm it I wouldn't even have believed it. Looking back up, I also saw something flicker through her dull eyes. It was just the edge of hope.

I felt a tight constriction in my chest—she didn't

know me, didn't even know what I wanted her for. But whatever her life was with Luca and Phillip, the complete unknown was preferable to her.

Luca saw it too, and his face darkened. He was definitely pissed off now. He looked past me, toward my mother. "Youth can only be pushed so far," he started. "Hospitality rules are clear—" I could feel movement behind me, and Luca broke off whatever he was going to say. Then Chivalry was standing next to my chair and leaning toward Luca.

"Let us not turn to rules and our elders," Chivalry said smoothly. "You have an item that has become nearly useless to you, and here is my baby brother showing an interest in it. Can we not resolve this, offspring to offspring?"

A muscle in Luca's cheek twitched sharply, but with obvious effort he cleared the expression off his face. "Your involvement surprises me," he said, his eyes raking over Chivalry, measuring and considering. Compared to Luca's skinny male model look, Chivalry practically looked like a Charles Atlas ad. The European vampire was looking more cautious now.

"Should it? Perhaps," Chivalry conceded. "But you have not had the pleasure of siblings, Luca. For my brother's delight is very much my own." Slowly, with clear intent, Chivalry leaned forward, toward the other vampire, invading his personal space. The tips of Chivalry's fangs slid out just enough to rest against the top of his lower lip, and his voice dropped. "Never would I deny Fort a treat he longs for." With that utterly untrue statement, Chivalry began reaching out for Maria.

Just before he could touch Maria's shoulder, Luca

moved suddenly and caught Chivalry's hand in his own. The tension in the room shot up as the two of them stared at each other, each pushing hard against the other vampire's arm. Both were wearing long sleeves, but I could see the muscles in both their hands standing out, and Chivalry's knuckles were whitening.

The pupils in Luca's eyes began expanding, darkening in a clear sign of aggression, but when he spoke his voice was still superficially polite. "I find myself longing for an older sibling, as you paint a compelling portrait. But this is my property, and I find some strong attachment to it." His fangs slid out as well, longer than Chivalry's. Against all apparent laws of physics, Luca's thin hand began to push even harder, and I heard Chivalry give a small grunt as he attempted to hold his ground. But, with agonizing slowness, Luca pushed Chivalry's hand back, bending it toward his own arm. I winced at the sight, and now Chivalry was sweating visibly. It was clear now that Luca was stronger, but Chivalry didn't let go, and Luca didn't stop pushing.

Chivalry glanced down at me, and I shook my head frantically, willing him to keep trying. He looked away from me, took a deep breath, then threw all his weight into it, and for just a second Luca's hand wavered. Against my hand, I could feel Maria start to shiver, almost vibrating as she stood, but I didn't dare look at her, focused on my brother.

Luca's eyes narrowed down to slits, and I could see just the slightest hint of perspiration at his temple. Then I saw his arm muscle flex against the shiny satin of his tight shirt, and with a hard push he threw Chivalry off balance and onto his knees. I was still sitting, my head now on the same level as my brother's. Chivalry's hair wasn't perfectly pomaded anymore, but was wet with sweat as Luca began once again forcing his hand backward, the wrist bending far past where nature intended. Chivalry's lip pulled back, exposing his fully extended fangs as he gave a sharp grunt of pain, but he kept his eyes locked with Luca.

Then there was a sudden scraping as a chair was pushed back from the table, and Prudence stood next to Chivalry, her hand around his bent wrist, stopping all of Luca's momentum. Everyone paused for a long moment of shock, while she stood there, not a hair out of place, her upper lip curled ever so slightly in disgust, though who that was directed toward was unclear.

Luca stepped backward, removing his hand from Chivalry's. The black of his pupils pulled in again, and his fangs slowly receded. He cleared his throat, and for a few tense seconds seemed occupied with adjusting his hair and shirt, smoothing out wrinkles and restoring his appearance. "And you, my lady Prudence," he said finally, with clear deference in his voice. "Do you also intercede for your brother?"

I didn't even breathe as Prudence's hard blue eyes trailed over to look up and down Maria, then shifted over to me. Chivalry pushed himself up from the floor slowly, watching her face, his expression unreadable.

"Please, Prudence," I said hoarsely, barely able to push the words through my suddenly tight throat. I hated everything she was, but I sought out her blue eyes and tried to beg silently.

She looked away from me then, back to Luca. "Perhaps I am too far removed from the nursery," she said in her coldest voice. "There are many pets with no devoted owner such as yourself. I see no reason to quibble further in this unseemly manner."

"How wise," Luca murmured with a small smile. With clearly regained confidence, he reached down and put his hand on Maria's arm, just above where I was holding her.

"Prudence—" I said urgently.

"No, Fort," she interrupted. "You are indulged enough." Then she turned and walked back to her chair, and I could hear her settle down, and then the little beep as she turned her BlackBerry on again.

I looked back up at Luca, whose smile widened, then at Maria. That spark was gone from her eyes, and she slowly turned her face away from mine, back toward Luca.

"Fortitude."

I looked over at Chivalry, standing next to me. His face was still flushed, and he was holding his abused wrist carefully with his free hand. He glanced at Maria, then back to me. "That's enough," he said, and I could hear the resignation in his voice.

I shook my head, not letting go of Maria's wrist.

Luca gave a loud huff, then squeezed Maria's arm tightly. Her high shriek cut through the thick air of the room sharply. I flinched, then hesitated. Luca lifted one expressive eyebrow.

I let go.

I stared up at Maria, desperately hoping that she'd look down at me, hoping that she'd show that she understood that I'd tried, but Maria turned her face completely away. Luca wrapped one skinny arm around her, pulling her close against his body, and I could feel acid at the back of my throat at how she closed her eyes and shut down, accepting it.

Luca gave one last nod to Madeline, ignoring the rest of us, then walked quickly out the door with Maria, Phillip following closely behind them. I could feel the buzzing in the back of my head growing weaker and weaker as they moved farther out of the house, on to the driveway, then out into the night, until at last it was just me and the family.

There was a long pause, a sudden scurrying sound, and then the entire kitchen staff seemed to burst into the room. There was a flurry of cleared plates and platters, and within seconds we were alone again. The rush made me very aware that Madeline's human staff had been completely absent for the entirety of Luca's visit.

Madeline got up to leave. I realized that to her, there was nothing left to discuss.

"Aren't you going to do something?" I burst out.

"About what?" Madeline asked. She glanced at the door to the kitchen. "If this is about dessert, there wasn't one planned, but you can always ask for a slice of pie."

Unbelievable. "About Maria!" I said loudly.

"Really, Fortitude, you're going to have to be more specific. What should I be doing about Maria?" Madeline eased back down into her seat. With a clear indication of settling in, she unbuttoned her ermine cape and draped it over the back of her chair.

"Saving her! He's hurting her, probably molesting her."

"Darling, I'd say it's rather certain that he's been molesting her. But her life has likely been a misery for long enough now that I'm sure she's looking forward to her inevitable demise, which from the looks of her will be happening rather sooner than later. Why on earth should I interfere?"

I stared at her.

Prudence gave a gusty sigh. "For Christ's sake, Fortitude, why must you try to make everyone else get worked up over nothing? So some girl is suffering. So what?"

"Her situation is unfortunate," Chivalry said quietly from where he was still standing behind my chair.

"That is so typical of you to take his side," Prudence snapped. "You don't give a damn about her either now that she's out of the room and we don't all have to see what a messy eater that idiot is, but you'll pretend just to make Fort happy."

Chivalry glared at her. "I think my actions this evening have shown that my commitment is more than just some easy facade."

Prudence's eyes blazed. "And I should've gotten involved in your little squabble, risking injury in that fight, for what? What use do I have for a drained girl with one foot in the grave already?"

"My little turtledoves," Madeline said, making a little simmer down gesture with her hand. "This is all academic anyway. I have welcomed Luca to my territory, and other than Fortitude's tender feelings, it is disturbing none of us for him to have his plaything. In a week he will be back merrily assaulting the young girls of Naples, and out of sight is out of mind."

"How can you say that?" I asked.

"Very easily. You are young, darling, and prone to foolishness, so let me be clear. You are not to interfere with the young Maria, and you"—her gaze pinned

Chivalry—"are expressly forbidden to have any involvement with Luca or his servants while he is in my territory. I will not have your little brother's distress drive you to imprudent action."

"And me, Mother?" Prudence asked. "Do you have any orders for me?"

"No, darling." Madeline smiled. "I am certain that I can trust in your dual senses of decorum and disinterest in this area."

I shoved back from the table, letting my chair fall back and onto the floor as I stood and stared at my mother. "You could've stopped him from taking her," I accused. "I couldn't, Chivalry couldn't, Prudence wouldn't, but just one word from you and he would've left her."

Madeline's smile stayed fixed on her face, but there was a clear warning in her voice. "For me to demand the pet would be to challenge Luca's father, and that would risk a war between our territories. We tend to be slow-moving creatures, Fortitude, but we can be riled. I doubt very much that you would enjoy a visit from Dominic, who holds closer to older ways than I do. Like your sister, I do not embrace direct confrontation when I am not certain of victory."

"I can't sit here and listen to any more of this," I said.

"You certainly could, darling, but I understand that you would prefer not to. Have a lovely evening. And"— Madeline glanced up at me, her blue eyes suddenly gleaming—"you are more vulnerable than your siblings, so while Luca is in town I have made arrangements for your protection."

"If that's so easy for you, why can't you protect Maria?"

"Really, darling, you are utterly beside yourself. You

are my child, while Maria is nothing. Why would I even dream of spending favors, money, or effort for her protection?"

I left, ignoring it when Chivalry called my name. I could hear the sound of Prudence's voice, probably starting in on Chivalry, but I needed to get out of that house, with its stifling air and pervasive attitude of superiority. It was too much like when Jill and Brian had died, and Madeline had acted as if I'd just lost a pet bunny.

I made the drive home primarily on autopilot, and since it was almost midnight on a Wednesday, the roads were almost deserted. I made good time, pulling into my parking space at just after twelve thirty. I sat in the car for a long minute. Inside the car, I was wrapped in a bubble of silence, left alone with my thoughts. That was the last thing I wanted. It had hurt to have my last illusions and hopes shattered so harshly. Madeline knew me too well—I'd always imagined that maybe other vampires were different from my family, that they had managed to retain more humanity, or at least more respect for humanity. That maybe they didn't have the ruthless self-interest that the vampires I knew, even Chivalry, had. That hope had sustained me for a long time, because it meant that maybe there was a chance that after I transitioned, I would still be me and I wouldn't lose those feelings that my mother and siblings saw as so foreign. Meeting Luca had shown me that by the standards of the larger vampire community, my family was actually a bunch of tree huggers. I remembered how completely unaware he'd been of what his entourage looked like, and how surprised he'd been when I suggested that they needed to eat as well.

Chivalry's slow destruction of his wives, or even the way Prudence had killed my foster parents with such brutal and heartless efficiency, suddenly seemed less vicious compared to Luca. I'd never seen a mark left on Chivalry's spouses, and dinner had been moved progressively earlier in the mansion to accommodate Bhumika's flagging energy. She sat at the table every night, and I'd seen Chivalry suffer without complaint through countless Bollywood movies, just to make her happy.

But that didn't make Chivalry less of a predator. And I still dreamed that someone would drop a house on Prudence. They weren't any less deadly than they were before dinner—all that this meant was that there was a much worse option.

I got out, stood next to the Fiesta, and looked up at my building. The lights in my apartment were on, meaning that Larry had returned home. I didn't want to talk with him, or even look at him. It didn't seem right to even think about the money he owed me when somewhere in the city, behind those shuttered eyes, Maria was experiencing a level of suffering that I couldn't even imagine.

I started walking around the neighborhood. Everything was buttoned down for the night, and I was only passed by an occasional car, but maybe if I walked long enough and wore myself down I wouldn't dream. I already knew that my dreams would be bad ones tonight. I circled around for maybe half an hour, until I switched directions and started heading for the twenty-four-hour 7-Eleven. The buses had stopped running, but it wasn't too far to walk, and if any night was one that called for a pint of Ben & Jerry's, it was this.

I was already planning to buy a bag of Doritos chips to go with the ice cream when I realized I was being followed. Three tall guys who looked eighteen or nineteen and were wearing matching Bruins jerseys and assorted ill-conceived tattoos and facial piercings had been walking about twenty feet behind me, talking to each other in that overly loud way that drunks tend to communicate in. I hadn't thought much of them, figuring that they were just heading home after watching the latest hockey game at a sports bar, but when I crossed the street, they crossed it as well. I glanced back over my shoulder—all three were looking right at me now, and they weren't talking anymore.

I started walking faster. They walked faster too. I broke into a jog. One of them laughed, a high, mocking sound that made me aware of just how quiet it was, and I didn't have to look back to know that they were moving faster now. I wasn't even halfway to the 7-Eleven yet. The streets were empty of cars, and all the windows were dark. It hit me suddenly that I was about to experience my first mugging, a landmark of city living that I had frankly not been eager to meet.

For once I regretted not being a true vampire, with the ability to hand out shit, or at the very least outrun people. During high school the only person I was able to outrun had been Alton Myers, who was morbidly obese and had asthma. The inevitable occurred when a hand grabbed the back of my collar and yanked me backward. I heard the tearing of cloth and felt the solid impact of concrete on my ass. One of them landed a kick on my side that knocked the wind out of me. As I rolled around on the ground, trying to protect my vulnerable areas of crotch, stomach, and head while the other two decided to join in on the kicking idea, I was struck with the very horrible irony that I was the one vampire in the northeastern United States and lower Canada who placed value on the lives of humans who I didn't directly know. Now those humans were about to show their appreciation by beating the crap out of me.

This was possibly either a life lesson or a comment on my overall philosophy. It was definitely going to leave bruises.

"Hand over your wallet, dipshit," one of the boys said.

"Fine!" I said, rolling over when another foot just missed my kidney. "Just stop kicking me!" The assault slowed to a few enthusiastic nudges as I scrabbled at my back pocket for my wallet. From the sharp crunch that I'd heard from my other pocket when I first fell, I could reasonably assume that my phone had passed on to join Frodo in the undying lands, and I really hoped that the thugs would run off before checking my billfold. Replacing my driver's license and canceling my credit and debit cards was going to be a bitch, but I somehow doubted that they would be happy to learn that my entire cash reserve consisted of three dollars and a ticket from my sandwich shop that was only two notches away from a free hoagie.

I handed over my wallet and my luck held. At shitty. There was a pause as they all looked in, then a chorus of three voices calling me a fuck-head. I had braced myself for a renewed kicking when a smooth, very husky, very female voice said: "Boys, why don't you hang on a moment?"

We all looked. The three guys from where they had surrounded me, and me from my defensive huddle on the ground. Then there was a long beat while we all tried to comprehend what we were looking at.

A woman had come out of the nearby alley and was strolling up to us, as if this were . . . well, actually I'm not sure in what situation a woman would stroll up to a trio of teenage malcontents and their hapless victim with just that level of panache.

She was Asian, with beautiful almond eyes, perfectly refined features, and a cloud of rich black hair that flowed over her shoulders. It was too dark to figure out exactly what color clothing she was wearing, but there wasn't too much of it and it was fitting very well. A sleeveless tank top was short enough to show off her flat stomach, and her dark pants were practically sprayed onto her legs, and tucked into knee-high boots with a very impressive heel. She was grinning at us, with a little strut in her step, and her hands rested on her hips.

It crossed my mind that we were having a collective hallucination. Maybe I was seeing her, and they were seeing a camel. Or I was dead and heaven consisted of an anime fetish. Except she wasn't wearing a schoolgirl's skirt and kneesocks, so maybe not that. Also, if this was heaven, the ground was really dirty, I still ached all over from the kicks, and frankly there was something kind of intimidating about the way she was smiling.

Apparently my assailants were also confused. "Bitch, what the fuck?" the leader asked. I was thinking of him as the leader because he had the most rings in his nose, and also he was the one holding my wallet. He also seemed to have the best command of the English language.

The woman thought so too, because she laughed. "Very eloquently put," she said. "Now do me a favor and run along. You're messing up my property."

She didn't even glance at me, but I gathered that I was the property in question.

My muggers didn't think much of her request. "Fuck you, bitch," the leader said. "And you'd better start running, because when we're done with this fucker, you're next." But none of them moved. Whatever sense of menace was emanating from the woman, who could barely have topped five-foot-five and probably got carded every time she ordered a drink, they felt it too.

Her smile widened. "This is your last warning. And now I'm not even going to let you keep his wallet."

"She's crazy," one of the beta thugs muttered.

"Yeah, get her," said the other one.

"Too late," she said. She lifted one hand off her hip and blew a kiss. For a long minute nothing seemed to happen, and I wondered if she actually was a crazy woman. I hoped not, because then I'd have to try to save her, and I'd already done an incredibly crappy job of saving myself.

But then the leader of the thugs let out an ear-piercing scream, echoed almost immediately by his cohorts. My wallet dropped onto my stomach, and they were running like track stars, still screaming, across the street and down an alley.

Their shrieks were disappearing into the distance. If

we'd been in a residential area, people probably would've been calling the cops, but here there was nothing but chained-up storefronts. I started to get up, but the woman had walked closer, and she pressed her boot against my throat, effectively pinning me down.

"Uh-uh," she said, leaning down closer to me. I got my first close-up look at her face, and felt my stomach give a flip that had almost nothing to do with the recent blunt-force trauma it had suffered. "I think I like you where you are. Maybe you'll cause less trouble like this."

Behind her, there was a small scuffling sound and then a rhythmic clicking. I tore my eyes away from the gorgeous woman and my brief hopes that this might go the way of a *Penthouse* forum letter to look and see what was causing the sounds. It was a fox—its brilliant red coat, dark feet, and pristine white throat and tail tip visible even in the weak light from the half-dead street-lights. The fox sat down next to the woman and looked at me with golden eyes. Then it gave a wide, deliberate yawn.

I looked back at the woman, who was still patiently standing with one foot balanced gently on my larynx.

"Oh, shit," I whispered. "You're kitsune."

She gave me an approving grin and tapped my nose with one finger. "Got it in one."

Chapter 4

The kitsune were shape-shifters and trick-sters. They were native to Japan, but one of them had come over right after World War II, and had petitioned my mother to live in her territory. Madeline granted it, and the kitsune had set up shop, quickly raising a horde (or, more accurately, a litter) of children. There were many types of supernatural creatures in her territory, but Madeline's ties were the closest with the kitsune, who were universally fe-male and could change from women to foxes. I'd only ever encountered them in their fox form before—after I was first brought back to live in the mansion, Madeline had hired the kitsune to guard the grounds. I'd had more than a few runaway attempts foiled by a fox's nipping teeth. They seemed to take a particular enjoyment in the task, and I still remember the sinking feeling in my belly whenever I was halfway through the border hedge and heard the high, amused yipping of a fox. The last time I tried to run away, they let me get completely through the hedge before four of them jumped me at once, pinning me to the ground un-der a furry, wiggling pile of fox. They'd then driven me home with nips and yips, taking every opportunity to trip me and smack my face with their tails.

My feelings toward the kitsune were not fond.

When Madeline decided that I needed protection with Luca in town, she'd apparently turned to tried-and-true methods of both containing and tormenting me, and had hired my current guard, Suzume Hollis, granddaughter of the original Japanese kitsune. While I limped and she strutted, the fox scampering at our heels, she took a lot of delight in telling me how she'd trailed me from my apartment and had watched my entire mugging.

I'd never seen their other ability at work before tonight, but kitsune could play with people's perception as well. Illusion isn't really the right word for it, since Chivalry said a kitsune could make something look so real that it would fool every sense, but it was what had driven away my attackers. Whatever had sent those three screaming for their mommies hadn't been there for me, but for them it must've looked as real as I did. And if something had been chasing them, I hoped for their sakes that they had outrun it. A fox's trick couldn't kill them, but it might be able to scare them enough to bring out any congenital heart weaknesses.

"What kind of bodyguard doesn't stop me from getting mugged?" I asked incredulously. My embarrassment that her first impression of me had been me getting beaten up by Bruins fans was offset by my anger that she hadn't prevented it. Between that and the growing consternation I felt about just how good she smelled, I felt really exhausted.

"The kind who wants to know exactly how much handholding this assignment is going to require," she answered.

"How much is that?"

"Apparently the same amount as walking a five-year-old girl across the street. Was assuming the fetal position and trusting that they wouldn't kick anything critical really your best plan?"

Fortunately we'd arrived back at my apartment, so I was saved the trouble of trying to come up with a witty comeback.

Occupying the sole handicapped spot in the parking lot was a low-slung and sleek little sports car, painted matte black and looking like it could break land-speed records. I felt a small cringe of embarrassment on behalf of my Fiesta, since it had to share the same lot as this automotive masturbatory fantasy. I silently promised to be a better owner and at least replace the bumper that was currently held on by wire ties.

"How did I not notice this when I pulled in?" I asked.

"Probably because you didn't even look around. I could've been standing naked and waving pompoms and you wouldn't have noticed." Suzume opened the trunk of the car and pulled out a duffel bag. She tossed it over to me and I grunted a little as I caught it. It was so stuffed that I was amazed she had been able to get it closed—as it was, the zipper was barely holding on.

"No, that I would've noticed," I muttered. Not low enough, because she snickered a little as she closed the trunk again. She unlocked and opened the passenger's-side door, then tossed her keys on the driver's seat.

She noticed my confusion. "My cousin Noriko drove me over."

The fox yipped and hopped into the car. A minute later a naked woman a little younger than Suzume sat up and began to pull a sundress over her head with leisurely motions. I slapped a hand over my eyes, but the image was already burned into my retinas.

"Do you have a problem with nudity?" Suzume asked, her voice coming just beside my left ear. A shiver made its way down my spine, but I kept me eyes shut until the car started up and I heard it pull out into the street.

"No, no problem at all." I said. "That's the problem."

Suzume laughed again, a warm, throaty chuckle that rubbed across my skin like fur.

I dropped my hand and glared at her. "Are you doing something?"

There was nothing innocent about her smile. "What would I be doing?" She stepped closer to me, and now we were nearly touching. She radiated heat. This close, she had to tilt her head up to look at me. I could feel sweat start to trickle down my spine. Her hair looked incredibly soft, and her full lower lip looked slightly moist. Everything about her said that she wanted a kiss.

I stepped back quickly, and the moment broke. "Fox tricks."

"Maybe a little." One step and she'd again bridged the distance between us, this time so close that her breasts just brushed against my chest, and I could feel the temperature rising again. "But aren't you enjoying it?" Her eyes were as dark and velvety as the night sky, dancing with amusement.

"No, so cut it out," I said, shoving her duffel into her hands and heading toward the building. I could hear her following me, and her eyes were practically boring holes in my back, but I refused to look back at her as I went inside. I was the master of my own body, I told myself. Then I told it to myself again, hoping that this time my body would actually listen. I also reminded myself that I had a girlfriend (admittedly one who had been cheating on me for the better part of two months), and that it would be wrong to let another woman toy with me. Fidelity required that I reserve the right to toy with me to Beth. Though it was somewhat disturbing that Suzume seemed able to accomplish with a single look what Beth only managed with knee-weakening kisses and a conversational style that skewed toward monologues.

My body didn't find that a very convincing argument, but I did manage to return to a presentable state as we marched silently up two flights of stairs and into the apartment.

Thankfully the door to Larry's room was closed and for once there were no sounds indicating the presence of company. Suzume roamed around, opening every cabinet, surveying my DVD collection, testing out each of the drums still clustered around my sofa, even riffling through the pile of junk mail that was on what ostensibly my eat-in kitchen table, and really just served as a catchall for stuff. Everything seemed interesting to her, but when she lifted up the trash lid to look inside, I smacked it shut.

"Does a bodyguard really need to know what I've thrown out lately?"

She looked surprised. "Of course not."

"Then why are you looking?"

"Because I'm nosy."

I stared at her, and she gave me that bright smile again that flashed very white teeth. "Bathroom that way?"

I nodded. She scooted in, and a minute later I could hear her riffling through the medicine cabinet, then each of the drawers in the sink. Resigning myself to her search, I pulled a bag of peas out of the freezer and pressed it against my ribs. With the adrenaline from my mugging and the sight of female nakedness faded, all of my aching spots from the night's misadventures were making themselves known. With Suzume out of sight, but not out of mind, since from the sound of it she had now moved on to ransacking my bedroom, I took the opportunity to stuff a bag of frozen corn down the back of my pants. My ass was strongly protesting where I'd hit it on the sidewalk, and I sighed in relief as the cold started numbing it.

"Feeling better?" Suzume's voice was right in my ear. I jumped about a foot, losing my grip on the corn, which dropped completely into my loosened pants. I struggled, much to Suzume's bright-eyed interest, to retrieve it without resorting to shoving a hand down there, but all I did was get it farther wedged down toward areas that really didn't need icing.

"Need a hand?" she asked.

"No, everything's fine. Go back to cataloging all my stuff." I managed to shift the bag into one of my pants legs, and now I could start shaking it out.

"This is more interesting than checking to see if your milk has passed its expiration date. FYI, it has."

The corn was wedged behind one of my knees now, and I had the choice of dropping my pants completely or snaking a hand up from below. By now the condensation on the bag was moistening my pants.

I looked at Suzume. She looked back at me.

"Can I have a little privacy?" I asked.

She considered that for a moment, then shook her head. "No, this is fun. I want to see what you do next."

I headed for the bathroom and shut the door in her face, flipping the old-fashioned lock on the doorknob. The mirror showed that I'd ended the night pretty worse for the wear. I was dirty, the collar of my shirt had been half ripped off and now hung drunkenly down my back, and my pants were more than ready for another round of OxiClean. I felt embarrassed for just long enough to remember that I wasn't trying to impress Suzume, and that from the rattling of the doorknob I had pretty limited time to retain a modicum of dignity. The lock held her off just long enough for me to free the corn and have my pants halfway zipped.

"Usually locks indicate that people want to be left alone," I told her.

"Usually do," she agreed. "But since I've been employed to guard you, normal social protocols don't apply."

"How long is this guarding going to last?"

"Until Madeline calls me off or her money runs out. Given how loaded she is, you should probably hope that the first happens." Suzume started yanking at the bottom of my shirt. Surprised, I smacked her hand. She smacked back, and hard enough that I gave up and let her get the shirt off. We both stared down at my torso. Normally I think I'd be more impressed at the bruises along my sides, but at the moment I was wishing that I'd spent more time at the gym.

"They got some good ones in, considering that they were only wearing sneakers," Suzume said. She poked one of the more impressive marks and frowned when I yelped. "I thought vampires were tougher than this."

"I haven't transitioned yet," I snapped, really irritated, and stormed out and into my bedroom. This had definitely been a night of people pointing out my frailties. My dramatic exit was completely ruined when Suzume simply followed me in.

While I pulled a clean undershirt out of my hamper,

Suzume tossed herself onto the bed and rolled around a little. She pawed the navy blue sheets, then hung her head over the side and stuck an arm under my bed, emerging with a pair of Beth's underpants.

"Huh," she said, holding them out and studying them with an air of scientific inquiry. "Boy shorts, Hello Kitty design, size small."

I longed for death in that moment. When she leaned forward, sniffing, I gave up all pretence and lunged for her, grabbing for the underpants. There was some rolling and another brief smack exchange. I ended up stretched out with her straddling me, holding the underpants above my head as I panted. There was a definite undertone of *neener, neener* to her expression.

"Now, important question time," she said. "Ex?"

"Current," I grumbled.

Suzume's dark, perfectly arched eyebrows climbed up her forehead. "Long-distance?"

"No."

"Is she traveling?"

"No."

Suzume leaned down so that we were nose-to-nose, and became very solemn. "It's dead, Jim. Time to make it official and break up."

"Thank you, Dr. McCoy," I said sarcastically.

Her face lit up again with that smile. "This is more like it, Fort. If we're going to be spending time together, it's very important that you be fun."

"I'll keep that in mind. Now can you please get off me? This is not helping my bruises."

In an instant, Suzume's whole attitude changed. She crouched down closer, with slinking movements. While a moment ago it hadn't seemed to matter, now I was extremely aware of where we were, and how close we were. Suzume slid her hands slowly up my arms to wrap around my wrists. Her thumbs stroked against my pulse points in a way that set my whole body on fire. I was breathing hard, but it wasn't from exertion anymore.

Suzume dropped down farther, and I could feel the heat of her body stretched above me, a feather's distance from touching. There was nothing playful in her face now, just rawly sensual. The tip of her tongue ran over her bottom lip, and my mouth went dry.

"I bet I could get your mind off your bruises," she murmured in my ear, each breath a teasing puff of air that sent a shiver down my spine.

I squeezed my eyes shut and counted to three, then opened them again. No, this wasn't a hallucination.

"Are you planning on actually following through on this?" I asked, trying to keep my voice as steady and casually inquisitive as possible.

That now very familiar smile stretched across her face again.

"Nope."

"You're just toying with me again?"

"Yep."

"Fine. New house rule: no fox tricks."

She laughed in my ear, low, throaty, and with all sorts of promises. "That's the best part, Fort," she crooned. "I'm not even having to use them on you."

Well, shit.

I woke up the next morning feeling every bump and scrape from my misadventure with the Providence nightlife, plus a few extra bodily protests as a result of sleeping on my futon, which had the distinction of being the cheapest that IKEA could offer. Suzume had gotten the bed. This hadn't been from any chivalrous offer on my part—she had claimed it with the same subtlety she had shown in every other aspect of her behavior as a houseguest—namely, none. When I'd put up a protest at being kicked out of my bed, pointing out that as my bodyguard she really ought to be putting herself between me and any threat that might come through the front door, she had conceded my point and then offered to share the bed. Then she'd started stripping down, at which point I had made a tactical retreat to the futon.

As I staggered to the bathroom to dry-swallow some desperately needed painkillers, Suzume bounced out of my room. She was already dressed in the same black boots and tight pants as yesterday, but now topped off with a loosely fit lime green T-shirt that hit her around midthigh. The sight of her had me shaking an extra Tylenol out into my palm. I had a feeling I'd need it soon.

"Your alarm went off about five minutes ago," she said, sitting on the edge of the tub.

"Did you consider waking me up?" I asked. I'd assumed that I'd gotten up early. Now I was going to have to hurry.

"You're up now anyway." She shrugged. "Didn't seem important." She kicked her feet lazily. "Are we doing anything fun today?"

I was starting to see why her ancestor had left Japan. If she was anything like Suzume, she'd probably been encouraged to leave with torches and pitchforks.

"*We're* not doing anything, Suzume. *I'm* going to work."

"As your bodyguard, I go everywhere that you go. Even the shittiest and most boring places. I hope you understand the sacrifice I'm making for you. You can make me an omelet to make up for it."

I stared at her. "You expect me to cook for you?"

"Aren't I your guest? I know that Americans have different standards of hospitality than the Japanese, but I was raised with the understanding that a host was supposed to prepare meals for his guests."

"You aren't my guest!" I yelled. "My mother hired you to protect me! Which so far you've been shitty at!"

She stared at me for a long moment. I'd startled myself with my volume, and as I looked at her, with that beautiful face and eyes like a kicked puppy, I immediately regretted it.

"So . . . no breakfast?" she asked.

I closed my eyes, told myself I was an idiot, and looked at her again. "I'll get something for you on the way to work."

Like a flipped switch, she was gleeful and excited again. "Excellent. You don't have eggs anyway." She sashayed out of the bathroom while I stared after her. Then her head popped back in through the open doorway. "You'll need to hit the grocery store today. It wasn't polite to mention last night, but you really are not prepared to entertain."

Then she was gone again. I closed my eyes and banged my head against the mirror.

Twenty-five minutes and two breakfast sandwiches later, we were finally on the bus to work. Naturally this was when she decided to interrogate me about Beth, much to the delight of two elderly women, who turned up their hearing aids and listened raptly as Suzume browbeat me into discussing highly personal relationship details and then insisted on analyzing them.

"No, I'm really sure that if you're going to have an open relationship, it has to be preagreed upon by both parties beforehand. Otherwise that's just postsanctioned cheating, which is still cheating." Suzume was sprawled across three bus seats. One of her booted feet tapped against my leg, and the other one hung down to sway back and forth with the motion of the bus. Since I've gotten evil looks for just resting a bag of groceries on adjacent bus seats, it was really frustrating to see everyone just give Suzume indulgent smiles, even though there were actually a few guys in business suits standing for lack of open spaces.

"If you're this curious about her reasoning, why don't you just ask Beth?" I said, trying to withdraw farther into my own seat.

"Already did," Suzume said. "I find her line of reasoning to be extremely defensive and ex post facto." She gave me a sly smile. "That last part means 'ass-covering.' Which she didn't seem to appreciate me pointing out, by the way."

"What? How? How did you ask her?" I sputtered. Across from us, a trio of adolescent boys in soccer uniforms leaned closer, fascinated.

"Facebook. Your settings don't log out when you close your browser."

"My computer is password-protected!"

"Which might have slowed me down if you didn't keep your passwords listed on an index card in your desk drawer."

Horror filled me. "You have my passwords?" I asked.

"Don't worry, I changed all of them for you."

Nothing was coming out of my mouth except strangled moans. Two seats down from me, a tall woman who looked like Pam Grier circa Foxy Brown, albeit in a linen business suit, leaned forward and said, "Boy, you are screwed." There was a general round of head nodding.

"I don't need help figuring that out," I snapped.

"Don't be snide, young man," one of the elderly woman scolded. "If you were foolish enough to keep dating that awful girl after she slept with Larry, then there's no knowing what you're foolish enough to think." A murmuring of agreement rose around the bus.

"Do you see what you've done?" I asked Suzume.

"Yes," she said, complete delight filling her face. "I've solicited audience participation. Now"—she turned to address a pigtailed girl in a Dora the Explorer T-shirt who was traveling with her mother—"what do *you* think Fort should do about Beth?"

The rest of the bus ride was a new experience in humiliation.

"You have to start talking to me again eventually," Suzume told me as we walked into Busy Beans. I glared at her and pulled on my apron.

"I think you got a lot of really useful advice," she continued. "What I can't understand is why Beth hasn't called you yet. She had a lot of strong feelings when I was messaging her last night." Correctly interpreting my look of horror, she said, "Oh, I was using your account, but she knew it wasn't you. Just the really hot chick sleeping in your room who had a certain interest in determining the rules and boundaries of your open relationship."

I pressed my hands to my face. "My cell phone broke last night when I fell on it."

"Oh." Suzume considered for a moment. "You should replace it. She's probably left a few voice mails for you by now."

"What god did I offend badly enough that you were sent into my life?" I asked her. I wasn't kidding.

She leaned forward and pecked a playful kiss on my cheek. "Didn't I tell you that this was going to be fun?"

It was hard to fall into my usual routine. Jeanine was fuming because Tamara had texted her resignation fifteen minutes into the start of her shift, and was now doing a very poor job at manning the register. Suzume was keeping herself entertained by seeing how many sad hipsters she could con into buying her a scone. Apparently she was also adding a challenge to this by not eating any of her loot—just leaving it displayed prominently on her table. Thirty minutes into my shift, she already had five piled up and was hard at work dazzling a poor specimen in a Green Lantern T-shirt into providing number six.

It wasn't until the eleven a.m. early lunch crowd from the retirement community two blocks over arrived in a wave of canes, walkers, and polyester that I realized that I hadn't put out the day's papers. Jeanine's hissed invective filled my ears as I ran back to the service door where they were piled every morning. We stock four different publications, but only about fifteen copies of each, so I was able to grab the whole stack and haul it in. There's a shelf built beside the main counter, and I glanced at the headlines as I put each pile in its place. The *New York Times* was all Middle East politics, the *Wall Street Jour-*

nal was raving about a dot.com company going public, the *Boston Globe* was apparently shocked that yet another giant construction contract had apparently been bid out in a shady and potentially illegal manner, and the *Providence Journal-Observer*—

Normally the local city paper led with either kittens rescued from trees or whatever shenanigans the mayor had gotten up to this time. Today, though, the front page was devoted to a police sketch of a young girl who I immediately recognized.

It was Maria. The moment stretched, everything else fading away except the sight of the sketch in the paper, that face looking up at me. For a second I felt her wrist in my hand again, felt myself loosen my fingers and let her go.

Jeanine was yelling for me to get back behind the counter and take orders, but I grabbed the first paper off the stack and scanned through the article. Her body had been found beside a Dumpster just before midnight. With no missing person reports and no ID available, the police were asking if anyone had any information about her identity.

My hands were shaking as I looked at the sketch. I wondered if somewhere back in Italy there were people still looking for her. Was she a face on a milk carton, or had everyone assumed that she was dead long ago? Would anyone ever find a connection across the thousands of miles between Italy and a dirty alley in Rhode Island?

"What's wrong?" Suzume was suddenly at my elbow, her black eyes sharp and wiped clean of teasing. Her body was tense and alert, like a startled animal deciding whether to fight or flee. For the first time I believed that she was actually employed to guard me.

I tilted the newspaper so she could see it. Her dark eyes absorbed it quickly, then flicked back to me.

"Who is that?"

"The girl from last night," I said. I'd already told her about Luca and all the events at the mansion.

"How old is the paper?"

"It was this morning's, so probably a few hours." It was hard to look away from the sketch. The artist had managed to make Maria look more lifelike than she'd been when she still breathed.

"More than that. There probably wasn't much information at all by the time they went to print. I'll go find out more." Then she was off, making a beeline toward a slightly greasy-looking hipster sitting in the corner with his laptop. I shook my head a little and headed back to the counter. That particular guy was a regular, and notable because he spent hours in here talking to no one, playing online games, and stubbornly ignoring the implied courtesy of at least buying a cup of coffee before sponging off a business's wireless.

"Get it together, Fort," Jeanine hissed as I leaned over to take an order.

"Sorry," I muttered. I hoped that Maria hadn't been scared when she died. I hoped that she hadn't been hurting.

"Hey!" I looked up and into Suzume's triumphant face as she shoved an open Mac in front of me. The browser was already at the *Journal-Observer*'s Web page, where Maria's picture was still headline news.

"Suzume," I said, startled. "This is great—"

"Paying customers only," Jeanine snapped beside me. "Fort is paid to work, not look at whatever LOLcat's picture you've found now."

"No problem," Suzume said, with a smile that was more teeth than good intent. She made a little "come here" gesture with one hand over her shoulder. "Dougie?"

Freeloader Hipster shuffled forward, a slightly glazed look on his face as he dragged his eyes up from Suzume's ass. "Uh, yeah?" he asked.

"Scone me," she said, never breaking eye contact with Jeanine.

"Oh yeah, sure. Uh, one scone, please."

This was impressive, and the expression on Jeanine's face was one to savor, but I took advantage of her distraction to scroll through the article. There wasn't anything new here. They hadn't released any information about Maria's body, just a renewed request for any information, and a few sound bite interviews with representatives from a local homeless shelter and youth advocacy groups.

I reached the bottom of the article, not sure what I was even hoping to find. There would never be any justice for Maria. Madeline had already made it clear that she wasn't going to do anything, and the one other person who might also be outraged by this, Chivalry, had been told he *couldn't* do anything.

Then the next headline on the page caught my eye: HOME INVASION ENDS IN MASSACRE. Rubbernecking instincts at play, I clicked on it, opening up the article. The first thing that loaded was a family photo—the portrait kind that was taken around the holidays, with a fake fire in the background and everyone in matching sweaters. Mom, Dad, tween sister, kid sister, and the dog. Even the dog was blond.

Suzume had performed some kind of miracle, because now Dougie the Freeloader was regaling Jeanine with stories of his triumphs as a fifteenth-level night elf assassin. I skimmed the article. The wife's jogging partner had gone over for their morning run and no one had answered her knock. Doors had been locked, and most people would've just assumed something had come up, but apparently this woman had been the nosy kind. She'd peered into the window, and the next minute she was dialing 911. Both adults and the dog had been killed, fairly gruesomely judging by the quotes the woman gave, and the girls—

That's when I felt a chill go down my spine. Both girls were missing. I looked back up at the photo. The article listed the girls' ages at thirteen and nine, but they looked a lot younger. Both were blond and tiny, with rosy cheeks and a porcelain-doll prettiness.

Maria had been found just after one in the morning. I checked the article again. Police were estimating that the invasion of the Grann home had happened sometime after two, when another neighbor remembered hearing the dog barking like crazy.

If Madeline had told Luca that his efforts with Maria were effectively useless, and she no longer held any physical interest for him, I could believe that he would've killed her. But I looked at the picture of the two girls and felt increasingly certain that he would've gone looking for a replacement.

I looked up and met Suzume's eyes. "I need to talk to my mother."

Chapter 5

Two hours later my employment was hanging by a thread and Suzume and I had just crossed the bridge into Newport. Had Tamara not already quit that morning, I think Jeanine would've fired me, but she settled for not paying me for the time I had worked and calling it a personal day. I had a strong feeling that she'd be conducting interviews, though, and that it would take a lot of groveling for me to stay a member of the Busy Beans team.

The only thing more depressing about a shitty job is having to struggle to keep that shitty job. But for once I was refusing to think about my employment situation. Besides, having Suzume as a driving companion had been a new experience. Suzume had immediately appointed herself as arbiter of the radio, and she operated much like a scan button gone mad. Then there had been a series of increasingly convoluted verbal car games. Then she began taunting truck drivers.

"Listen," I said to her, distracting her from her current efforts to make the golden retriever in the car beside us go insane with barking. "I have a question for you."

"Go ahead."

"You think I'm right about the Grann girls and Luca, right?" Somewhere between having to sing "Ninety-Nine Bottles of Beer on the Wall" in a round and watching her flash an elderly female driver, I had begun to suspect that she was not entirely committed to this trip. Or that she had the attention span of a gnat. It was also possible that both were true.

"Absolutely not," Suzume said, not even glancing away from the window. "I think you're going Nancy Drew on two unrelated articles. And, yes, I do mean that as a diss on both your investigative abilities and your masculinity."

I felt nostalgic for that younger, more innocent time in my life twenty-four hours ago, when I hadn't met her. "Then why are you in this car with me, driving down to Newport?"

"Good question. First, remember the part where I'm being paid to guard you? The exchange of currency for services requires that I be in this car, even though it does not have functional air-conditioning. Second, hanging around in that coffee shop was making me regret my life choices, and the only person who needs to be doing that is you. Ten more minutes and I probably would've been forced to either set a fire or get you fired."

There was a short moment of silence while I digested that.

"I kind of appreciate your honesty," I said.

"You're welcome," she replied. Then she squealed, "Ooh, lobster special at that restaurant! After your mom slaps you down, let's go there for lunch!"

"I'm right, though," I told her. "I can feel it." I could. Every time I remembered the way that Luca had looked at Maria, and the way he'd subtly sneered when he'd told us about his disappointment in Maria hitting puberty. She hadn't been a person to him; she'd been a toy to be replaced when it broke.

"Keep feeling that, Fort. Just remember that I like extra butter, and I'm going to want a few extra of those lobster bibs to take home."

"Do I want to know why?"

"Most likely not."

When I had parked in Madeline's driveway and was getting out, I was surprised to see Suzume stretch out in her seat and prop her feet up on the dashboard, clearly settling in for a wait.

"Aren't you coming in?" I asked.

She looked surprised. "And guard you from what? My employer? Go in, get laughed out, and I'll wait out here."

"You should look into becoming a life coach, Suzume," I said. "I don't know what I did before having you and your support and positive feedback in my life."

"Made poor relationship choices," she said, sticking her hand out. "Keys, please."

Suzume, my unsupervised car, and the keys. The thought struck me as almost certainly disastrous. "No."

Surprise filled her face, chased quickly by hurt. Her lower lip trembled. "I just want to listen to the radio while I wait. You don't trust me?"

I forced myself to ignore the large part of me that now felt like an absolute jerk. "No."

She grinned. "You're getting smarter."

There just wasn't a good response for that one.

I knocked lightly on the door to Madeline's suite, and

went inside when I heard her immediate call. It had been years since I'd seen her this early in the day, which she always spent in her private rooms, tucked far away from the sun.

Inside, Madeline was partially reclined on her pink satin chaise longue. There was the ever-present cup of tea on a small table positioned precisely at her elbow. She was dressed in light brown slacks and a cream blouse, with flat orthopedic shoes, like any fashionable old lady ready for a casual day around the house that she didn't have to clean. Her deceptive granny glasses were back in place after their absence last night, and there was an open book of half-completed Sudoku puzzles on her lap. Her flat-screen television was normally concealed by a large custom-built cabinet inlaid with mother-of-pearl, but today the doors had been opened and she was watching Wolf Blitzer reporting from the Situation Room.

"Why, Fortitude!" she trilled with exaggerated surprise. "Three visits in three days! I must admit, all of this attention is quite going to my head."

"This is serious, Mother," I told her. "I think that Luca murdered two people last night and kidnapped their daughters."

Madeline gave a large sigh. "My darling, one day you will simply have to learn how to work your way up to news. I understand that conversation is a dying art, but it isn't yet in its grave, despite your best attempts. Now." She patted the chair next to her. "Why don't you have a seat and walk me through this slowly?"

I sat down in the spindly little chair she had indicated. I'm not a particular fan of antique furniture, a fact that is due almost entirely to spending most of my adolescence absolutely surrounded by it. Damaging a normal piece of furniture is upsetting, but whenever I accidentally bumped or stained an antique it was always treated as some sort of deliberate assault.

I explained about Maria's body and the Grann home invasion to Madeline. She put CNN on mute and listened without any comments, giving me her full attention. Her attitude surprised me a little, and in response I tried to be as analytical as possible, knowing that she'd respond best to that.

When I finished, she took off her glasses and gave them a thorough cleaning with a linen napkin. She held them up to her lamp, looking for any remaining dust or streaks, then carefully put them on again.

"I can see why you brought this to my attention, Fortitude," she said. "The two events are very suspicious, and both your timeline and suggestions of Luca's motives do make sense. But have you also considered that this might simply be a figment of coincidence and your suspicious mind? Tragic events have been known to happen without the help of vampires. Why are you so certain that a human wasn't the cause of the Grann family's misery?"

"Because it's not what a human would do," I told her. "I have thought about this, Mother, I truly have. A human wouldn't act like this. Someone trying to break in and take money might've killed the parents and the dog, but he would never have grabbed the kids. That's too much trouble. He would've either killed them too or locked them in a closet for the police to find. If it was a pedophile, he would've grabbed the girls out of the backyard, or on the way to school, or maybe even out of their bedrooms if he could. But he would've avoided the parents." The more I talked, the more certain I felt.

"Perhaps. But humans are infinitely variable, Fortitude, and a sociopath could have done this." Madeline was watching me intently.

"Maybe," I conceded. "But everything about this would make sense if a vampire did it."

Madeline's eyebrows raised. I flushed a little, but pushed forward. "If Luca saw the girls, and wanted them, then the parents are just impediments to what he wants. Killing them makes sense to him, because they're just obstacles and don't matter. Also, vampires avoid attention. A murder-kidnapping is a big splash, but vampires think long-term. If he grabbed the girls while they were going to school, or took them out of their beds, then the parents would spend the rest of their lives looking for their daughters. Other people might give up or lose interest, but not the parents. So they would always be a little bit dangerous. It makes more sense to kill them and grab the girls at once. Then it's just one shocking tragedy that the community will eventually forget about." I was shaking a little when I finished.

Madeline nodded slowly. "Very good, Fortitude. Very, very good. I am impressed. You forced yourself to stop thinking like a human, and to think like a vampire, even though that is what you spend all your waking hours avoiding. Yes, I am quite impressed."

"So you agree?" I asked. "You think I'm right?"

Madeline said nothing, simply looked at me. I felt a deep sinking in my stomach.

"You knew," I whispered. My throat was tight, and I had to force the words out. "You knew before I even got here that Luca took the girls."

She nodded once.

"You're not going to do anything about it. He killed two people. He's probably already raping two little girls. And you're not going to do anything at all."

"I granted him hospitality," Madeline said softly. She didn't look at me; she looked at the television, where the muted Wolf Blitzer was gesturing at a series of graphs. "Hospitality grants him the same rights that my children enjoy. To move freely in my territory. To engage with those who live within my borders. To seek prey as he wishes." She shot a look at me from slitted eyes. "I had not claimed that family, either as prey or as servants. To interfere with his hunt is to break hospitality. I will not do that."

I could taste the acid edge of bile. I got up and walked to the door. I was slow. Every bone in my body seemed to ache, as if I'd aged a hundred years in that chair.

"Fortitude." Madeline's voice stopped me when my hand touched the doorknob. I glanced back. There was something unusual in her expression as she looked at me. It almost looked like regret. "I'm sorry that this hurts you so much, my darling," she said. Her voice was gentle. "I don't understand what it feels like to care for the lives or the suffering of people you have never met. I will not break our oldest laws for you. But I am sorry for your pain."

She'd never apologized like this to me, not even when she ordered the deaths of my foster parents. Something had changed between us in the last few minutes. I opened my mouth to say something, I'm not sure what, but then I remembered the Grann family portrait, and the big smiles on the faces of the daughters. Maria had probably smiled like that once, before Luca took her.

I turned away from Madeline, saying nothing, and quietly left. Behind me, the sound returned to the television.

Outside, I didn't even hesitate before reaching back inside myself and plucking the mental string that tied me to Chivalry. I felt it resonate, and let my feet carry me to him.

The artificial light in Madeline's suite was designed to mimic sunlight, but nothing could substitute for the real thing. I followed the tug of the string downstairs, through the house, and onto the back stone veranda, where I was left blinking in the brilliant afternoon light of a perfectly cloudless day. Looking down the immaculately trimmed emerald back lawn, I could see the waves on Narragansett Bay extend until they met the blue horizon. I walked down the steps and hung a right, heading unerringly into the rose garden.

Calling it a rose garden was a bit of a misnomer, suggesting a few unwieldy bushes. This was a huge garden, constructed like a Renaissance folly, with probably at least a hundred different bushes, all meticulously maintained and constructed in a maze. The bushes were all high enough that you couldn't see over them, and big fuzzy bumblebees wobbled drunkenly from one bush to the next. Roses burst out from every direction in every imaginable color and variety, and the air was thick and almost unbreathable with their heavy fragrance. The walking lanes were paved with large slabs of slate gray stone and wide enough that four people could walk shoulder to shoulder comfortably. I'd spent hours in the maze, and now I made my way quickly to the center.

The center of the maze was paved with more stones,

with a few little wrought-iron tables and chairs set here and there. There was a small fountain featuring a modest mermaid sniffing a stone rose, and the water burbled and splashed soothingly. Bhumika's wheelchair was parked in one of the corners of the center, on the edge of the flagstones. She was dressed in a bright red sari, the edges of the cloth draped over her shoulder and hanging almost to the ground. Someone had sunk a large beach umbrella into the grass, and so she was shaded from the sun. All of her attention was fixed on Chivalry, who was barefoot and dressed in faded jeans, a white T-shirt, and a wide straw hat, looking ready for an Abercrombie & Fitch photo shoot. Under her direction, he was pruning a lilac rosebush with daggerlike thorns.

"Like this?" he asked, making a cut.

"A little more angle, honey," Bhumika said. "You want a clean cut at around forty-five degrees." Chivalry gave a heavy sigh, and she said encouragingly, "You're getting better." Before she'd been confined to the wheelchair, she'd spent all her time in the summer out here with the roses. Not just pruning and caring for them, but also crossbreeding them to try to create new varieties. Their suite of rooms in the mansion was stuffed with huge pots filled with grafted roses and all of her experiments in new varieties. Two years ago, at Chivalry's request, Madeline had had the old house conservatory renovated and expanded so that Bhumika could work with her roses even in the winter.

My foot scraped on the stone, and they both looked over at me. Bhumika was surprised, Chivalry was grim and resigned. He would've felt me coming.

Bhumika glanced over at Chivalry as he got up and

walked over to me. She was concerned, and I knew why. I'd never just dropped by the mansion before—I'd only ever come after campaigns of nagging. I wondered how much she knew about what was going on.

Chivalry kissed the top of Bhumika's head as he passed her. "This will only take a minute, honey," he told her.

"You know too," I said. "You know about those girls." I didn't even try to keep the accusation out of my voice. Chivalry wrapped a hand around my upper arm and began hurrying both of us away from Bhumika, and I let him. Behind us, Bhumika turned back to contemplate her roses, shutting out our conversation.

"Yes, I know," Chivalry said from gritted teeth. "And there's nothing I can do about it. You heard Mother last night. I am under direct orders not to have anything to do with Luca or his activities."

"And you're just going to do that? Let those little girls get hurt, be raped, when you could stop him?" I was yelling at him now, and I saw something spasm in his face. His pupils began to bleed out, his eyes now huge and black with temper.

"Yes, Fort!" he screamed. It shocked us both, and we froze. He drew in a long breath, and closed his eyes. When he opened them again, the hazel was visible again, and there was nothing that would've suggested he was anything but human. "Fort," he said, his voice quiet and controlled. "I know that this is upsetting, and that Luca's actions are disgusting and wrong. But you have to let this go. I'd help you if I could, you know that I would, but Mother has forbidden me."

"Let it go," I repeated. I looked away from him. All

around us it was roses, green grass, and sea breezes. It seemed almost impossible to imagine that anything wrong could happen here.

"Yes," he said. "Just let it go. You can't help them. You can't save them. You're going to live for centuries, Fort. You have to stop thinking like a human or you're just going to break yourself."

I turned my back on my brother and walked back into the maze. With one turn, Chivalry was completely obscured by bushes.

"Fort!" Chivalry called to me.

"Go back to Bhumika," I said, knowing he could hear me. "Go back to pretending that people don't matter."

The grounds are large, and it was a long walk back to my car. I was sweating as I opened the car door and dropped myself into the driver's seat. I sat and stared at the steering wheel, trying to sort through everything I knew.

Suzume had put her seat completely back, and was napping in the sun. The newspaper was stuffed up on the dashboard, open to the crossword puzzle, partially completed. I pulled it down and reopened it to the front-page sketch of Maria.

Suzume opened her eyes and watched me with mild curiosity.

"How much of all that did you spy on?" I asked.

"Rooms without windows in mansions stuffed with staff members are a bitch to get to," she said, not showing any surprise or even bothering to deny it. "But two people yelling in a rose maze is pretty easy."

"So you know that I was right."

"Yep. What are you planning on doing next, Miss Marple?"

"Miss Marple?"

"I've promoted you from Nancy Drew."

"Ah." I thought for a long minute. "Suzume, do you think you could take on a vampire?"

She gave a lazy, arrogant smile. "You guys don't seem so tough."

"But would you?"

"I'm being paid to keep you safe. If you decide to go knocking on a vampire's door, keeping you safe would probably involve kicking his ass."

"Good to know." I thought for another second. "Luca isn't like my siblings. I can't just figure out where he is, and I don't know how I'd find him in a place as big as Providence."

"I know someone who could probably help us with that," Suzume said.

I slanted a suspicious look at her. She gave me wide, innocent eyes.

"Why are you being helpful, Suzume?" I asked bluntly.

She gave a little shrug and pulled her seat out of the reclining mode. "This sounds interesting." She held up one cautionary finger. "But there's one condition."

I braced myself, trying to imagine what she would demand. "What?"

She held out her hand. "I get to drive."

I took a deep breath and handed over the keys. Her gleeful smile told me that this had been a mistake.

Suzume's driving was erratic and frightening, but I realized that if I could pry open my eyes and stop trying to push the invisible passenger brake, she tended to slow down. Her reflexes were a lot better than mine too, and she did seem to have a good understanding of just how fast she could get the Fiesta to go around turns without breaking loose. All the windows were down, and she'd found a radio station that played frenetically paced punk music, which she now had cranked up loudly enough that conversation was rendered impossible. We were both a menace and a public nuisance as we blared our way over bridges and through idyllic towns

At one point we were sitting at a red light and I turned down the music enough to ask her who we were going to see. After a few Wizard of Oz jokes that weren't nearly as funny as she seemed to think they were, she finally gave in and told me that it was her grandmother.

"That's who you think is going to help us?" I asked. "Are you nuts? My mother says that she's not going to get involved, my brother won't cross her orders, and you think going to one of her flunkies is going to have better results?"

A slam of Suzume's hand and the radio was silenced, and with a sudden right turn that left my insides shaking she pulled into the parking lot of a derelict Blockbuster. The car was thrown into park before it even fully stopped moving, and then Suzume was up in my face.

"Flunkie?"

I thought I'd seen every expression on Suzume's face, but until now I hadn't seen her really pissed off. There was a curl to her lip and a burning intensity in her eyes that made me take a few mental steps backward from my estimation of her as an ADD party girl. Her voice was flat and quiet, and the way she looked at me made me nervous. I'd seen house cats look at bottle caps like that.

"Maybe I misspoke," I said, backpedaling. "I'm sorry."

Suzume never blinked, just kept staring at me, but

slowly she seemed to calm down, and the threat level in the car began to diminish. I still didn't look away from her, and my eyes began to water with the effort of not blinking. It didn't seem like a good idea to break eye contact.

Finally she eased back in her seat and gave one slow blink. I took a deep breath and blinked about fifty times, trying to rehydrate my starving corneas.

Suzume pulled back out onto the road, but she drove slower now, and she didn't turn the music back on.

"How much do you know about the relationship between the kitsune and your mother?" she asked.

"Not much," I admitted. "I know that your grandmother had to ask permission to live in the state, and I know that Madeline has hired you from time to time to do stuff. I guess I assumed that . . ." I trailed off, not quite sure how to phrase it without setting Suzume off again.

"You assumed that we worked for your mother," Suzume filled in. I watched her closely, but now she seemed completely calm. But there wasn't any hint of her usual playfulness, and I still felt nervous.

"Yes," I said cautiously.

"I thought you were being deliberately insulting. I didn't realize that you didn't understand. But before you come into my grandmother's house, I should make sure that you don't make another mistake like that." She glanced at me with hard black eyes. "That would be very bad."

"Right," I agreed.

Suzume settled down a little more in her seat. Now that we weren't flagrantly breaking traffic laws, I could relax as well, enough to see that Suzume was actually a better driver than I was. Even when people were stopping short or pulling out suddenly, she always seemed as if she was expecting it.

"In Japan, the kitsune live in family groups," Suzume said. "Each group has its own territory, and to cross into another family's territory is an act of war. My grandmother grew up in the traditional way, surrounded by her mother and aunts, sisters and cousins. They lived in the city of Nagasaki, and they were known as a very famous family of geisha."

"They were—"

"More like courtesans than prostitutes. They were primarily artists and entertainers. My grandmother was a dancer, and people came from all over Japan to see her. Then World War Two happened. My grandmother's family decided to stay in the city instead of fleeing to the countryside, and they had enough connections that even when the war began turning against Japan, they had plenty of food and comfort. Then—"

"Oh," I said, seeing where this had to go.

"My grandmother wasn't at home when the bomb was dropped. One of her aunts was sick, and my grandmother was traveling to a doctor for medicine, a specialist who lived on the edge of the city. She saw the flash from miles away, and heard the explosion. She ran home, but there was no home left. Their house had been near the center of the blast, and there was nothing left. Her entire family was killed in an instant, and she was on her own."

There was nothing to say, so I just listened. Suzume's voice was completely calm, as if she was reciting a story that she'd heard a hundred times.

"Some of the highest-ranked officers in the military had frequented their home, so my grandmother was very aware of politics. She looked around the city and knew that if the Americans could do this much damage with just one bomb, then Japan couldn't keep fighting. She made her way to Kyoto. After the next bomb was dropped on Hiroshima, the emperor had agreed to surrender, but there were a number of officers who refused to give up. They attempted a coup to stop the orders from going through. My grandmother made sure that it didn't happen. Japan surrendered, and the Allies moved in. No more atomic bombs were dropped."

The car slowed, and we pulled into the town of Exeter. It was small and rural, a sleepy community under the canopy of green maple leaves.

"My grandmother stayed in Tokyo for a while, but with her family all gone, she wanted to leave Japan. An American GI fell in love with her, and she married him. He brought her to Rhode Island, and she met Madeline. My grandmother understood everything in Japan, but this was a new land. Its dangers were unfamiliar to her, and she was all alone. She and your mother struck a deal—Madeline would provide protection until my grandmother had created a strong, fortified position, and then my grandmother would return the favor." Suzume looked at me. "We're not subordinates, Fort. More like adjacent rulers."

"Thank you for explaining," I said.

"You're welcome. Just remember that when you're talking to my grandmother, you're talking to Atsuko Hollis, the White Fox. And she can fuck you up."

"Well, who the hell *can't* at this point?" I muttered. But Suzume heard me, and I was rewarded with a flicker of her usual smile, and I relaxed. There had been something unnatural about having her mad at me, and despite everything I might've expected, I didn't really like her serious side.

The house we pulled in front of was what's referred to as a New Englander. From the front it looked like a cute little farmhouse from the late eighteen hundreds, with white clapboard siding and neat black shutters. But then you stepped to the side and realized that someone had built a long addition off the back, probably when the farmer's wife had twins. And then a few wings had been slapped on by someone else about fifty years later. Then the second floor had been extended to cover the new ground floor, and the whole thing ended up looking like Salvador Dali had been the architect. I could see a trimmed yard in the back, but what really took the eye in was the forest. Tree management had apparently not been a priority for the kitsune, and huge old trees towered over their house on three sides, pruned back only just enough to keep them from actually leaning on the roof.

There was a wide poured-asphalt parking area, and a small barn that had been converted into a garage, but I couldn't see any cars.

"You didn't call ahead. Are you sure that your grandmother will be home?"

"Utterly certain. Look."

I looked. One of the downstairs windows was open to let in the breeze, and a small red fox was pressed up against the screen, watching us. When it realized I was looking at it, there was a flick of a bushy tail and it was gone. As we walked closer, I could hear the sound of small, scampering feet and soft yips.

Suzume led me away from the front door, to a small

side door that led us into a tiled laundry room that also seemed to double as a mudroom. She directed me to take off my shoes while she did the same, unlacing her boots and setting them neatly against the wall. I toed off my sneakers, then looked to her for more directions.

She was standing in front of the next door that apparently led into the main house.

"Okay," she said. "Now brace yourself."

She opened the door fast, and three fox kits tore into the room. One was the red fox we'd seen in the window, one was gray, and the smallest one was a kind of mottled cream. They were about the size of cats, but they were fast, and determined to sniff everything. Apparently the sight of us was a little too stimulating for the gray one, who was leaving a suspicious trail of droplets.

They surrounded us in a swarm of quick paws and fluffy wagging tails. Suzume just got a courtesy sniff, but apparently I was new and exciting, because quickly all three were balanced on their hind legs for extra height while those long wet noses snuffled at my hands and pockets.

I stood there under their furry assault. "Um, what should I be doing?" I asked Suzume, who was watching with great amusement.

"Petting them would probably be a good choice." Then her voice snapped, "*Riko*."

The red one froze, and I realized that she had a mouthful of fabric. She opened her mouth, and released my T-shirt and one of the tails of the long-sleeved flannel shirt that I wore over it. Both now had holes forming exact imprints of her teeth. I pointed at it and looked at Suzume.

"Yeah, the kits can be a little destructive if you don't

watch them. And if you don't start distributing head rubs, I think your shoes are next."

Yep, the cream kit currently had her entire long snout stuck into my sneaker. I began rubbing Riko and the gray kit behind the ears, and they immediately collapsed into puddles of contented kit. Jealous, the cream kit yanked her nose out of my shoe and came barreling back to get in on the petting. This began the unsolvable problem of two hands, three kits. I discovered that the kits were extremely willing to bodycheck and nip each other, and occasionally my hands.

Though I do have to admit, they were really silky, and it was like playing with puppies, except they understood what you were saying. Mostly. Riko really wanted to chew my shirts.

As I was rubbing, though, I did notice something. "Do foxes get the white spot on their tails when they grow up?" I asked. I'd seen wild foxes crossing streets, as well as Suzume's cousin in fox form last night, and they'd always had white tips to their tails. But all three of the kits in front of me were solid colors, with black stocking marks on their legs and a few black streaks on their muzzles.

"No," a new voice said from the doorway. There was a tiny Japanese woman standing there in a peach kimono with black flowers embroidered on it. Her hair was pure white, not even a touch of silver or gray, and she was obviously Suzume's grandmother. But she wasn't wizened or decrepit—there was a little wrinkling to her face, but she still had the remains of what must have been incredible beauty, like in pictures of Sophia Loren. Her shoulders didn't have any stoop at all, and she stood confidently and gracefully.

Meanwhile, I was crouched on the floor covered in kits, lightly sprinkled in something that I was a little suspicious was urine. Let it never be said that I don't know how to make a first impression.

"A natural fox has a white-tipped tail from birth," Atsuko continued. "But a kitsune must earn her white." Her gaze was steady while she evaluated me. Apparently done, with no indications at all what she thought, she looked over at Suzume, and her expression became exasperated. "Have you been fired already, Suzume-chan?"

Suzume looked hurt. "Grandmother, why would you think that?"

Atsuko sighed. "Because I know you, Suzume-chan."

We relocated to the living room. Atsuko had a very minimalist decorating style. The hardwood floors in all of the rooms were polished and gleaming, with as little furniture as possible. There were a few decorations on the wall—a few painted fans, a few framed photographs. It looked a little weird in an old sprawling farmhouse, but after the overgilded clutter of my mother's mansion, this was soothing. There was a wide fireplace on one side of the room, the old kind that used to function both for warmth and cooking. Its oak mantel was massive, and completely bare except for one small sculpture, made of bone white china. It was a man in long, old-fashioned Japanese robes, standing on the backs of two foxes.

The living room had two low, long sofas around a low coffee table, and a few wide light brown cushions pushed up against the walls. When the kits climbed onto those and promptly conked out for naps, their purpose was pretty clear.

"Grandmother has had to adapt to our Western aversion to sitting on the floor," Suzume explained as we settled onto one sofa and Atsuko knelt on a mat beside the table.

"And I have had to mourn the poor posture of all my children and grandchildren as a result," Atsuko said. What followed then was a forty-five-minute tea ceremony that was beautiful, ritualistic, and nearly had me screaming with frustration. If Suzume hadn't warned me in the car about her grandmother, I probably would've broken in and tried to start talking about the Grann girls, but I forced myself to be patient. Ceremony had been important last night when Madeline offered Luca hospitality, and I could only assume that this was also important, so I followed Suzume's lead.

Every move Atsuko made seemed weighed with importance. She had incredible powers of concentration too. At one point the kits woke up again, and began to play with a small squeaky tennis ball. This involved a lot of yelping, tumbling, and biting. It was pretty clear that Atsuko's lack of knickknacks and extra furniture wasn't just a decorating preference. For three small kits, they seemed capable of an incredible amount of destruction.

Atsuko was finally pouring the tea when the gray kit propped her head on Suzume's knee and gave a loud whimper.

Suzume looked down. "Do you need the potty, Yui?"

The kit nodded.

"You know what to do."

The kit whimpered and nudged Suzume with her nose.

"No, I'm not going to open the door for you. You're a big girl now."

The kit slumped back on her haunches and gave a loud, high crying sound. Then she looked over at me hopefully.

"No," Suzume said sharply. "He's not going to open the door either."

Some more whimpering, a very betrayed look at me, and then the kit opened her mouth widely and gave a loud, hacking cough, like a cat with a hairball. Her back arched, and her tail began spasming. As I watched, her long muzzle began to retract, her fur slowly withdrew into her body, and then she was a writhing ball of something that I finally glanced away from, looking at Suzume and Atsuko. Neither of them looked remotely concerned. I glanced back, and there was a little girl, maybe three years old, and stark naked, sitting on the floor and panting. Her eyes had the same delicate tilt as the older women's, but her facial features were much more softly rounded, and her hair was an almost shockingly bright shade of red. Apparently Atsuko's progeny had been crossbreeding pretty heavily with the locals, because other than her eyes, Yui looked like she could've stepped right out of a South Boston Sunday school playgroup.

She made a very foxy squeak.

"Human words when you're human," Atsuko said with a firm discipline that reminded me of my third-grade teacher, who could control an entire classroom of children just by frowning.

"Not nice," Yui said to Suzume, then pulled herself off the floor and walked out of the room, followed closely by the cream fox. Left alone, Riko claimed the tennis ball and made a few victory laps around the room.

"Is that what it looks like when you shift?" I asked Suzume.

"I'm a lot faster," she said. "It's kind of like tying your shoes. Little kids don't have good motor control, so it takes a long time, but an adult can do it without even thinking about it."

"And the business about the door?" From down the hallway there was a loud splash, a child's shriek, then the flush of a toilet.

"They need a human hand to open the bathroom door. But when I was her age, my sister and I would wait until the other one had to go human to pee, and then we'd try to push her into the toilet and flush it."

Atsuko gave a loud snort. A minute later Yui walked in, leaving a long trail of water. The cream kit followed, looking extremely smug.

"I guess Tomomi knows that trick too," Suzume said blandly.

The tea ceremony continued. Yui didn't change back into a fox, but the other two continued to play with her. No one seemed interested in suggesting that she get dressed, so I assumed that being dressed in a state of nature was normal for the kitsune children. My foster mother had kept a baby book of photos of me, and I remember that there'd been plenty of me running around naked, apparently my favorite state of dress as a toddler. Yui quickly curled up and took another nap on the cushions, which seemed to serve equally well for kit or baby, and the other two kits curled up with her.

Finally all the tea was drunk and the cups were neatly stacked up on the tray again.

There was a long moment while Atsuko arranged the long sleeves of her kimono just so, and then she gave a small nod. "Now why don't you explain why a son of the vampire has sought me out?"

So I told her everything, starting with when I met Luca and ending with my last visit to the mansion. She didn't say anything, just listened to what I said and watched me closely. Finally I finished. There was a long silence, and my stomach clenched. If Atsuko didn't help me, then my last chance to help those girls was gone.

Atsuko closed her eyes and sat. We waited. At one point I thought that she'd fallen asleep, and I glanced over at Suzume, who shook her head. So we waited. Finally she opened her eyes again.

"A troubling situation," she said. "Made more troubling by Madeline's promise of hospitality. By the terms of our alliance, I do not interfere when she or your siblings hunt humans. To become involved overtly could threaten this alliance, and so I cannot become directly involved. But"— she spoke over my blurted protest—"Madeline herself requested that I assign you a protector. To keep my granddaughter fully informed about these matters is a reasonable action. If she passes this information on to you, she is not responsible for what you choose to do with it." Atsuko nodded, her decision made. "Suzume-chan, use the phone in the kitchen and call Commissioner Phelps. Vampires rarely exert themselves much, particularly if they aren't planning to stay long in an area. If you get the addresses of the attacked family and where the girl's body was found, that should be an area for you to start looking."

Suzume nodded and went into the kitchen.

"Thank you," I said to Atsuko. "I really appreciate this."

"Do not thank me too quickly," she said with a thin

smile. "We have not yet discussed what you will give me in return for assisting."

"But you said you were just giving information—"

"That is my justification if this turns out poorly, which it almost certainly will. You are too weak to even hope to reclaim these girls by force, and I highly doubt that Luca will hand them over if you ask him to."

"Suzume—"

Atsuko cut me off, her voice hard. "My granddaughter has been paid to guard you, but she is not one to risk her life for another's. If the situation becomes dire, she will abandon you to your death and refund your mother's money."

"How can you say that about your own granddaughter?" I asked.

"Because it is the truth. She is the offspring of my most beloved child, and her sister is my chosen heir. She is clever, and she is strong, but she is a trickster, a *nogitsune*, and if you choose to trust her when the situation is no longer amusing, but is threatening, you will rue the outcome."

I didn't say anything. Atsuko tilted her head in a way that looked more like a fox than a woman, and considered me.

"But you have no choice but to trust my granddaughter, do you?" the old woman said shrewdly. "She is your only chance to save the girls. Who you seem very intent on rescuing. How curious."

"You know, today everyone seems to find the desire to get two small girls away from a murdering molester *weird*," I said. "It seems to me that maybe this is opposite-day, because I would think that everyone would be just a *bit* more worried about their own lack of empathy."

Atsuko gave a dry, almost coughing laugh. "You seem to misunderstand. I have spent sixty-five years in the shadow of vampires, and it is the fact that *you* have empathy that is so surprising. This is unusual behavior from a species whose actions tend to be predictably narcissistic."

"I'm not fully a vampire yet," I said.

Those bright dark eyes saw a lot, and Atsuko laughed again, a full belly laugh this time. "And you think that is the reason why you feel this way? Then you are a very foolish creature, vampire-child, like the tadpole crying that he does not want to become a frog because he does not wish to lose his tail."

"But tadpoles do lose their tails," I said, confused.

"Of course they don't." Atsuko smiled. "They are still there, just on the inside."

"Grandmother, if we've gotten to the riddle section of the visit, then it's time to go." Suzume came back in, carrying a Providence city map. She leaned down and kissed Atsuko's forehead. "I offered the police commissioner one free hour and he was more than happy to give me the addresses. We've got to run."

"I'm glad," Atsuko said. She gave Suzume a sharp look, then asked, "And did you also call Keiko? Your sister has been looking for you today, and has been most insistent that it is simply personal, and has nothing to do with the business."

Suzume grinned. "Oh, you're very clever, Grandmother. Yes, I called her, and yes, Keiko screwed up. But look at it this way—if she called me to take care of it, and I will, then does it really matter if you aren't supposed to know about it? And won't you probably be happier in the long run if you didn't?"

Atsuko frowned. "When I was a girl, a fox like you would've been beaten and left out for demons to eat."

Suzume's smile widened. "But I'm too useful to serve as demon chum. Also, too pretty."

Atsuko muttered something in Japanese, then focused on me again.

"What will I owe you for the information?" I asked her. I was hoping that she would settle for free coffee at Busy Beans.

Atsuko was thoughtful; then a look crossed her face that was very sly, very foxy, and not very nice at all.

"A favor," she said. "A big one, to be owed to me and mine from you, to be redeemed at a time and place of our choosing."

Oh, that sounded bad. But when I considered Jessica and Amy Grann, who were depending on me, it sounded worth it.

I agreed; then Suzume and I hit the road, driving back to Providence.

Chapter 6

"Can't this errand of yours wait until after we track down Luca?" I asked. We were back in Providence, after a brief fast food pit stop to make sure that neither of us passed out from low blood sugar, and Suzume was driving. Apparently she'd never been to this destination before, so I'd been crouched over the map trying to give her directions as we slowly prowled through a series of extremely affluent residential neighborhoods. I made a mental note that if I ever got money out of Larry, the first thing I would buy was a GPS.

"Nope. Business trumps philanthropy. I'm pretty sure Andrew Carnegie said that."

"No, I think Scrooge McDuck said that. And what kind of business is this anyway? Real estate? Ponzi schemes?"

"You can say that we're in the service industry."

"The what? Like waiters?" A woman with one of those insane triple-long baby carriages was crossing the street in front of us, and Suzume was able to turn completely away from the street and give both me a suggestive eyebrow waggle and a very salacious leer.

"No," I said in horror. "No, *no*. *Not*—"

"Oh yes." Suzume was thrilled by my reaction, and pulled a business card out of her pocket to hand to me. It was a Rolls-Royce of business cards—the glossy card-stock was the kind usually reserved for wedding invitations, it was engraved, not printed, and in beautiful scrolling font, so restrained and elegant that it screamed old money, it read *Green Willow Escorts*. A phone number was listed at the bottom. And that was it.

"I thought your family got out of the geisha thing," I said, feeling a little stunned. I didn't doubt that Suzume could con men out of their pants, but somehow I just hadn't pictured that she would be doing it so literally.

She laughed. "You look so appalled. I wish I could take a photo of this and make it your new profile picture. And why should we have gotten out of the business? Grandmother already knew how much money and power you could accrue. What kind of free hour do you think I traded to the police commissioner for the information you needed?"

"But you . . ." I struggled to find the words, and failed.

Suzume executed the kind of perfect parallel parking job that I could only dream about (parallel parking tended to be a forty-point sweaty endeavor for me), and then leaned into me, invading my personal space and sending my core body temperature skyrocketing.

"What?" she asked, and my head began to spin as I inhaled the smell of her skin. She traced my jaw with one long finger, leaving a trail of fire. "Don't you think I'd be good at it?"

I took a deep breath and tried to marshal my thoughts, refusing to acknowledge the frantic signals being sent from my lower body, all along the lines of "now, dude, *now!*" I saw that glitter in her eyes that only seemed to appear when she was particularly fucking with my head, and I was beginning to catch on that this didn't have anything to do with sex.

"You're not a hooker, are you?" I said.

"What makes you think that I'm not?" That sassy grin, that beautiful face, the body that right now seemed to be making a million promises. I felt even more certain.

"Because," I said, forcing myself to relax instead of tensing up. Okay, that wasn't even close to happening in my pants, but I could try to lie with my upper body. "You'd be a terrible hooker." Her eyebrows shot up, and I continued. "You always have to let me know that I've been had. You have to see me actually realize and acknowledge how awesome you are. You would never get a single repeat customer, unless he was a masochist."

Suzume slid back into her seat in a sinuous maneuver that made her look like her bones were made of jelly, dropping all the seduction. She gnawed her lower lip and tilted her head thoughtfully. "I wouldn't discount the masochists. They're willing to pay pretty well for discretion. And our employees are a bit more refined than your average streetwalker, so we like to call them escorts instead. But you are right, my temperament wouldn't exactly be a good fit. Besides." She shrugged. "Even high-level escort work here in America is a pretty far cry to what the geisha were in Japan. Atsuko moved from labor to management, and the nice thing about a family-owned business is that no one expects you to work your way up from the bottom." She gave a little Beevis and Butthead–style snicker, and I couldn't help smiling a little. Humor that immature was hard not to delight in.

"Yeah, about that." I held up the business card. "Shouldn't this be a little more, you know . . . explicit? I mean, aren't you trying to entice people into buying sex?"

Suzume gave me a look that was equal parts pity and condescension. Apparently I'd just wiped out all the respect I'd just gained. "Fort, anything that advertises itself as either VIP or exclusive just isn't. If all you want is a blow job, you can get that for the cost of dinner and a movie. The people who can afford our services are buying a lot more than that."

"They're buying sex, right? Because I'm with Bill Clinton—sex is more than a blow job."

"Okay, let's try a new example. There's a restaurant in New York City where dessert costs a hundred dollars."

"What, really?" I tried to imagine spending a hundred dollars on dessert, but couldn't. "Is it like that eight-person bucket of ice cream that you can get at some ice cream parlors, where if you can actually finish it it's free?"

"No. This is a two-scoop sundae."

"Is it made out of gold?"

"Okay, kind of. It has gold leaf in it."

"Then after you finish it you can go panning for gold in your stool and recoup some of the cost."

Suzume slanted a suspicious look at me, but I kept my face as innocent as possible. Of course, as a product of a liberal arts college, I'd spent whole classes discussing the idea of perceived value, but I wanted to see when Suzume would lose patience with me.

We made it through sunglasses, purses, jeans, and

high school cheerleaders before I finally realized that we'd been sitting in the car for almost thirty minutes.

"You did this deliberately," I accused Suzume.

"Or we were having a pleasant conversation about market economics," she said.

I glared at her.

"Okay, I did this deliberately," she admitted. "But if I hadn't, then you would've spent the entire thirty minutes bitching about how much time we were wasting. Instead now you only have to wait another ten minutes."

"What?"

She pointed across the street at a middle-aged man with salt-and-pepper hair and one of those perfectly angled jaws that are rarely seen outside DC comics or network news anchors. His suit could've paid my rent for two months. He'd just gotten out of a chauffeured black Lincoln and was walking up to one of the restored brownstones that lined the streets. When the door closed behind him, the idling car started up and left.

"Okay, so some guy we've apparently been waiting for has gone into his house. Why do we have to wait ten minutes?"

"If we knock on his door now, then he definitely knows that we've been watching for him to come home and he'll get suspicious. If we wait more than ten minutes, we run the risk that he might've just been getting ready to go out again, and we might miss our window. Ten minutes is just enough time for him to pee and get out another set of clothes."

Suzume leaned into the backseat and began riffling through her duffel bag, which she'd thrown into the car before we drove down to Newport. Dragging my eyes away from the curve of her rear, which was a medal-worthy achievement in itself, I considered what she'd told me.

"Okay, better question," I said when she wiggled back into her seat, holding a black women's suit jacket. "Why are we stalking this man?"

"We're not stalking," she replied, pulling on the suit jacket and smoothing out a few wrinkles. Then she flipped down the sunshade and began to use the vanity mirror to arrange her hair in one of those smooth uptwists that professional women on television always seemed to be wearing, and that I'd rarely seen in person outside of my senior prom. "We're providing customer service."

"Green Willow Escorts does door-to-door customer service?"

"Green Willow Escorts charges five thousand dollars as the flat nightly fee, and this particular client is the CEO of a Fortune Five Hundred company. That means boatloads of personal income, and even a little more if he likes to cook the books at work. So not only do we do door-to-door customer service, but we also send our clients birthday presents."

"Like a stripper-gram?"

"Like monogrammed ties, Fort. Ashtrays if they're smokers." A quick application of eyeliner and she gave me an urgent gesture. "Come on, time to go."

"Fine," I grumbled, getting out of the car. "But can you at least make this quick?"

"I'll do my best, but artistry can't be rushed," she responded.

As we walked across the street I realized how different Suzume looked. It wasn't just the jacket and the hair, though they did make an impact. But she wasn't walking with the long, almost strutting steps that I'd become used to. She'd shortened her steps almost to a mince, and her posture became completely straight rather than casually slouched. Her head dipped a little, and her eyelids seemed heavier. There was something weirdly . . . submissive about her suddenly.

"Suze," I asked, feeling very disturbed by the change. "What's going on?"

She looked over at me beneath those heavy lids, and gave me a quick wink. "Just roll with this, Fort. It'll be fun." She rang the bell, and I had to swallow what I would've said, which was an observation that every time she said that, what followed was never fun.

"Will he have a butler?" I whispered as I heard footsteps approaching. "If he spends that much money on hookers, he's got to be loaded."

"No," Suzume said, her lips barely moving. "This guy likes privacy."

Sure enough, it was the man we'd seen on the street who opened the door. He didn't look happy at all to see us, but before he could say anything Suzume gave a formal head dip that almost looked like an abbreviated bow, and held out one of the Green Willow business cards she'd shown me earlier.

"Mr. Delaney," she said, and I almost jumped out of my skin at the change in her voice. It was as soft as if she were whispering in my ear again, but something about the tone was wrong. It was higher, almost girlish. "It has come to my employer's attention that there was a difficulty in your appointment last night, and that it was possible that we had failed to meet all of your needs. If you have a few minutes to spare, I would like to discuss this with you."

A lot of emotions had gone across Delaney's face while Suzume talked. At first he seemed a little worried, but as she kept talking, he relaxed a lot. By the end, there was that look of smug superiority that I tended to associate with people who worked in high finance and didn't like waiting in lines to order their coffee.

"I was planning on going out, so I don't have much time," he said.

"I understand that you are an extremely busy man," Suzume said, almost seeming to shrink within herself while somehow remaining perfectly poised. "But the topic is a"—her voice became hushed—"*delicate* one, and if my driver and I could just step inside . . . ?"

Delaney looked over at me for the first time, and I tried to follow Suzume's lead and look submissively nonthreatening. It probably wasn't too much of a stretch. Delaney looked me up and down, sneered, and dismissed me as useless. Even though it was what I'd been aiming for, it pissed me off.

"Fine, come in, but this will have to be quick." Delaney stepped back, and we both entered the house. It was decorated like a photo shoot from *Esquire* magazine—all dark leather sofas, parquet hardwood, oil paintings of English hunting dogs. All it lacked was the pop star pinup model in the middle of the room.

Delaney started up as soon as he had the front door shut. "Your service was highly recommended to me, but I have to say that I was extremely disappointed by the quality of what I received last night. I *might* consider using you again, but only if I receive a personal apology, a full refund, and a steep discount on any future transactions—"

He was interrupted when Suzume slammed her fist into his throat. One minute she was nodding, and the next she was moving. I stared. She was slower than a vampire, but that still left her a lot faster than a human. Delaney gave a strangled sound and started turning purple, instinctively clasping both hands to his neck. That left him wide open for what she did next, which was to slam a booted kick into his left kneecap. There was a very audible crunching sound, and if Delany had had enough breath he would've been screaming. As it was he gave a low croak as he collapsed onto the floor. She approached him fast, and he swatted out with his right hand, trying to ward her away. One quick move of her hands, a sharp snapping sound, and his wrist was hanging at a wholly unnatural angle. She repeated the action on his other wrist, and Delaney was able to let out one loud howl of pain before she'd slammed him onto his back and crouched beside him like a demented gargoyle, one knee wedged up and pressing on his abused throat.

I was frozen in the spot I'd been when the assault had started. "Suze?" I asked, incredulous. "What the hell kind of customer service is *this*?"

"The very necessary kind," she crooned. Her voice and body language were all back to normal, but her bright dark eyes never wavered from Delaney's purpling face. "Mr. Delaney," she said, "you were less than honest when you described your needs to us. You told us about your need for power, and for a woman's submission, but you neglected to also mention how you needed to elicit pain and fear." Suzume pulled a short black rectangle out of her pocket, and with a quick flip opened it to reveal a very long, very shiny knife. Delaney's struggling doubled when he saw it, but all Suzume had to do was increase the pressure on his throat and his struggles stopped. "Oh, none of that, Mr. Delaney. We were very concerned about what your escort, Shauna, told us about your requirements. She needed a number of stitches, Mr. Delaney. That's not the way we prefer to do business. We were also less than pleased when she told us how you had threatened her." Suzume pressed the flat part of the knife blade against Delaney's face and gave a long, almost tender stroke, removing a small section of afternoon stubble. He whimpered, and a dark puddle began to form on the hardwood beneath his legs.

"Suzume," I said. I wasn't sure what I meant to do, or what I even wanted her to do. Delaney had hurt that woman, and probably hurt her a lot worse than Suzume was suggesting. But I wasn't sure I wanted to see her kill this guy.

"My companion counsels lenience," Suzume told Delaney. "It seems that you are very lucky today. But I do wonder." And the knife turned, so that those long, slow strokes were now just cutting his skin, leaving very thin lines of red behind. Delaney's eyes were open and staring, driven past fear into some kind of animal stasis. "How many have there been before Shauna? No." She shook her head at him. "You don't have to answer me. You were very practiced at what you did. There have been quite a few. You're a monster who hides behind good looks and money. I won't kill you today, but I think I'll make it a bit easier for people to see the monster in the future."

Suzume smiled widely. Her mouth wasn't human

anymore—that was a fox's jaw and teeth that weirdly warped her face. Delaney screamed at the sight; then he screamed again when she struck.

He was rolled up in a corner when we left, his hands pressed against the ruin of his face.

"What an unfortunate car wreck you were in, Mr. Delaney," Suzume called brightly as she shut the door. "Just as unfortunate as the one you told Shauna that she had been a victim of. It would be quite sad if you found yourself in another car wreck. The next one would quite certainly prove fatal."

I drove. Suzume tossed her jacket into the backseat and took down her hair, letting it blow around her face in the wind from her open window. She closed her eyes and basked in the late afternoon sun. I watched the road, not sure where I was driving, just making certain that I put a lot of distance between us and that brownstone. Neither of us spoke for a while.

"Well?" Suzume finally asked.

"Well what?"

"You're a very puritanical sort of vampire, Fortitude," she said, not opening her eyes. "Am I a monster now to you?"

I thought about it for a minute. We sat in rush-hour traffic, but for once I didn't mind. Despite the poorly merging drivers all fleeing their jobs and determined to cause as many automotive close calls as possible, it felt like Suzume and I were wrapped in an untouchable, strangely lazy bubble.

"What happened back there?" I asked quietly.

"We screen all of our clients. It makes the service a

little more like an elite country club, so the clients are willing to pay even more, but it also is supposed to help keep the escorts safer. My sister, Keiko, is in charge of meeting the clients, figuring out what they want, and if they should be someone we do business with." She paused, then opened her eyes. "She fucked up."

"And Shauna?" I asked.

"She'll live. We're paying her medical bills, and Keiko said that the plastic surgeon is optimistic. But we can't take the memory of last night away from her. And so I don't know if she'll ever be okay. I hope so. But I don't know."

Around us horns blared as a Mass-hole driver attempted to force his SUV across three lanes of bumper-to-bumper traffic. Curses were screamed out windows and many insinuations about his mama were made. But our car felt peaceful.

"Don't think I did it for Shauna," Suzume warned. "Don't believe that I'm a defender of wronged women. It kept my sister's error from being brought to my grandmother's attention. It made good business sense to frighten him badly enough that he wouldn't cause the family problems later down the line."

"Okay," I said. I looked over at her. "Would you do what you did to Delaney to Luca?"

"Yes." No hesitation. "You and my grandmother have made a deal, and I'll hold up our end of the bargain. If I can make him suffer, I will."

I nodded. "You're not a monster," I said. "You're no angel, but you're not a monster."

Those dark eyes brightened a bit, and a small smile tugged at the edge of her mouth. "So we're okay?" she asked.

"Yeah." And I realized that it was the truth.

"Okay." Energy returned to her face, and she began wiggling in her seat. "I have to call my sister. Then we have to wait until it's dark until I can track your vampire, so let's get out of this traffic cluster fuck and get some dinner."

My increasingly limited funds eliminated Suzume's first three restaurant selections, and we finally settled on a corner pizzeria that was trying to hold the tide against the pressures of having both a Papa John's and a Domino's within a block by dropping their prices through the floor. It was mostly pizza by the slice, but they also had some rickety tables and stools set up in the back for anyone willing to brave their uniformly sticky surfaces and questionable hygiene to eat in. Even though they actually still had a pay phone in the back, Suzume conned the teenage, acne-ridden worker to let her use the staff phone by the simple method of blatantly flirting with him. What was sad was how little it took—just one of those lazy, naughty smiles and reading his name tag in a husky voice and he practically shoved the phone into her hands.

"That was cruel," I told her when she finished and came back to the table where I'd been waiting. "Poor little guy. It's probably going to be years before he has sex. You could've at least flashed him or something."

She grinned at me, then made a big show of looking slowly over her shoulder at the guy. The moment she made eye contact, he froze like a deer in the headlights. Suzume winked at him, and he dropped a stack of pizza pans onto the floor.

Suzume looked back at me. "I'm not sure he could've handled a nip slip," she said blandly.

"So mean," I said, shaking my head.

For my wallet's sake, we ended up splitting a pizza. Vegetarian on my side, meat lover's on hers. On a few bites I got forbidden mouthfuls of pork that were so good that I almost moaned.

"Come to the dark side." Suzume taunted me with her slice. "We have pepperoni."

I turned her down and returned to mine, reminding myself that zucchini on pizza not only tasted good, but had less morally suspect farming practices. My brain agreed, but all body parts below my neck seemed determined to want things that they shouldn't.

We'd both built up appetites, and practically inhaled the pizza. Soon all that was left was one last, lonely piece of the meat lover's. Suzume swore that she was completely full, but from that gleam in her eyes I knew that she was just taking another opportunity to torment me. I adjusted the beer list so that it blocked my view of the slice. Out of sight, out of mind. Suzume smoothly bumped the serving platter with her elbow, moving the slice back into my line of vision. I glared at her and moved the beer list again. This time she knocked her knee against the edge of the table, knocking the list completely over.

"Are we really going to do this?" I asked.

"Do what?" she answered, giving me those huge, innocent eyes, which were completely negated by that wide, canary-eating smile. "I'm just sitting here, making pleasant postdinner conversation. You're the one getting all worked up. Self-denial isn't good for you, Fort. There's science on that."

I snorted. "Oh, really? I'd think that the average waistband in America would suggest otherwise."

"I'm not surprised that you're taking such a poorly nuanced approach." Sitting up straight, she tilted her head in a way that made me know, just *know*, that somewhere in her house she had a pair of nonprescription glasses that she kept around for the days when she wanted to look pseudointellectual. "As a student of history"—and here I almost choked on my soda as she blithely continued—"I can point you to clear evidence of this. Just look at the Shakers. Complete nutters for self-denial. No booze, no fun, no sex. Just a lot of furniture construction. That reminds me of a certain fellow I've been hanging around with lately."

"The beer is five dollars a bottle, Suze, I told you that before," I protested. The shop might've been practically handing the pizza away, but they were charging an arm and a leg for the drinks. Sneaky bait and switch.

She was having far too much fun, and just ignored me. "Ah yes. You, Fortitude. You probably have some illicit stash of woodworking tools back at the apartment, right in the spot where your porn *should* be. But brace yourself, because I'm about to lay some truth on you that will blow your mind." She took a significant breath, which did things to her chest that I absolutely should not have been noticing.

"The Shakers died out," I cut in.

She shook her head. "Not even close to the lesson."

"Huh?" Okay, now I was confused. That was always the lesson when someone mentioned the Shakers.

Suzume repeated her significant breath and pause. I swear, this time she even added a completely gratuitous wiggle, just to mess with me. Well, me and the table of frat guys to our left who'd been staring at her since she sat down. She'd made at least four unnecessary pork jokes, probably the reason why two of them had suddenly untucked their shirts in unison. As for our unfortunate pubescent worker, his manager had banished him to the back room after it became clear that he was going to be unable to safely handle any objects with Suzume in the vicinity.

Her rich dark eyes locked with mine, and she lifted one eyebrow. Unwillingly fascinated, I leaned closer.

"The Shakers died out," she said, completely straight-faced.

I threw my napkin at her and she laughed, bright and happy that I was playing along.

"So, this sister of yours," I hinted.

"Yeah, Keiko." Suzume picked up the pizza and made a big show of biting into it. Like an opening shot of a porno show. One of the frat guys actually whimpered. Suzume rolled her eyes at the sound and muttered, "Dude, pathetic."

"Okay, Keiko," I repeated.

She shrugged. I huffed a little. A few hours ago I wouldn't have pushed it, but after the shared mutilation of a sexual sadist, I felt like we'd bonded. I nudged her with my foot under the table. "When you were calling the police commissioner, your grandma mentioned that your sister was her choice for heir, something like that. Is this the same one?"

Suzume made a small sound of annoyance and a bigger "yakky-yak" gesture with her hand, but scrubbed her mouth harder than necessary with a napkin and gave in. "I only have the one sister, so, yeah, she's the same. She's six minutes older than me, which is one of the reasons why she got the inheritance nod."

I paused, feeling a sudden pang. There'd been several times today when I'd wished that Suzume would either disappear or completely drop dead, but I hadn't wanted her hurt. "Sorry, is that a sore subject?" I asked.

Suzume blinked for a second, surprised, then laughed out loud. She opened her mouth to answer, but was overcome by a wave of snorts and giggles so extreme that she could barely breath. It took a few seconds of gulping air before she could finally edge her answer out. "Oh man, no. *Hell* no. Believe me, I'm grateful as fuck that Grandmother picked Keiko instead of me." She dabbed her eyes, then waved her napkin for emphasis. "Being heir means getting all the shitty jobs and having to behave all the time. Definitely not for me. I like being the heir's sister just fine—I get to have fun and kick ass all I want." Another spurt of laughter, then, "No, really, I appreciate you trying to be all sensitive, but that's not the problem."

Maybe I should've been offended by having her dissolve into a puddle of hilarity at my attempt to respect her feelings, but my stomach had unclenched as soon as I knew that I hadn't hurt her. And I didn't get the sense that she was laughing at me—there was something in the way that she snorted, with absolutely no attempts at sexiness, that made me smile. Okay, and she was as cute as a picture of a kitten sitting in a teacup. And that comparison was threatening enough to my masculinity that I cleared my throat and asked, "Then what was all the not-wanting-to-talk-about-it business?"

"Apart from not really wanting to chat about fox business to a vamp?" She grinned, and it took some of the sting out. Then she cocked her head and seemed to rethink something. "Okay, well, I guess you don't completely count as a vamp anymore. Grandmother likes you, and when you forget to be all emo you can actually be fun. New category for you, then: category Fortitude. Special rules." She shrugged, oh so casual, but she must've known how much that meant to me. Her attention focused back on the table, fussily brushing off some crumbs, clearly trying to lighten or at least move past the moment. "Keiko and I have been having problems lately. She's been the perfect granddaughter since we were ten and she got the tap from Grandmother. Then in the last few months she's decided to have a little teen rebellion. Which I guess since she's twenty-seven was kind of overdue, but she did the classic good girl thing and just went completely overboard. I've been covering for her, but now it's actually starting to bleed over into work, and that's no good."

"What did she do?"

She sighed, and reached across the table to pat my cheek lightly. "You're good peeps, but even category Fort has a rating system." She mimed locking up her mouth and throwing away the key. I snorted. As if that was even possible.

"You're not going to tell me?" I asked, torn between just being surprised and being somewhat miffed.

"Nope." This time she was serious.

Two could play at her game. I picked up the pizza slice, which now was sporting a giant Suze-size bite hole, and dared, "Even if I totally broke vegetarian commandments and ate the rest of that slice?"

Her wide grin was back. I'd known that she'd love that offer, and the sheer happiness she exuded at being played along with radiated through me. But she still shook her head. "Even then, buddy. Sorry." At least she meant that sorry.

"Fine." I tapped my fingers on the table and something from what she'd just told me popped its way back to the front of my brain for review. "Your sister was picked to be the heir when she was ten?" Talk about an early achiever. When I'd been ten it had been a big deal to have a teacher ask you to wipe the chalkboard down. It was years before I realized that they'd been totally Tom Sawyering us.

"Yeah." Suzume didn't look eager to discuss it.

I pushed her. "She must've been one amazing little kid."

"You'd think that, right? But not really. Well, she was amazing, I mean, how could anyone that closely related to me not be amazing, right? But she was just normal."

"So why . . . ?"

"Well, a couple reasons. None of this is really a secret, so I'll tell you. One, Grandmother has a little bit of a, shall we say, genetic preference. My aunts all went local, if you catch my drift, so the cousins, they're all quarter Japanese. I mean, you saw Yui's hair. Grandmother's first great-grandchild, and she's only an eighth Japanese. It's kind of like a shot of sake being poured into a vat of Baileys. But my mom, well, she was kind of an over-achiever. First of all, she was Atsuko's oldest, so there was always a little favoritism. But then, when she wanted to get pregnant, she slept with this total Tokyo-grown guy who was getting his doctorate in something or other over at MIT. Believe me, the heritage thing doesn't make any difference where it matters—a kitsune is a kitsune.

There are one or two caveats, but we pretty much breed true. My cousins shift just as quickly as I do, doesn't matter how diluted things are. But to the White Fox, it kind of does matter. So Keiko being three-quarters Japanese was big for Grandmother. Then"—Suze shrugged— "once our mother died, Grandmother decided that Keiko was the heir."

I paused, taking that all in. Or, mostly, filed it in the back to think about later, while I focused on the important thing to come out of all of that. "I didn't know your mother was dead." I knew what that felt like. Who knew what the circumstances had been? But I knew what it had felt like to lose Jill.

"I know. It's okay." She wasn't smiling, and wasn't trying to laugh this one off. But she wasn't giving me "back off" vibes either. We both just paused a second, letting it all sink in.

"What was her name?" I asked. That felt important.

"Izumi." And I knew from the way that she said the name that Suzume had loved her mother.

I reached across the table. I didn't take her hand, I didn't think she would've accepted anything so Hallmark channel, but I did brush the back of my fingers against her forearm. Not much. Just enough that I could feel her and she could feel me, and that she knew that I was being sincere in what I said next.

"I'm sorry, Suzume."

"It's okay." She nodded, letting me know that she meant it. Then she glanced back to the front of the store, and the moment was over. "Come on, it's dark enough now to start hunting."

With a total of eleven dollars in my wallet and even less

in the bank, we drove to the address where Maria's body had been found. It was in one of those areas of the city where the mayor had offered incentives for business investors to go into derelict factory areas and revitalize them into trendy lofts, chain store shopping, and unhygienic nightclubs. Parking in one of the maintained lots was expensive, so I circled around until I finally found a spot that was far enough from the main drag and poorly lit enough that no one had wanted to chance it. There was a spray of shattered glass under my door, indicating that someone had parked here before me and regretted the decision.

"Lock my duffel bag in the trunk," Suzume said.

"No one is going to bother to break into the Fiesta," I said, a lot more confidently than I actually felt. There were more expensive cars closer to the clubs that I hoped would distract potential thieves. But I put the duffel into the trunk just to be on the safe side, along with my CD collection.

"Hold on," Suzume called from inside the car. "Open up the side pocket and pull out what's in there."

I unzipped it, then sighed. "Suzume, these are your underpants."

"No, under the underpants."

Muttering, I looked under the tangle of bikini briefs and thongs, telling myself over and over that it was just fabric. Just silky, brightly covered fabric that happened to have a narrow string that went right into a certain place on Suzume's body—

Then I found the gun.

"Suzume, I'm not going to carry this," I called.

"Why not? Don't worry, it's stolen. No one's tracing that thing."

I sighed. "Not really the point."

"Fine, you want to go hunting a vampire with your bare hands? Be my guest."

I considered the gun in a new light. I'd once seen Prudence punch through a wall without breaking a nail. Having a projectile weapon to threaten Luca with did have a certain basic intelligence to it.

I pulled it out. It was a .38 pistol packed with hollow-point bullets. That was the same size as a standard-issue police revolver, so it had stopping power, but I wouldn't risk removing an arm if I shot someone with it. Hollow-point bullets, though, are designed to mushroom out when they make contact, maximizing damage, and that suggested that Suzume might've stolen this from someone who hadn't exactly been owning this for the right reasons. While I might've been a regular voter for Democrat candidates, I didn't inherently dislike guns, and I wasn't unfamiliar with them.

My foster father had strongly believed that if he locked his service gun in a box and hid it away from me, then it would just be something forbidden that I'd be driven to explore whenever I got the chance. So instead he'd made sure that I understood what it meant to him, and that it was a tool rather than a toy. He used to take me down to the gun range a lot of weekends, and I'd watch him work on his aim. He taught me how to shoot at the range, even though my scrawny little-kid arms had barely been able to lift his gun, and the recoil would've knocked me on my ass if he hadn't always been there, his hands wrapped around mine, his body bracing me against the kick of the gun as it fired. We'd even done one of those father-son gun-safety courses that had been held in a more rural area of the state. It had been kind of like Boy Scouts, but with more guns and flannel. About the same number of s'mores and sing-alongs.

I checked to make sure the safety was on. It wasn't, which made me shudder at the memory of how Suzume and I had been tossing the duffel around. Between this and the knife I'd seen her flash at Delaney's, I made a mental note to ask Suzume how many more deadly and concealed weapons she had stashed.

Which reminded me that right now I was the only person standing on the dark street. Suzume had seemed really confident that she could track Luca from the dump site, but as I closed the trunk I couldn't even see her in the car.

"Come on, Suzume," I bitched. "This isn't the time for a postmeal nap."

I walked around to the passenger door and looked in, then jumped back.

A coal black fox sat on a pile of clothing in the car seat. Seeing me, Suzume wagged her long dark tail ecstatically and began bouncing up and down in place. Little whining noises emerged from her throat, but those bright button eyes were full of human intelligence and her retracted switchblade was clutched tightly between her teeth.

There was no doubt in my mind—this twenty-pound ball of fur was ready to kick ass. I tucked the gun in the back waistband of my pants, checking to make sure that my flannel overshirt concealed it and trying not to remember how many different state firearm laws I was currently breaking, and opened the door.

Suzume hopped gracefully down, then gave me a little grunty "ugr" sort of yip, slightly muffled behind the switchblade, and began walking down the middle of the sidewalk toward our destination. I followed, praying we wouldn't bump into anyone. Looking at Suzume walking in front of me, I realized that there was the same kind of implied strut to her step as a fox as there was when she was a woman.

In the car, with the sense of camaraderie surrounding us, I'd been completely confident in what we were doing, and that Suzume would back me up. Now, as we walked through the dark streets of Providence, I had to work hard to ignore Atsuko's warning. I reassured myself that, from the prance in her steps, at least Suzume still seemed to be having fun.

It took a while to make our way to where Maria's body had been found. Suzume's large pointed ears were cranking around on her head like independent satellite dishes, and every time she heard someone approaching we had to duck into the nearest alley until they passed. There wasn't a single spot of white on Suzume's body, so she could drop into small shadows and practically disappear, but I had a harder time. Usually there were some empty boxes or a Dumpster for me to hide behind, though on a few occasions I just hugged the walls and hoped no one glanced the wrong way. Along the way, I stepped into many things that I regretted.

It made sense for Suzume to avoid being seen—after all, someone would have to be intoxicated to the point of brain damage to mistake her for a dog, and the last thing we needed was someone calling animal control. But I was hunkering down for another simple reason—we really didn't have time for me to get mugged again.

After a lot of close calls with drunken sorority girls

(who, given my luck the last few days, would still probably have mugged me), we reached the spot. There were a few strips of police tape still clinging to the side of the alley, and I ducked under them. I looked around. There was a closed-down bar on one side of us, and a florist's shop that closed at the end of normal business hours on the other. It was more of the same across the street, so Luca had minimized his chances of getting caught.

Suzume was canvassing the alley, nose to the ground, crossing and recrossing as she formed what I realized was a grid formation. I tried to imagine how many different smells there must be in this alley, and how she could possibly sort through them, and I could feel my hope start waning. We were basing everything on Suzume's ability to sort out one single thread of scent that was almost twenty-four hours old and that she'd never even encountered before. I hadn't even been able to offer her Luca's old pillow case, like in movies where bloodhounds were being used.

A thought occurred to me. "How are you even going to be able to figure out which scent you should try to follow?" I asked.

Suzume gave a deep sigh, then set down her knife. She hunched up her shoulders, rolled her eyes, and lifted her upper lip to display her impressive canine teeth. Then she gave a long hiss and dragged herself forward a few steps. Then she dropped down to her belly, covered her nose with both front paws, and whimpered.

I'm not usually that good at charades, but, "Vampires smell bad?" Well, that was a bit of a hit to the ego. I made a mental note to slap on a little Old Spice tomorrow, then gave myself a mental slap to remember that was definitely not trying to get a fox interested in me. If she thought I smelled bad, then that was a good thing, right?

Suzume bobbled her head back and forth in a so-so sort of gesture.

"Okay, we don't really smell bad . . . we smell different than humans?"

Suzume nodded, and I felt relieved. Then she shot me a long-suffering look.

"Sorry," I apologized. "I won't interrupt you again."

She gave a little huff, picked her knife back up, and returned to the important business of sniffing.

I leaned up against the alley wall and watched. A few times Suzume would backtrack, her eyes slitted in concentration. Her tail was low to the ground now, held only just high enough to keep from dragging, all business. Once she licked the ground, and I shuddered. If the sight of that didn't convince me that wanting to kiss this woman was a bad idea, nothing would.

It was a warm night, with just enough breeze that I was grateful for my flannel shirt. Suzume's fur was sleek and thin, a fox's summer coat, but she seemed completely at ease. I wondered if Maria had been cold in her last minutes, or warm. Were these alley walls the last thing she saw, or was she already dead by the time she was brought here? The police commissioner had promised to e-mail Suzume scanned copies of the reports, but in all our running around this afternoon there hadn't been time to grab time at a computer. My phone was dead, and Suzume wasn't even carrying one. She said that she'd broken so many of them that now her cell phone lived in its charger in her apartment. If this didn't work, hopefully we could tease out some sort of clue from the accident reports.

A low yip brought me out of my depressing thoughts. Suzume was staring off into the distance, in perfect profile to me, executing a pointing position worthy of an oil painting. When she saw that she had my attention, she carefully set down her switchblade, then dropped her jaw open to loll her tongue in a foxy grin. Her tail was flipping in a way that could only be described as smug.

"You got something? Something real?" She bobbed her head. "You're amazing, Suzume!" She gave a little shrug of her shoulders and wiggled one paw as if to say, *Tell me something I don't know*.

Now she was tracking something, and Suzume moved fast, running through alleys and along sidewalks. I jogged to keep up with her, and as we moved farther and farther away from the dump site, the trail never going openly into streets or buildings, but always hugging the edges, I took great comfort in the gun stuffed in my waistband, reaching back to press my hand against it. The flaws in my plan (or, rather, lack of a plan) were feeling very obvious as I followed a fox toward an unknown destination.

Chapter 7

We'd left the revitalized strip of nightclubs behind, and entered a block that was primarily day businesses with a few small restaurants, mostly the sort that catered to lunch crowds or early dinners, mixed in. Suzume was tracking steadily when the wind shifted. I could feel it in a strong gust that made me shiver, but it hit her like an electrical current. Her head snapped up sharply, she inhaled, and then she had switched directions and went tearing across the street. Startled, I began to ask what she was doing, then gave up and chased. She had outpaced me before we even crossed the street (which fortunately in this area was mostly deserted, lacking the evening entertainments that drew crowds and cars elsewhere), so I had to concentrate on following her tail. A few times she paused and glanced back toward me, and I could see her impatience as she hopped in place until I'd caught up enough for her; then she'd be off and running again.

I was sprinting hard and gulping air. Clearly my usual workout sessions of standing still and pouring coffee were not enough to keep pace with a fox. I was concentrating so hard on not being left behind that I didn't slow down the next time she stopped right in front of another alley, and I almost barreled over her when she failed to start running again like all the other times. She gave a low, muffled yip, but I was already stumbling, and barely avoided falling on my knees. I made a lot of noise, and when I saw what Suzume was looking at I could've cursed myself.

We were between a bakery and one of those small satellite bank branches that just consist of an ATM in one of those controlled-access rooms that's supposed to make people feel like they're less likely to get mugged when they get money late at night. There weren't many streetlights in this area, but there weren't any clouds tonight, and there was enough moonlight that I had a clear view down the alley that ran between the two buildings. Signs of the bakery were very evident in a pile of empty cardboard boxes and a nearly overflowing Dumpster.

Phillip, Luca's host, was standing right next to the Dumpster. My skid and near fall had startled him, and he was looking up at us with eyes that gleamed too brightly, almost glowing in the moonlight. The expensive clothes from the night at the mansion were gone. Now he wore plain shorts and a sleeveless T-shirt, with thong sandals on his feet. Everything was matted and filthy, with so many tears that it was a wonder that it hadn't fallen off him. He was carrying something wrapped in those white trash bags you buy at the grocery store, something long that he had been carrying with both arms. He shifted a little, hissing at us like a startled cat, and I saw that there was long blond hair hanging down from one end of his bundle.

It was one of the Grann girls; I couldn't tell which.

There were dark smears on the white trash bags, and when I looked closer I could see that it was blood. I couldn't tell if it was hers, because it was covering Phillip's hands, and it smeared wherever he'd held her.

"Put her down, Phillip," I said loudly. I couldn't remember drawing the gun, but it was in my hands now, a solid and comforting weight. At my feet, Suzume growled loudly, dropping her switchblade onto the ground and opening her mouth to display those sharp white teeth.

"Mine, Master said," Phillip gibbered. He'd never spoken at the mansion. His voice was hoarse, almost broken, garbling and chewing at each word. His eyes were rolling around wildly, showing the whites, and I wasn't sure if he recognized me from the other night, or if he even knew what was standing at the mouth of the alley, just that something was there. Spit flew with every word he said, and there was dirty foam caked in the corners of his mouth. "Master said, Master gave. Mine!" He crouched down low, almost squatting, even though he never looked away from where we were standing. His arms tightened on the bundle in his arms, and even though the girl didn't make a sound, I could see the bunching of his arm muscles and knew how hard he was gripping her.

"Put her down and back away!" I raised the gun, holding it two-handed for better control, and sighted down at him. My legs had spread without even thinking about it, and I could almost feel Brian's hands on my arms, feel him behind me, holding my body in the right position. The years fell away and the stance felt as natural as if I'd been doing it every day, instead of not since I was nine. But I hesitated. The girl was in his arms, held low to his chest, but if I missed I could hit her. I hadn't been to a range in years. I couldn't trust myself to make this shot.

"No, no, no, *no*!" Phillip screamed. "Mine! You cannot take!" He squeezed harder. I heard something crack, and knew it was from one of the girl's bones giving way.

There was no time to trust myself. I squeezed off a shot before the echo of that crack had even left my ears. I felt the gun kick in my hands, but I held it steady. The bullet caught Phillip right where I'd aimed, exactly where Brian had always told me to aim when my targets had been paper outlines of bodies. Just at that midpoint between neck and shoulder, where it stood a good chance of breaking the collarbone. Painful enough to stop someone, but not fatal. There was a spatter of blood from the wound, and Phillip toppled back, dropping the girl in the process. She bounced once on the concrete, then was still.

Phillip screamed again, and there wasn't anything human in the sound. He lunged forward, arms swinging widely, and now was coming straight for me. I was still holding the gun, but now I froze. That had been a stopping shot—he shouldn't have jumped back up from that.

Apparently he didn't know that. I moved my target to his other shoulder and squeezed off another shot, but he was right in front of me and one long arm slammed into me, knocking me off my feet and making the shot go wild. The blow knocked the wind out of me, and I hit the ground hard, gasping. Phillip followed me down, his huge, blood-smeared hands grabbing at my shirt, then at my neck. Panic ran through me as his hands wrapped around my throat, and I began fighting hard, kicking up at his body and knocking my fists against his hands, trying to break his hold. But I couldn't knock his hands loose, and he squeezed. I gasped for breath, and my vision started to blur. Phillip's face was close to mine now, those gleaming eyes now all too focused, and I could feel his wet saliva hit my skin as he babbled.

Then there was a scream of pain and his hands suddenly let go. I pulled in breaths of air desperately, and my vision cleared. Suzume was on his back, her jaws locked deeply into the back of his neck. Phillip shook himself, but she hung on tenaciously, her teeth digging in deeper. He reached back and started smacking his fists into her, and she let go with a yelp. She fell, twisting as she went so that she landed on those catlike paws. Phillip had turned and was lunging for her, and she nipped hard enough at his hands that he pulled back with another scream. She'd left gouges across his palms, and one finger was almost severed, spurting blood as it hung back grotesquely, held on by only a thin strip of skin.

Phillip kicked her, and even though Suzume jumped back fast, he made partial contact, and the force of it threw her hard, and she hit the alley wall, her small head smacking against the bricks. He moved in closer, and my fingers scrabbled frantically around the ground. The gun was gone, and I couldn't find it, but when my hand found an old brick that had been knocked out of the wall and half-covered with garbage, I gripped it. Phillip was closing in on Suzume as she stumbled almost drunkenly, dazed from slamming into the wall. She was trying to hop backward, shaking her head, and she didn't seem to realize that she was blocked by the wall. I slammed the brick down on the back of Phillip's head with everything I had. I could feel the impact all the way up my arms, the hard surface of the bone giving way to a sickly softness, a hit that should've had him out like a light, if not dead, but Phillip turned and lunged for me. There was blood seeping out his ears and nose, and he was moving slower, but he was still coming. I pulled back far enough that his grab missed, but I stumbled on something, and his fist slammed into my side. Suzume moved in. There was blood matted in the fur around her head, but she was moving with intent again, biting wildly at the back of his legs, blood flying and staining her white teeth. He pulled up sharply, kicking again, and this time catching her full in the chest, sending her hurtling backward. I still had my brick, and now I slammed it straight into his face with as much force as I could muster. His nose crushed inward, but his eyes didn't even seem to register that. He grabbed for me, and I had to stumble back again.

Then Suzume was there again, running hard. She changed shape so fast that it was as if I blinked and a woman replaced the fox between one step and the next, going down to her knee, grabbing down with one hand, and coming back up with her switchblade completely extended. She buried it in Phillip's throat, shoving it in and then tearing it back out again, releasing a flood of blood as it sliced completely through his windpipe. Phillip went down on his knees, his mouth opening and closing soundlessly. I was flat on my ass, staring, and Suzume was in a half crouch, blade ready. A long moment stretched as Phillip rocked forward, braced on all fours. His head dropped down, and I let out a heavy breath.

Phillip's head rocked back up, bobbing wildly on his

half-ruined neck, and those unnaturally rolling eyes were fixed directly at me. His lips pulled back to bare his teeth, and he started crawling toward me, mouth working in a silent biting motion.

"Just *die* already," Suzume yelled, and shoved her knife into his right eye, both hands on the hilt as she put all her weight behind the strike. The blade went completely in, stopping only when the butt of the hilt knocked against the bone of the eye socket. Blood and awful, viscous things squirted out of the wound, and Phillip fell backward, landing sprawled out. His mouth snapped open and shut twice more; then he gave a huge shudder and didn't move again.

There was a long moment while we both stared, unable to move, tensed and ready in case he suddenly pulled another slasher movie stunt and came back for one last hit. But the glow of his one remaining eye faded, leaving it dull and dead, and I became aware of the ragged sound of our breathing. The adrenaline faded enough that I also felt every hit that he had landed in one almost blinding rush of pain, and I let out a very unheroic whimper of pain.

"Are you okay?" Suzume asked. There was blood running down her face from where her head had hit the alley wall, and she had one hand pressed against the right side of her rib cage, where a truly massive bruise was already starting to spread. She was also completely naked, which seemed like an impolite thing to notice after what we'd just experienced, but there it was. Even covered in both her and Phillip's blood, banged up, and rather dirty from rolling around in a filthy alley, it was still an impressive sight. I pulled my mind back to what was important.

I rolled from my back to my stomach. My body gave me a very clear signal that standing up wasn't a good idea yet, so I started crawling on my hands and knees over to where the Grann girl was wrapped in white plastic, still lying where Phillip had dropped her.

"Don't, Fort," Suzume called. I ignored her and pulled at the plastic around her face. It had been wrapped tightly, and my hands were coated in blood (both mine and Phillip's), but I was able to tear at them enough that they started to give way.

"She's already dead," Suzume said, not moving from where she was kneeling beside Phillip.

"No. No, she's not." I yanked harder, and the plastic finally lifted away and I could see her face. It was Jessica Grann, the older girl, but she didn't look like the smiling girl from the photo anymore. There wasn't any mistaking this for sleep. There were bites all along her face and throat, bites that had taken chunks of flesh. The plastic was still wrapped cocoonlike around her lower body, but I could see the top of her chest. She was wearing a little flannel pajama shirt, bright yellow, with cheerful daisies. Her eyes were still open, glassy, blue, and staring.

"She was dead before we got here," Suzume said. "I smelled it when Phillip dropped her. She's been dead for hours, maybe even all day."

"Why would he steal her?" I asked. It didn't seem right for her to be wrapped in trash bags, like junk, and I kept ripping at them, trying to get them off her. "Why didn't he just kill her with her parents?"

"I don't know. I don't speak crazy." Suzume yanked hard at her knife, but it was still lodged in Phillip's eye socket. She braced a knee on his chest and pulled again, harder, and this time it came free. "Don't touch her body, Fort. The last thing you need is for a CSI team to pull one of your fingerprints off her."

"I won't leave her like this," I said.

"Take the plastic off if you have to. We can dump it somewhere else, but just don't touch her, okay?"

"We can't just leave her here." Not after everything that she'd been through. We couldn't just abandon her again.

"Yes, we can." Suzume's voice was hard. "You can't help her, Fort." She glanced at Jessica's small face, and her voice softened. "We're right next to a bakery, and judging by the smells from the Dumpster, they use it regularly. Tomorrow morning someone will be taking the trash out and they'll find her. She won't be here long."

It hurt to do it, but I nodded. "Fine." I'd gotten all the bags off, tugging them out from under her, and I wrapped them into a ball. Jessica was lying on the dirty ground now, staring up at the sky. Her feet were bare, clean, and untouched. Somehow that was the worst part of this.

"Her sister," I said urgently, remembering Amy with a rush. "Suzume, can you track Phillip back from where he came from? Amy—"

"Is probably also dead. I can smell another little girl on Phillip."

That sudden flare of hope died. I looked down at Jessica and wondered if somewhere her little sister was lying in another Dumpster, wrapped in trash bags, waiting to be found. If she'd suffered as much as Jessica had.

"I need a little help over here," Suzume called, and I made myself pull back from Jessica. There was nothing left I could do for her. Beside her I saw the gun, half hidden under the Dumpster where it had landed when Phillip knocked it out of my hand. I pulled it out, thumbed the safety back on, and tucked it back in my waistband.

I was able to stand, despite shrieks of protest from my gut, ribs, and left knee, and I walked over to where Suzume was still crouched beside the body. She'd been busy while I was distracted. First she'd cut away what was left of Phillip's shirt, and had wrapped it around her hands like cloth mittens. Then she'd carved open Phillip's chest, and was now cutting out his heart.

"Suzume, what the fuck?" I asked. I didn't feel outraged at her desecration. Right now, with the knowledge that the girls were dead still seeping into me, everything was dulled, though I doubt I ever would've spared much outrage on Phillip's behalf. Mostly I felt tired.

"To kill an older vampire, you have to destroy the brain and the heart," Suzume said, sawing away at the last stubborn ventricle that held the organ in place. "Otherwise he can regenerate and come after you. Usually it's a good idea to torch the body too, just to be sure. Now, our buddy here might not be a vampire, but he stayed up long after we should've put him down. He was faster than he should've been, and I have some cracked ribs that say that he was also a lot stronger than a scrawny guy should've been. So we're just going to be a little cautious here." She freed the heart, and dumped it on the ground carelessly, where it lay like discarded meat partially wrapped in the fabric she'd used to help keep her hands clean. "Do me a favor and crush that with your brick."

"You're serious?" I asked.

"Do *you* want to just leave it unsmushed?"

Well, when put that way . . . I grabbed the brick and gave the heart a few good whacks, until now it was a very flattened piece of meat.

"And the brain?" I asked.

"It's already dribbling out his ears thanks to when you nailed him during the fight. Now help me haul."

Suzume grabbed his shoulders, I grabbed his feet, and we started moving Phillip from the middle of the alley-way to one of the back corners. While Phillip wasn't particularly heavy, neither of us was feeling very good after the fight, and we were both grunting and cursing a lot whenever we hit a sore spot, which we both had in spades. At one point Suzume surprised me by calling for a break halfway there. We both crouched down and wheezed a little.

"How do you know how to kill a vampire?" I asked. "I didn't know any of that." Not that that was a subject that was likely to come up over dinner, but I couldn't help feeling slightly miffed at how ignorant I was of our own basic biology. I'd always assumed that we were just like humans, only a bit faster and stronger. I did know that a wooden stake to the heart wasn't a great idea, but only because Chivalry always muttered a lot whenever he watched *Buffy the Vampire Slayer* reruns with me. I'd asked him once if it took a stake to kill us, and he'd told me that at my age having a wooden stake hammered into my chest would certainly prove fatal, but I could also get the same result with stakes of any other substance. Or by getting shot. Or stabbed. Or run over by a car. Or even eating bad shellfish. I'd assumed at the time that the takeaway on that lesson was meant to be that we were all fairly vulnerable. In retrospect, it apparently was meant to be that I, personally, was really vulnerable to everything, and the rest of them were just careful to avoid any aggressive movements directed at their chests.

"My grandmother told me."

"How does *she* know?"

"Oh, she asked around." For the first time, there was the hint of a smile. "Purely academic curiosity, of course."

"Of course."

We finally got Phillip's corpse to the spot Suzume wanted; then we spent another few minutes fussing around until he was situated the way she wanted. Now he was rolled up on his side, knees pulled up to his chest, with one arm under his head like he was napping.

I looked at our handiwork.

"Oh yeah, this looks like a completely natural death," I said. "As long as you ignore the gunshot, the smashed head and nose, the empty spot where one eye used to be, and, oh yeah, the *gaping chest wound*."

"I like the sarcasm. You must be feeling better. Now gimme your shirt."

I stared at her, slightly confused.

She spread her arms and wiggled her shoulders. "Naked, dude."

"Oh, shit, sorry." I found that I was still able to blush as I hauled off my flannel button-down and handed it over to her. Clearly I must've incurred some kind of head wound to not only manage to ignore her nudity during the entire heart-smushing and body-moving ordeals, but fail to volunteer my shirt before that. Clearly I was lacking in chivalrous moral fortitude. So to speak.

She took my shirt with a little smirk and a completely

gratuitous wiggle that had a chain reaction on some of her more interesting body parts. To my surprise, she didn't put the shirt on. Instead she turned it inside out and began to scrub off the blood that was still liberally coating her from the fight and her postmortem activities.

"Did I get everything?" she asked.

"Um, one more spot on your face."

"Thanks." She wiped it off, then handed the shirt back to me. I held it away from myself and looked at her, confused. She held her hand out expectantly.

"T-shirt, please."

"Oh, hell no," I said. "I gave you a perfectly nice shirt. It wasn't my fault that you decided to make it a washcloth."

"Fortitude," she said in a reasonable tone that set my teeth on edge. "We need to get back to the car without having someone call the police. That means that we can't be obviously coated in blood, and I really shouldn't be naked."

I couldn't really argue with her reasoning, though I did try as I stripped off my T-shirt and handed it over. She pulled it on, and it completely tented her, falling almost down to her knees. Then she grabbed my flannel and proceeded to mop me off as well. It did get most of Phillip's blood off, though it revealed more than a few scrapes and cuts, plus my own set of blooming bruises that seemed to completely coat my torso.

"So I have to walk back to the car shirtless?" I asked.

"While that would be lots of fun, no." Suzume turned the shirt right side out again, and held it out to me. The inside was covered in blood, and only the fact that it had started the night as navy blue kept it looking even semi-passable on the outside.

"You're kidding," I said.

"Very often, but not this time."

"It's *wet*."

"On." I knew that implacable look on her face. While it usually involved a demand that it was a meal-time, I knew that it again meant that I was going to have to give in.

In a night of increasingly gross occurrences, putting on that bloody shirt was right near the top. Patches of it stuck to my skin, and I shuddered as I buttoned it up. There was also some relief that I'd fed from Madeline so recently. Three nights ago, there would've been no way for me to feel anything but hunger when presented with this much blood. I hated to feed, but I had to acknowledge in this moment that putting it off the way I had been doing was more than a little stupid.

Then again, maybe it hadn't been entirely clever life decisions that led me to stand in an alleyway at night, accompanied only by a fox and a pair of bodies.

"Are we done?" I asked.

"Not quite," Suzume said. She crouched down again next to the body, and rested her right hand over Phillip's staring eye. She took a deep breath in, and for a moment it was if my entire body was filled with that pins-and-needles feeling that comes when your foot is just on the edge of falling asleep. Then Suzume breathed out again slowly, and the feeling passed.

She got up slowly, brushing off her knees. Her face was completely colorless, and she shook. "Okay, now we can go."

"What do you mean? How is that going to keep them from finding Phillip?"

"Phillip where?"

"Right there!" I pointed at where we'd dumped the twisted and ruined body, then stared. Phillip wasn't there anymore. Instead it was an old man, dressed in rags with a little hat sculpted out of tinfoil. He was curled up on his side, eyes closed peacefully. Flies were converging around him, and the smell of him made me reel backward. I knew without question that the old man must have died here days ago, probably when his heart gave out.

I looked over at Suzume, who had braced herself against the wall. She was still shaking slightly, and her head almost drooped with exhaustion, but there was that familiar smirk on her face.

"What did you do? How could—" I looked back again. The old man still lay there. "You changed him!"

"No," Suzume said. "I just changed the way you see him."

"What do you mean?"

Suzume slid a little, and when I reached out a hand she took it gratefully, using it to pull herself back up. "Everyone who looks at him will see an old homeless man who died a few days ago, and everyone will agree that his heart must've given out. The coroner is going to see the same thing, even if he opens up the chest. The morticians who keep him in storage while they try to find his family will all see an old man, not Phillip. The people who bury him weeks from now will still see an old man. Every camera will record the old man. People will walk in his blood and never realize it. Someone can stick their hand inside his chest and never realize that there isn't a heart left."

"My God," I whispered.

"Not quite, but I am pretty awesome," Suzume said. She started to slide again, and this time I wrapped my arm around her waist. "It's hard to do," she said, resting her head against my shoulder. "It has to trick a lot of people for a long time. It has to trick machines too."

"Are you going to put one on Jessica too?"

"I only had enough in me for one." Her voice was soft, almost thin.

"Why him?"

Apparently she wasn't tired enough for sarcasm, because she rolled her eyes at me. "We have two bodies. One is a vampire spawn whose body isn't quite normal anymore, who both of us have bled on and who has my saliva all over him. The other is a murdered little girl who every police officer in this city is looking for. Which one would you rather have CSI technicians crawling all over?"

"Valid point," I muttered.

I looked back once as we left. Jessica was shadowed by the Dumpster beside her, but her blond hair and pale skin were bright in the moonlight. I hoped someone would find her soon, and that they would put a blanket over her. She looked so small and vulnerable, lying there in her daisy pajamas.

We made slow progress back to the car. Suzume was so tired she was practically sleepwalking, and I was still bruised and sore from the fight, with one knee that ached sharply with every step. I dumped the trash bags down a storm drain a few blocks away from the alley, and by that time I was practically carrying Suzume.

This should've been my opportunity for a display of masculine studliness as I swept the gorgeous woman off her feet and carried her to safety, but unfortunately—

"Christ, you're heavy," I bitched to Suzume. We'd finally given up all hope that she could walk back to the car, and now I was carrying her piggyback style. Her head lolled on my shoulder, hair falling down to tickle my nose, and I heard her quiet snicker in my ear.

My rest breaks were getting longer and longer by the time we finally reentered the neighborhood we'd parked in. It was almost midnight now, and there were lines out the door in front of most of the clubs. People were dressed to impress, with short skirts and shiny shirts.

"Oh, come on," I moaned, staring at the hordes from the shadow of a closed building's awning. "This was completely deserted a few hours ago."

"Thursday is ladies' night," Suzume muttered in my ear. "Just get to the car."

"Yeah, fantastic idea. You're wearing a T-shirt and look like I've just roofied your drink. I'm going to get arrested, and then they might start wondering why my shirt is soaked in blood."

"Idiot," Suzume whispered. "They'll see a drunk girl being carried home by her boyfriend. No one will worry, and no one will care."

I cranked back and looked at her. Her eyes were barely slitted open, and she looked even paler than before. "I thought you didn't have the energy for any more illusions," I said.

"I'm showing dumb, mostly intoxicated and hormone-driven twits exactly what they expect to see at this time of night. This is barely a scrap of an illusion that only has to hold up at a distance. But unless you'd like to test your own bloody date-rape concept, I'd suggest getting us to the car before I lose even this."

I shut up and hauled us down the street to where I was parked. A few people laughed at us, and one guy yelled some advice about making sure she vomited before I put her in the car, but no one seemed worried, and no one came any closer to investigate. I hurried as fast as I could anyway, the back of my neck creeping at the thought of what we'd look like without Suzume's illusion. That meant that we were moving at a pace just faster than a crippled giraffe.

The Fiesta had not fared well in our absence. The rear driver's-side window had been smashed, and my radio had now joined the free market economy. I was too exhausted to even feel pissed, and I practically poured Suzume into the passenger seat. I had just enough awareness to put the gun into the trunk, where Suzume's duffel bag and my CD collection had managed to survive unscathed. I opened up Suzume's duffel and after some rooting around managed to unearth a pair of shorts for her. I might've been half-dead from exhaustion and pounded to a pulp, but I still knew that I'd feel calmer if she was wearing more clothing.

I shouldn't have bothered. A black fox was sound asleep on the seat when I got into the car, her head and neck still threaded through the appropriate holes in my T-shirt. She woke up enough to give a few halfhearted grumbles when I pulled it off her, but then her head dropped back down and she was out again. I stripped off my flannel shirt, stuffing it under my seat and shuddering at the way the saturated fabric squished, and pulled the T-shirt over my head.

The drive back to my apartment was awful. My brain felt like it was mired in molasses, and at one point I forgot and tried to turn on the radio to keep myself awake. My already cut knuckles scratched against a few of the ripped-off wires, which did manage to wake me up a little. Night wind howled in from the broken window, and I hoped that it wasn't supposed to rain. There was no way I was going to tape plastic over that tonight.

At least Suzume was a lot easier to carry as a fox. She hung limply in my arms as I hauled myself up the stairs to my apartment and tucked her onto my bed. I thought about just collapsing, but there was a more urgent concern.

The pipes in my building are old, and they make a banging sound whenever someone takes a shower, but for once I didn't give a crap about being a polite neighbor or roommate. Under the bright fluorescent lights I looked like I'd been playing in a slaughterhouse. My chest was caked in dried blood, along with a number of black fox hairs from Suzume's brief period in my shirt. Under good light, I could now see all the smears of blood and dirt on my jeans as well, and I dumped them straight into the trash. The water running into the drain was pink as I scrubbed myself down with soap, and the hot water ran out long before I'd finished. I shivered as I scrubbed, feeling the sting as soap entered into the dozens of cuts that I found on my face, arms, back, and knees.

Finally I felt marginally cleaner and turned off the water. My teeth were chattering as I dried off and dry-swallowed a pair of Tylenol. I turned the light off without looking in the mirror, figuring that I'd have to see my bruises again in the morning anyway. I shuffled into my room like an old man, wincing with every step. On the bed, Suzume opened those bright button eyes and looked at me for a long minute, then scooted over an inch and gave a soft yip of welcome.

I pulled on a pair of old brown cotton pajama bottoms that were worn smooth and thin from a thousand runs through the laundry, dropped the wet towel onto the floor, and crawled into the bed. I was asleep almost before my head hit the pillow.

I woke up at one point in the night, confused. There was a furry body snuggled against my chest, and my body was one throbbing ball of hurt. Then I remembered what had happened, and I remembered the way Jessica Grann had looked the last time I saw her.

I lay awake in the dark, thinking about what had been done to her, and remembering the way her blue eyes had stared up at me. Maria's eyes had been a deep chocolate brown, but I wondered if they had looked the same way to whoever had found her—empty, yet somehow accusatory. I felt moisture on my face and scrubbed hard at my eyes with my hand. That wouldn't bring Jessica or Maria back, or take away the image of their broken bodies. It was a long time until finally exhaustion and the soft whuffling of Suzume's breathing pulled me back down into sleep.

Chapter 8

I woke up slowly, a lazy drift into consciousness. There wasn't any confusion about where I was—I was in my bed. I had had the shit beaten out of me. I'd helped kill Phillip last night. Jessica and Amy Grann were dead. I had failed.

And judging by the furry weight on my chest, either I had a kitsune on top of me or feral cats had invaded the building.

I opened my eyes and looked directly into Suzume's black button eyes. She whimpered happily and wagged her fluffy tail back and forth. I sighed deeply, feeling the soreness in my chest as I inhaled.

The sunlight was very bright in the room. An awful suspicion filled me, and I looked over at my bedside clock, then back at Suzume.

"I was supposed to be at work three hours ago," I whispered.

Her fluffy head nodded vigorously, tail still wagging. I looked back at the clock. Sometime last night it had acquired small tooth marks around the alarm button.

"You turned off my alarm?"

Suzume's tongue lolled out of her mouth; then she gave two sharp yips. She looked really proud.

"You're trying to get me fired," I said, the horror fully sinking in.

The fox snorted loudly, then hopped off my chest (that didn't do my bruises any favors) and dropped down over the side of the bed with a soft thump. A minute went by; then Suzume's head and shoulders popped up, fully human. The height of the bed cut off my view of anything really exciting, but it was very obvious that she was naked. What was also both sad and obvious was that the sight of her bare shoulders was much more erotic to me than it should've been. I focused on how she was trying to ruin my life. It shouldn't matter how good she looked while she did it.

"Idiot," Suzume said with another snort. She folded her arms on the bed and laid her head down to look at me sideways. "If I wanted to get you fired, I would've come up with something a lot more creative than just making you sleep in."

"Oh yes, I never meant to impugn the artistry of your trickery," I said sarcastically. "But after the way I cut out of work yesterday, how is missing the entire first half of my shift going to somehow convince Jeanine that I'm employee of the month?"

"I called in earlier and said that you'd had a family emergency and couldn't make it in today." She looked curious. "Do you actually want to go into work today?"

"No," I admitted. If it had just been how badly I felt, and just how insane the bruises that I'd acquired last night probably looked right now, I would've dragged in no matter what. But failing the Grann girls so badly, and with the memory of Jessica's body so fresh in my mind . . . no, I definitely didn't want to go anywhere near the banality of Busy Beans. Of course, there were other concerns. "But I really can't skip work."

"Because you're broke," she said.

"How do you know that?" Given the way that Suzume had treated me as her source of free food since she'd met me, I was pretty surprised that she'd known.

"A few subtle clues were evident." Suzume mimed inhaling on a pipe, then began ticking them off on her fingers. "First, there was your car. It's rusty, old, doesn't like to start in the morning, and the bumper drags enough that I'm sure that one more speed bump is going to rip it right off. Second, there were your clothes. They suck. Third was your unspeakable cheapness in not buying me a beer last night to go with the pizza. I mean, pizza and beer. They just go together. You don't mess with nature. But probably the most striking clue was when I accessed your online bank statement and looked at your balance."

My jaw hung open, and I wasn't able to force anything other than strangled sounds out of my throat.

"Really, it was elementary, my dear Watson." Suzume mimed tucking away her pipe. When I continued to stare at her and blither, she sniffed, irked that I wasn't praising her skills of detection. "Honestly, Fort, you shouldn't use the same password for everything. Don't worry. I changed it for you."

I closed my eyes and let my head fall back against the pillow. There was a short silence while I could feel her looking at me, then the soft crinkling sound of a paper bag being opened, and the ambrosial smell of a toasted bagel filled the room.

I cracked open one eye. Suzume had a bag from Dunkin' Donuts in one hand and a fresh bagel in the other.

"Hungry?" she asked.

"You went out and bought bagels?" Clearly the shocks were just going to keep coming this morning.

"Of course not." She looked offended. "I stole them from Larry."

I paused and considered. Then, "I'm okay with that," and I snagged the bagel she offered and began to eat it. As soon as the first bit went down, my stomach remembered that in addition to being extremely traumatized, it was also extremely empty. I pretty much inhaled the entire bagel. Without even being asked, Suzume handed me another bagel, along with a container of cream cheese. Bliss.

While I was eating, Suzume ducked down behind the bed for a minute, then reemerged wearing my old Brown T-shirt and a pair of my shorts. They completely dwarfed her, but instead of making her look ridiculous, they just made her look more adorably pixieish than usual.

Too adorable, actually. For a woman who last night had been sporting enough facial contusions to have earned a free ride to a battered women's shelter, plus a deep head cut that bled profusely and a few cracked ribs, she was now completely unmarked, without even the slightest suggestion of a bruise or discomfort.

"Suzume, are you messing with me again?"

Her eyebrows lifted in surprise. I gestured to her face. "Are you keeping me from seeing your bruises?"

"Oh." She grinned. "Nope. We heal faster in our natural states."

I frowned. "But you went fox when we got back to the car. Did you change back after I went to sleep?"

The grin wiped off her face, and she leaned closer to me, menace suddenly seething in her dark eyes. I pulled back in surprise, the quick change from warm amusement to this icy anger startling me.

"Keep one thing in mind, Fortitude," she hissed, low and dangerous. "I'm not some were-critter. I'm not a woman who can turn into a fox when she feels like it. I'm a fox who can become a woman. Try to remember that."

"Okay, okay," I said. She glared at me for another minute, then pulled back and scooted to the far side of the bed, pulling another bagel out of the bag and giving it a vicious bite. We ate in silence. After a few minutes she slowly seemed to thaw, even offering me the last bagel in the bag.

We were almost finished when she asked, almost normally, "So, why have you been paying all the rent for the last few months?"

I didn't like talking about this, but I could see that this was Suzume's version of an olive branch after how she'd lashed out, so I answered.

"About six months ago Larry said that he was having money trouble, and he only gave me a partial payment. The next month he gave me even less, and since then I haven't gotten anything at all."

Suzume chewed thoughtfully. "Are you friends with him?"

"No." Definitely not. I hadn't been too fond of him even before he'd slept with Beth.

"So make him pay it."

I stared. She made it sound so simple, as if I'd just been letting it slide this whole time. "How would you suggest I do that?" I asked.

"Threats of violence have always worked very well for me," Suzume said, completely serious.

I sighed. "And if threats don't work?"

"Then use violence." Suzume gave a smothered little laugh. "Jeez, Fort, you seem to *like* making things more complicated than they really are."

After breakfast in bed, it was hard to get moving. Showering and then falling straight into bed might've been what I wanted to do last night, but apparently it hadn't been the best thing for my bruised body. Everything was stiff, and even lifting my arms up enough to get a T-shirt over my head turned out to be a really bad idea. I eventually had to suck it up and ask Suzume for a hand.

She looked at me critically after I lay panting on the bed following my return to a toddler-era style of dressing.

"You look like shit," she said.

"Fuck, Suze, can you pretend for a minute that you care about my ego?"

She ignored me. "Your mother will dock my pay if she sees you like this. And my family will never let me live it down if they know I let someone wipe the floor with you when it was my job to keep you safe."

"I'm so sorry. I never stopped to think about how my pain was going to inconvenience you."

"I understand, Fort, and you're forgiven."

I sighed as she rattled on. There were some areas of sarcasm that went right over her head.

"But I refuse to let you be a stain on my record. Get in the car."

"What?" I blinked at her. "I thought you said that we were going to have a casual day. Not move any further than the couch? Let me cuddle up to some ice packs?" I was definitely harboring some carnal thoughts about a few bags of frozen vegetables. Plus . . . "What about *Star Wars*? You said you'd watch the original, undigitally fucked-over *Star Wars* with me!"

"No, this is way too serious. We're going straight to a doctor's office."

Straight to a doctor's office didn't exactly happen. Suzume's standards of hygiene were a bit higher than mine this morning, and while she indulged in the kind of thirty-minute shower that would knock out our ancient water heater for the rest of the day, I hobbled over to my computer to check the news. A bakery worker had found Jessica's body in the early hours of the morning, just as Suzume had predicted. The hunt for Amy Grann was headline news, and I felt a sharp pang as I wondered how long it would be before they finally found her body, and where it had been dumped. I scrolled through the article, not reading the text too closely. The press had gotten more photos since yesterday, and in addition to the Grann family portrait, there were now several that were just of Amy. I saw her playing with the family dog, posed in her Sunday best, and giving a gap-toothed smile in her softball uniform.

I spent the most time looking at that picture. A few of her teammates were standing around her, and it was clear that she was the short one on the team. I'd played on Little League teams at around the same age. Because

I'd been about five inches shorter than all the other boys, I was front and center in every team photo.

My foster father had coached my Little League team. I was incredibly bad at sports, and would've been a lot happier spending my Saturdays sitting at home watching TV, but Jill and Brian had been determined to give me the perfect childhood, over my own objections if necessary. So I'd spent hours of time in left field, the place where I had the least opportunity for missed plays and throwing errors. There were a lot of hot afternoons when I'd stared at the sky and counted clouds while mosquitoes feasted on my exposed flesh and I waited impatiently for the innings to just be over already so that I could return to an air-conditioned environment. I wondered if Amy's dad had coached her team. I wondered if her mom had been in the stands for every game, like Jill had always been for me.

My maudlin mood was broken when Suzume came out of the bathroom. She'd changed clothes, and was now dressed in what were apparently her standard bodyguarding clothes—black boots, close-fitting black pants, and a thin body-hugging T-shirt. Today the T-shirt was fire-engine red. She'd clipped her hair up so that half of it was in some kind of sleek twist, and the other half was falling around her face in little feathery strands. She practically glowed with vitality and good health.

By contrast I was wearing a much-laundered and half-faded Dalek shirt (*exterminate!*) with a few holes in the shoulders and the same cotton pajama bottoms that I'd worn to bed. Bending was really not agreeing with me right now, and so I'd chosen to turn down Suzume's extremely generous offer to help me change pants (having suffered through more than enough commentary on my physique when she helped me with my shirt) and hope that no one noticed my sartorial sins. Since my face looked like I'd just gotten into a fight with a city bus and lost, I was betting that my pants were going to be the least of my problems today.

We then spent a few minutes taping a plastic grocery bag over the shattered window in the Fiesta. My karma had finally decided to stop shitting on me full-time, and it hadn't rained last night. Of course, the trade-off of that was that the bloody shirt I'd stuffed under my seat last night had spent the morning baking in the sun, much to the apparent delight of the neighborhood's entire fly population, which had found a nice access point through the open window.

I hauled out the shirt, along with my ruined floor mat, but Suzume stopped me just before I would've tossed them in the trash.

"Trash collectors seem to take dim views on finding blood-soaked clothing. I'll bag them and put them in the trunk. Then we can throw them into the medical waste trash at the doctor's office."

While that was an admittedly good solution to the bloody evidence issue, there was one small matter that I'd now spent half the morning trying to explain to the very image-conscious kitsune.

"Suzume, seriously. I don't have health insurance and I have no cash. How the hell am I supposed to afford a doctor's visit?"

"A human doctor?" Suzume sputtered with outrage. "You think I'm taking you to a *human* doctor? Why would I bother? So they can write the words 'Icy-Hot' on a prescription pad? I'd slap a case of concealer on you before I wasted my time with a human doctor."

I leaned against the hood of my car and sighed as Suzume continued her rant. When she began winding down, I asked, "So, what is the alternative to a human doctor? A vet?" I really hoped it wasn't a vet. I could totally see Suzume taking me to see a vet. She'd probably ask if there were any weekly specials on castration.

Suzume shook her head sadly. "You have no faith in me at all. Get in the car and I'll give you another ice pack for the trip."

Since that was probably the best offer I was likely to get, I took her up on it.

Twenty minutes later we were driving through the rarified air of Barrington, one of the wealthiest of the Providence suburbs. While a town like Newport consists of an interesting mix of the superwealthy who live in gated mansions and the ordinary and everyday people who filled out the rest of the population, Barrington was very much exclusively the golf and country-club set. The average income was in the hundred-thousand-dollar range, and a few years ago *Money* magazine had ranked it as the sixth-best town to live in in the United States. Subdivisions filled with McMansions lined the roads, and every time we had to sit at a stoplight I could see people in the cars around us looking utterly appalled at the sight of the Fiesta, which, like me, was not at its aesthetic best just now.

"One of these people is going to call the police on us," I predicted dourly.

"What for?"

"Driving while poor." I glared at a woman in an Audi

next to us who apparently spent my yearly income on tanning beds. She sneered, but I noticed that she turned down a side street pretty quickly.

"Don't be such a crab," Suzume said. She pulled into one of the small plazas filled with professional buildings of the medical variety—dentists, eye doctors, that sort of thing. "Look, we're here."

There were apparently a lot of doctors clustered in each building, so I scanned the posted sign for any likely candidates, then looked again.

"Okay, I give up," I said. "The dermatologist or the urologist?" After all, I had pissed a little blood this morning, which at the time Suzume had assured me was a perfectly normal by-product of being punched in the kidneys.

Suzume pointed. I stared, then looked at her wide grin, then read it again.

"Absolutely not," I said.

Five minutes later we were sitting in the peach-toned waiting room of Lavinia Leamaro, doctor of obstetrics, gynecology, and reproductive endocrinology. The sofas were upholstered in brightly flowered fabrics, and the little side tables were covered with copies of women's parenting or pregnancy magazines. There was an enormous framed sepia-toned photo of a woman breast-feeding an infant dominating one wall, which I had very deliberately chosen to sit beneath so that I wouldn't have to struggle to avoid looking at it. On the wall I was facing there were at least a hundred individually framed four-by-six photos of infants, each labeled with name, birth date, and apparently critical information about their weight and length. At the top of the wall the words

OUR SUCCESS STORIES! were painted in elaborate teal calligraphy. There were three women also sitting in the waiting room, all in their mid-thirties to early forties and very visibly not pregnant, and when they weren't shooting me confused and somewhat hostile glances, they were staring fixedly at that wall of infant photos with an almost rabid hunger.

I was feeling a bit out of place.

Suzume was conducting a very spirited conversation with the registering nurse, but pitched just low enough that it didn't carry. Since I had a feeling that whatever story Suzume was pitching was unlikely to present me in a flattering light, I was extremely grateful for that. Conversation completed, Suzume strolled back and dropped down onto the sofa next to me. The three women all started shooting covert glances over at us as Suzume grabbed a magazine and flipped through it.

"Now, look at that," Suzume said, stopping at one page. Since I somehow doubted that there was anything in a magazine entitled *Modern Pregnancy* that was going to interest me, I very studiously avoided looking. "Now, that is not all baby weight," Suzume continued. I tried, but I couldn't help myself and I glanced over, and immediately regretted it. "No, wait," she said. "She's pregnant with triplets." She tilted her head. "Bold of her to get photographed in just underpants, though."

"She's wearing underpants?" I asked, wishing that I could scrub that image from my brain. That looked less miracle of life and more *Alien*.

"They're mostly hidden by the belly. But that's still a bit big if you ask me. When my cousin Yuzuki was pregnant with triplets, she didn't look anywhere near that big."

"Your cousin had triplets?"

"Yeah, you met them at my grandmother's house. Riko, Yui, and Tomomi. My grandmother's first, and so far only, set of great-grandchildren. Yuzuki was always a suck-up." Suzume tilted her head the other way, considering. "Of course, Yuzuki did stay fox for pretty much the whole pregnancy, so that probably had an effect. The human body is really built for singles rather than litters."

"So your cousin had triplets and you and your sister are twins? Jeez, multiples really run in your family."

"We're *foxes*, Fort," Suzume said, *how many times do I have to spell this out?* not really even bothering to stay subtextual. "Litters are more natural to us than single births. If we stick to our natural form for most of the pregnancy, we get a couple kits in one go. Stay in human shape, though, and the body has to protect itself by reducing. Are you getting this, or do I need to break out hand puppets?"

"Okay, okay. This is really fascinating, Suze, but"— mindful of our audience of women, who seemed uncertain of whether to shoot Suzume glares of death for being a decade younger than they were or feel sorry for her because she was presumably having fertility issues but were definitely trying their best to subtly scoot close enough to overhear our conversation, I dropped my voice to a whisper—"*why the fuck are we here?*"

She looked surprised. "Because you can't dodge a punch and you heal like an immuno-compromised grandma."

I was saved the indignity of trying to respond to that when the nurse called, "Suzume Hollis? Dr. Leamaro will see you now."

We got up and followed her in. Behind us, the three women who had been waiting before we arrived finally decided what the correct response was, and their nasty glares bored holes in our backs.

Instead of leading us into one of the examination rooms for the standard medical practice of a second round of waiting, the nurse escorted us to an office, where a statuesquely attractive middle-aged woman with curly salt-and-pepper hair that was thoroughly restrained in an elaborate French braid, save for one corkscrew curl escaping at her temple, rich dark skin, and a white doctor's jacket sat behind a mahogany desk that would've been a lot more imposing had it not been completely overflowing with file folders, charts, loose paper, and at least three partially consumed coffees.

Her eyes were a shocking contrast to her skin and hair, an almost acid green that made me wonder if she used colored contact lenses. She fixed those eyes on Suzume and gave her a very chilly glare that made me certain that they'd met before—only someone who'd already been subjected to Suzume's presence would have that level of animosity.

I couldn't help saying it as I limped in. "Dr. Lavinia Leamaro, I presume?"

Now the good doctor offered me a little of that glare.

Suzume sprawled bonelessly in one of the chairs parked in front of the desk. "Don't be so formal, Fort. She'll respond to Lulu."

"Dr. Leamaro is fine," she bit out in sepulcher tones. I decided to attempt a little discretion, and I stood just behind Suzume's chair. The fact that the chairs were really low and I was still aching from getting up from the sofa in the waiting room had absolutely nothing to do with my decision, of course.

"Why am I being subjected to your presence?" Dr. Leamaro asked Suzume. Oh yeah, she'd definitely spent some time with the fox before.

"Well, it's very personal, but"—Suzume leaned over the desk, and dropped her voice—"I just have this . . . *longing* to be a mother, but Fort's sperm don't swim! Help me, Lulu. You're my only hope!" Then there was some loud fake sobbing as Suzume threw herself face-first into the mound of papers.

Dr. Leamaro stared down at Suzume. "I really hate you," she said.

"Don't lie, Lulu, you *looove* me." Suzume popped back up, sunny smile in place.

There was a loud sigh and Dr. Leamaro made a show of checking her watch. "My appointments are backing up as we speak, so can you please tell me what you want so that I can just give it to you and you'll leave?"

"My tagalong got himself broken"—Suzume pointed at me—"and he's not old enough to wear big-boy pants yet, so no vampire healing." At my horrified gasp, she waved a hand casually. "Don't get your panties in a twist, Fort. Lulu's no more human than you are. She's an elf. C'mon." Her voice turned coaxing as she looked back to the doctor. "Flash him an ear. Do it. Do it."

"Absolutely not." Dr. Leamaro curled her lip in distaste.

"You're an elf?" I asked, unable to help myself. Keeping myself away from Madeline's business and as far into the human world as possible meant that I didn't have much contact with the supernaturals outside my immediate family, and I'd never seen an elf outside of storybook illustrations and *The Lord of the Rings* movies. "Really? I thought elves were . . ." I stopped myself just in time.

"Were what?" Dr. Leamaro's voice was as toasty as Antarctica during a cold snap. Apparently I hadn't stopped myself soon enough.

". . . Irish," I finished lamely. The doctor didn't look remotely appeased.

Suzume snickered. "She's a halfsie, Fort. I meant it when I said that she's about as human as you are right now. You're more likely to meet an A-cup Playboy bunny than a full-blooded elf. But her daddy was running around the Emerald Isles before Saint Patrick, so you're half right. And your mom is from Chicago, right, Lulu?"

"I have no desire to chat genealogy with you," the doctor snapped. "Your vampire lacks a visible vagina"—I suppose I partially deserved that one—"so I have no idea what you expect me to do."

"Well, certainly not what you usually do to your patients, that's for sure." Suzume snorted. "I want to borrow your witch."

Dr. Leamaro suddenly stopped being pissed and started looking cagey. "I have no idea what you're talking about," she said primly.

Suzume gave a full belly laugh. "You expect me to buy that you're actually practicing medicine here? An *elf*? Next you'll be offering me a great deal on a bridge in Brooklyn. Get the damn witch in here."

I couldn't keep thinking of her as Dr. Leamaro, and Lulu definitely didn't like what Suzume was saying. "I graduated from Harvard," she bit out. The battle cry of a thousand Ivy Leaguers with their credibility questioned.

"Yeah, yeah, I saw the diploma, Lulu. I'm sure you rocked the MCATs. Witch, please."

"Infertility medicine is a *science*. I don't need any magic to do my job."

"And it's a good thing, because elf magic blows. You had to hire a witch for the magic part. Because the *science* of medicine never has a hundred percent results. We checked your stats a few months ago after you got that big write-up in the med journal. Every woman who walks through your door is knocked up within a year."

Lulu's mouth snapped shut and her eyes widened.

"Kind of sloppy, actually," Suzume continued. "Did you have to be perfect because your ego demanded you be the most awesome doctor in the state, or because your odds of real success are so low? My bet is both."

Lulu slumped back in her seat, all the fight out of her, and looked ready to vomit. "What are you going to do?"

Suzume laughed again. "Nothing, you dummy. Like the foxes give a shit about the operation you have going here. We were just curious. Have your witch patch up my vampire and I'll get out of your hair."

"Um, excuse me," I cut in. "But what exactly *is* she doing?"

"Oh, sorry, Fort. I forgot that you need the Junior Reader version." I gritted my teeth as she continued. "The elf population was in the crapper even before Christianity washed up on their shores, thanks to a few good wars in antiquity, then a few more wars just for good measure, and then they inbred so heavily that most of the younger elves were sterile before Rome was even mildly concerned about Visigoths. Visit an elf outpost and you practically hear the banjos in the background." Lulu gave a sharp huff, but didn't interrupt. "Full-blood elves might not die of old age, but they sure liked to kill each other, and when you mix those two together with sterility you end up with the same thing that happened to the dodo bird. So they had to start breeding with humans, which for them was kind of like you making it with a sheep." Suzume's grin was wicked. "Big superiority issues for elves. Big *sociopath* issues for elves. I mean, seriously, dudes like a body count, but mainly there's the superiority problem. The thought of extinction finally got them in the mood, but not enough to actually form relationships with those repellently lower forms of life. This resulted in a long and idyllic period where males would seduce a human woman, then check in nine months later to see if things worked out. If they had, they stole the baby. Easy-peasy. Then, though, the real tragedy happened." Her voice dropped, and she whispered, "*The pill*. Suddenly those seduced maidens weren't getting knocked up like they should've, and then add safe and legal abortion to the mix and you have a *huge* problem for a teensy-tiny population that not only relies on one-shot knock-ups, but breed true pretty rarely."

Suzume paused and seemed to do a mental count, then said, "Lulu, I counted twelve babies on your wall of triumph that had crappy glamours on them. You've got, what, like a five percent success rate on breeding halfsies?"

"Seven percent," Lulu snipped.

"Let me see if I've got this straight," I said slowly.

"Seven percent of the women who come in here get a shot of elf semen?"

"Idiot," Suzume said affectionately. "*All* of them get it."

"Okay, I'm lost," I admitted.

Finally having enough, Lulu sat up straight and jumped in. "It's very simple, Fort," she said. "Elf genetics are difficult. Inseminate a woman with elf semen, and you have a small chance of getting an active hybrid. Usually, though, all you end up with is a human with some latent genetics that we've never figured out how to trigger. You can even try breeding two latent half-breeds, and all you'll get is another latent. Only hybrids that are active at birth will ever carry the traits that those of us who are part of the elf community value. The women who come to my clinic have usually had multiple rounds of in vitro and other treatments with other doctors, with no success. They are desperate for a pregnancy, and I can offer them a guaranteed success. I won't be using their husbands' semen, but for women in the middle of reproductive hell, that's an entirely workable deception. There is a very small possibility that their child will not be entirely human, but since I'm the one who delivers them I can place a *solid*"—her calm sales pitch broke for a minute and she glared at Suzume, who smiled condescendingly—"glamour on the infant. The baby is left with the family until it begins approaching puberty, and then a false accident is arranged that leaves the child with the elves and the parents none the wiser."

I stared. "That's horrible."

Lulu looked surprised, and shot a confused look at Suzume. "Are you sure this is a vampire? He sure doesn't sound like one."

"It's amazing, isn't it?" Suzume said conversationally. "You'd think that his mother had fucked Jiminy Cricket. And I'm serious, Fort, what *is* horrible here? These women have a ninety-three percent chance of that never happening."

"But some of them will think that their kid has been killed!"

"Only seven percent of them. And that's a kid they never even would've had without Lulu."

"If they'd gone to another doctor—"

"Fort, these women *are* infertile. No science is going to get them pregnant. It took magic. And"—she turned back to Lulu—"not that story hour hasn't been *fascinating*, but am I going to get a shot at this witch of yours?"

"What's in this for me?" Lulu asked.

"Firstly, I'll start giving your business card to all our rich customers who have wives with infertility issues. So that's some cash down the road for you. Secondly, I won't tattle to Madeline Scott about the operation you've got going here, because I just *know* that you haven't been forking over a cut of your profits. But more importantly, if you let me use your witch I'll take the judgmental bloodsucker away and you can get back to squirting elf juice in vajayjays."

"I really hate you," Lulu said, those stunning green eyes slits of malevolence.

Suzume smiled. "I almost believed you that time."

Lulu took Suzume's offer, and we were stuffed into a small examining room that was covered with yet more photos of kids. These ones were a lot older than the ones in the waiting room. Apparently Lulu's clients were encouraged to keep sending in birthday photos, and the painted words on each wall noted the ages. I was kept company by HAPPY THIRD BIRTHDAY! HAPPY SEVENTH BIRTHDAY! and HAPPY THIRTEENTH BIRTHDAY! There was a noticeable drop in cuteness between those last two age groups.

Lulu's witch was a short man in his late fifties with a receding hairline, an impressive beer gut, the vocabulary of a particularly foulmouthed sailor, and a general attitude of being extremely put upon. He had me strip down to my underwear, which was accompanied by many unwelcome observations, wolf whistles, and encouraging "woo-woo" noises from Suzume, who was slowly spinning herself around in a little wheeled stool, and then I was liberally coated in a pastelike substance that was orange and smelled very sharply of fish guts.

"Is this seriously magic?" I asked when he also told me to drink a clear concoction that had the consistency of ketchup.

"What, you think I'm wasting my time with useless potions?" the witch asked, very offended. "Do I look like some Gaia-hugging twat with a Coexist bumper sticker on the back of my Saab? Man up and drink the fucking potion. Buddha's balls, kid, doing fertility spells all damn day might be goddamn-ass boring, but at least the fucking women don't mouth off when they're told to drink something. You tell those broads that it'll get them a baby, and they will put that potion back so fast that you would swear that they had a damn beer bong implanted in their jaw."

"Sorry," I muttered, and started to choke down the drink under his gimlet glare. I gagged a little. "Maybe you should serve this with a spoon," I suggested. With a few more snarled curses, the witch stormed out with a shouted "And don't wipe that stuff off for twenty god-damn minutes or I'll mix up one that has to be taken in suppository form!"

The door slammed.

"Witches take it pretty personally when you insult their potions," Suzume said mildly.

"How was I supposed to know that?" I asked. Suzume's expression spoke volumes, so I poked at some of the orange gunk currently hardening on my face and changed the subject. "So, what's an elf glamour?"

"Third-rate illusion magic. Pretty much all that most of the halfsies can manage. Just enough to make a kid's pointy ears look round."

"And your illusion magic is . . . ?"

Suzume snorted. "Awesome. Seriously, have you checked me out while I'm working? I should have my own daytime show."

"What's the difference?" I asked, fascinated enough that I was willing to enable Suzume's ego trip.

"I give the mind a nudge and let the brain fill in cracks. Elves try to wrestle brains into submission. Much less ef-fective. Consider my kick-ass job with Phillip last night. If there had been a dozen of those Keebler wannabes there, putting all their sissy mojo together, they still would've failed completely, because they would've tried to make the body invisible. All it takes is one person tripping where he shouldn't, or two people who keep bumping into something that isn't there, and they start looking closely. And the moment someone starts looking closely, an illu-sion will start unraveling. You need to give the mind something that it will accept and even work to maintain.

Crazy homeless man dead in alley? Check. Guy carrying drunk girlfriend? Check. An elf glamour spends its time screaming, *Round ears, not pointy ears, round ears!* If I pulled fox magic, mine would just say, *Of course these ears are normal.* You know, all Obi-Wan. *These aren't the droids you're looking for* is a lot more effective and easy than *these droids are completely invisible.*"

"What about the night you scared off my muggers?"

"Oh yes. Good times." Suzume smiled nostalgically, then winked. "If a trick just has to work long enough to scare someone off, then it's not as important for it to hold up. Their minds were working the whole time to tell them that what they were seeing couldn't exist, but they were too focused on running to stop and listen."

I nodded. That actually kind of made sense.

"So, why didn't you try to trick Phillip last night?" I asked.

Suzume snorted. "Yeah, why didn't I also try to stop and juggle?" I raised an eyebrow, and she explained. "Fox magic is a little like calculus. I can do it if I have a minute to think it over, but if I had to do it in the middle of a fight, my answers would be really off. And last night, every time I was starting to stop and take a breather, you thought it was a great idea to become Phillip's punching bag."

This time it was my turn to roll my eyes. "All my fault. Suuuuure, Suze. That headfirst trip you took into a brick wall had absolutely nothing to do with that decision to keep trying the love bite approach to stopping a fight."

Suzume stuck her tongue out at me, then pointedly turned around and began ransacking through the medical supply cupboard. I couldn't hold back a grin.

I looked back at the walls. There was something kind of creepy about being surrounded by all those kids with posed smiles. It was the kind of décor that belonged in a Stephen King movie.

"For a place dealing with infertile women, don't you think it's kind of, you know, insensitive to plaster pictures of kids on every wall?" I asked.

"Yes." Suzume had just found the tongue depressors, and was laying them out end to end across the floor.

"Then why do you think they're doing it?"

"*Because* it's insensitive."

"That makes no sense, Suze." I propped up and looked at her.

"Haven't you ever bothered to learn anything about the wider world, Fort?" Suzume asked.

"Let's assume that I haven't, and that you've already made a few more condescending remarks, and skip to the part where you just tell me the answer."

Suzume gave an offended sniff. "As if I've been anything but a patient instructor." That her pants didn't spontaneously combust at that statement was complete proof that there is no higher power. "It's for the witch."

She paused, and I made a little *go on* gesture.

"Witches need payment that's more than just cash. More than half the reason Lulu's success rate is so high is that she's using women who have spent so long trying to have a baby. Their desperation feeds into the witch's magic and makes it stronger. The pictures"—she gestured at the wall—"are like waving a red flag in a bull's face. It keeps all those emotions stoked, probably with a nice dollop of envy and a little soupçon of resentment. All good stuff if you're a witch cooking up a brew."

"You mean this is black magic?" I looked in horror at the now-empty cup of sludge that I'd just finished downing. It had a chililike aftertaste.

Suzume laughed, cutting me off before I could stick my finger down my throat. "Black magic, white magic, that's all New Age horseshit. It's just magic. Witches learn magic like a lawyer learns the law. It's all the same stuff that goes into it. Witches are bad or good like lawyers are nice or douches—it's all in how they're applying it. And I don't know about you, but helping sterile women get buns in their ovens and patching up whiny vampires isn't exactly a rain of toads."

"Oh, okay." Silence fell for another moment, broken only by the sound of Suzume playing with the tongue depressors. Another question had occurred to me, and I gave the conversation another poke. "So, have you seriously been spying on Lulu?"

"Googling someone's name every once in a while isn't spying, Fort. It's just keeping a cautious eye on the neighbors. And you should be grateful we're bothering, which is more than your mom and siblings have managed lately. Lulu might come off well, but she's like all the other halfsies. A piece of work with daddy issues. Considering how closely she works with the full-bloods, she's got to be carrying around some serious head trauma."

"What do you mean?"

"Don't let her 'those of us who are part of the elf community' bullshit fool you. The full elves still kicking around and jerking off might spend all their time trying to make halfsies, but they never let those halfsies forget that instead of immortality, they've got Mommy's life span. Instead of the magic that had Druids planning Stonehenge, they get a few basic parlor tricks. Worst of all, no amount of crazy breeding is ever going to bring back the world that those elves lost. They're like dinosaurs trying to pretend that they aren't doomed by saying that the platypus now counts as one of them. It's not going to really help, plus they still hate everything with fur."

"Okay, that does sound like the holidays would be awkward."

"Exactly. And it's the halfsies like Lulu, trying so hard to win Daddy's love and approval, who end up going off the deep end. Which is, sadly enough, still only the kiddy pool compared to full elves."

I was starting to pick up on Suzume's theme. "Because full elves are crazy?"

"Completely bat-shit." Suzume pushed a few more tongue depressors around with her foot, then turned back to the supply cabinet.

I poked at the orange gunk again. "I am starting to feel better."

"My heart quivers with delight. You've got ten more minutes with that stuff, so stop poking it."

I've never been very good at not poking at stuff. I was always the kid who had to pull off Band-Aids early, and I have a few scars from where I wouldn't stop scratching at my chicken pox, no matter how many times Jill and Brian told me not to. I looked back at the wall of thirteen-year-olds to distract myself. Why a series of photos depicting pouty faces, the incipience of acne, and the prevalence of orthodontia would make someone yearn to get pregnant, I had no idea.

"It's hard to believe that some of these kids are thirteen," I said, scanning over the photos. "A couple of them look like they still wear footie pajamas to bed."

"Puberty is an uneven taskmaster, but it catches up to everyone in the end," Suzume said, her voice lazy as she started in on the cotton balls.

Something in the back of my mind tickled when she said that, and I looked back at the wall of thirteen-year-olds. Something about this had bothered me since I first saw it, and I tried to figure it out, but just as easily it seemed to squirrel away again.

"Say that again," I told Suzume.

"Puberty is a bitch."

"No, no, you said something else."

"Puberty is a variable bitch?"

That was it, that was what was important. I looked back at those photos. All these kids had just turned thirteen, but not all of them looked it. I scanned through them. Birthday parties, cakes, lots of braces . . . I stopped at one of the photos. A girl was lying down, wearing a tiara that had BIRTHDAY GIRL written on it in rhinestones, faking sleep so that her dog would sniff her mouth. She had a big smile on her face, clearly a bad faker, but she looked young. Young like . . .

Young like Jessica had looked last night, lying on the ground of the alley. So that's what was bothering me, and I started to relax. I hadn't been thinking of her for a while, and my conscience was probably kicking me for letting Suzume's constant banter and my aching ribs distract me from her death.

But my eyes pulled back to that photo, and I frowned. No, that wasn't it. There was something else. Something about puberty. I remembered Chivalry saying something. Except he'd phrased it differently . . . mature women, that's what he'd said. I kept picking at it, trying to figure out how my brain was trying to link these things together, and then I remembered *when* he'd been saying it and suddenly everything seemed to come together in a flash.

"Suzume!"

She looked up from her efforts at creative disorganization and glanced sharply around the room for whatever had gotten me so excited. "What?"

"Suze, girls hit puberty around twelve or thirteen, right? Like, periods and stuff?"

She stared at me, completely flummoxed. "Aroundish," she agreed slowly, clearly trying to track my conversational non sequitur. "Some a little earlier, a few a little later, but most have it by thirteen. I could lend you my old Judy Blume books if you're curious."

"Can you tell?" I asked urgently.

"Huh?"

It was all so obvious suddenly. Why she'd been stolen, then killed. "Luca said that Maria lost usefulness for him when she hit puberty. That he wasn't sexually interested in her anymore. And Jessica looked really young, but the newspaper listed her age as thirteen. So would she have hit puberty?"

"Oh." Suzume paused and seemed to think, then nodded decisively. "Yes."

"You're sure."

"She was menstruating. I could smell the blood on her last night, under the rest of it. The blood is different, so the smell is distinct." She gave a little *so what?* shrug.

"But don't you realize what this means? Luca didn't kill Jessica because he'd planned to all along. He killed her because he thought she was younger and she turned out not to be! But Amy's nine—she actually *is* really little!" Suzume's eyes widened, and I nodded, feeling stunned. "You said you smelled another little girl on Phillip—was that other girl dead?"

Suzume shook her head slowly. "No," I said. "We just assumed because Jessica was dead. We didn't realize why. And that means . . . that means Amy might still be alive. We can still save her."

Chapter 9

"You can find Amy, right?"

Suzume hadn't said much since I'd realized that Amy could still be alive. She'd called the witch back in, and the two of them had scrubbed the orange paste off me. Well, most of it. Apparently there was the unfortunate side effect of staining the skin, but the witch assured me that it would wear off. In about four weeks. In the meantime, my body looked like I'd gone paintballing naked, and lost. But since I now felt better than I had at any point since my mugging, I wasn't complaining. The witch said that I still had a little surface bruising, though how he could see any around the bright orange blotches was beyond me.

We'd had to make one slight stop on our way out to dump our bag of bloody and possibly incriminating clothes. Apparently the good doctor maintained an incinerator in her building for just such occasions. Convenient, and moderately suspicious. But now we were finally back in the Fiesta and ready to hit the road to save Amy. Or at least that should've been the plan. Suzume was sitting in the driver's seat, tapping her fingers on the steering wheel and frowning.

There was a distinct lack of her usual balls-to-the-wall decisiveness and eagerness for conflict. I gave her a nudge.

"So we should head back to where we killed Phillip. You can go fox and sniff his trail back to wherever it leads—that will probably be wherever Jessica was when she died. And if Luca was originally planning to keep both girls, then there would've been no reason to keep them separate. If we're lucky, then Luca hasn't moved and Amy is still there." I was almost shaking. An hour ago I'd been convinced that Amy had died, and now she was probably only about twenty minutes away from me. Sure, it wasn't perfect—if Luca moved to a new spot, it might be hard for Suzume to track, especially if he'd made that move by car, but I felt like my odds were good that he'd still be in the same place. If he didn't know that Phillip was dead yet, maybe he was even out looking for him. Leaving Amy behind for us to grab.

"Fort, do you have a plan on this one?" Suzume asked finally, still drumming her fingers.

"I just told you," I said, impatient. "Find the trail, follow it to wherever Amy is, get Amy."

Suzume sighed. "You're missing something, Fort. And much as it grieves me to be the voice of caution in this area, I must ask—do you remember the part about how the little girl is being held captive by a vampire?"

"I thought you said that vampires weren't so tough."

Suzume's face reddened, and I knew that she was having to force out the words. "That was when I'd just been hanging out with you. After a vampire flunky nearly wiped the floor with us, I reconsidered my position. If that's what a hybrid mongrel can do, I'm not going anywhere near his daddy until we have some serious backup."

I hated that she was right. I really didn't want her to be right. But, "Fine. Call your grandma."

"You weren't paying very close attention, were you? You've got exactly one fox in your corner right now, and that's only because your mother is cutting me checks to keep you alive. My grandmother is not risking an alliance that keeps her people safe."

"I can't go to Chivalry," I said. "He won't disobey orders. Madeline's the one who made the damn orders, so that takes her right out as well."

"True." Suzume's eyes glittered. "Now, who does that leave?"

I hesitated, and thought. When I began to glance back to the doctor's office, Suzume made an exasperated clicking sound with her tongue. "Are you high, Fort?"

"Okay, maybe not specifically her," I said defensively, "but I can't be the sole supernatural creature in this state who feels that child-molesting vampires are a bad idea!"

"No, there do exist a few more bleeding hearts who will go out of their way to take out a creature whose habits, while repugnant, have not yet endangered their own kind. But there's still an itsy-bitsy problem there."

"And I'm sure you're going to tell me about it."

Suzume ignored my sarcasm. "Yes. Tell me, Fort, who do you think is the controlling power in not only this state, but for anywhere in the next few hundred miles?"

"The vampires." I was reluctant, but it was the truth.

"Exactly. So even if we tracked down a few more people who, like you, aspire to follow the example of Dudley Do-Right, they wouldn't tangle with a vampire who has your mother's protection. Because even if we could somehow hoodwink them into believing that your mother isn't that fond of this guy, and wouldn't care if we tangled with him, do you really think that she's going to be very happy about someone in her territory setting the precedent of fucking with vampires and getting away with it? Every supernatural creature in four states sits in the shadow of Madeline Scott, and we didn't exactly vote her there."

"You're saying that we shouldn't go after Amy?" I didn't bother to try to stifle the outrage in my voice. At this moment, I didn't think I could handle having yet one more person treat Amy Grann's life as dispensable. It was all too easy to imagine what was waiting for Amy if I stepped back, stopped caring, or accepted this as not my business. That smiling little girl from the photos would look like Maria had—hopeless, empty, dead while she still breathed. I remembered seeing all those ragged scars on Maria's neck and arms, and that sick feeling of knowing that those hadn't even been the worst abuses that she'd been made to live through. There was no clean death waiting for Amy if I turned away—just degradation and pain until the day that she was no longer amusing for Luca, and that was the day that she'd be literally thrown away in the trash. I slammed my fist hard against the Fiesta's dashboard, which was old, dried out, and worn, and it split under my hand. Looking at it, I knew that I should be feeling guilt about taking my frustration out on the Fiesta, who had certainly already suffered over the last few days, but I couldn't.

"No." Suzume was all business. "That's not what I'm

saying. I'm saying we need backup who can kick a vampire's ass. Who is the one person who we haven't eliminated?"

I thought. I thought again. I was already shaking my head before I'd even fully grasped the answer.

"No," I said. "Not her. Never her."

"Put-up or shut-up time," Suzume said, so merciless. "Do you want to save this girl's life or not?"

I did. But it still took me a long, hard minute to accept what I had to do.

Suzume and I switched seats. I turned the ignition key and hesitated again. Then I got a hold of myself. This couldn't be about me anymore. Amy was alive right now, and could be saved. That had to mean more than events in my past that I couldn't change. The way that I felt, all that old pain, it had to take a backseat to keeping her alive. That's what my foster father would've told me, I knew. I could feel down to my bones that this was what Brian would've expected me to do. Even if it meant going to see the person I hated most in the world and asking for a favor, how could I possibly consider that more important than Amy Grann's life? If saving her life meant doing this, how could I live with myself if I didn't? Brian would've told me to do everything I could to save her, even if it meant asking his own murderer for help.

I turned the key, then waited while the engine floundered and turned it again. This time the engine caught.

Then I drove us to my sister Prudence's house.

South Portsmouth, where Prudence lives, is one town over from Newport. I guess that for Prudence that was just far enough to declare some independence from Madeline, but not so far that it would be real independence, which would suggest that she was leaving the nest and trying to claim territory for herself. And while Chivalry lives at home and is Madeline's right hand, handling almost all of the day-to-day duties and tasks that occur, Prudence is Madeline's left hand. She doesn't get sent out when diplomacy is in order, or even when threats are. Madeline sends in Prudence when there's a high likelihood of violence ensuing.

Of course, it had occurred to me in the past that there could be an inverse correlation there. That when Prudence went in to handle something, there was a far greater chance that there would be deaths than if Chivalry had gone. I'll probably never stop wondering if Jill and Brian would still be alive today if Chivalry had been sent over to the house instead of Prudence. And it's because of that nagging question, that doubt, that I'd never sought Prudence out for anything in my life. Our paths had to cross from time to time at the mansion, but I'd never wanted any kind of closer relationship with her, and Prudence obviously felt the same. There were a lot of questions I'd had about myself, about what it meant to transition to full adulthood, but when Chivalry or Madeline hadn't answered them I hadn't bothered to go to Prudence.

Now the Fiesta sat on the shiny asphalt driveway that led up to her very modern town house. Prudence likes new construction, and she usually moves every decade or so. The town house was light gray with white trim, three stories tall, harbor views, and was surrounded by about fifty buildings that were completely identical except for the numbers above their garages. It was just after noon, but there were no kids playing, no mothers pushing baby strollers around. The only sign of life was a guy in a lawn-service T-shirt who was mowing the already rigidly uniform grass.

This wasn't the kind of place where young families moved. This was where single professionals lived. There was something incredibly antiseptic about all of those uniform buildings, and I could see why Prudence had moved here. It was her kind of place.

I stared at the door, not making any moves to get out of the car.

"Do you think she's home?" Suzume asked quietly. We hadn't talked very much during the drive. I hadn't liked what Suzume had told me, even though I knew that all it had been was the hard truth, and my temper was still simmering just under the surface. It wasn't helped in any way by having to come see Prudence and ask her for a favor. For once, Suzume had been almost respectful of my mood, not trying to cheer me up or antagonize me into a reaction. Now her tone was almost polite.

"Yes," I said, not looking away from the door. I didn't elaborate. I could feel Prudence waiting inside, and I knew that she could feel me sitting out here. All of the windows had those expensive bamboo-slat blinds, all closed against the sun that Prudence was old enough to have to avoid. I watched, but there weren't any movements—she wasn't peeking out the window. She was just waiting to see what I'd do next.

"Do you want me to come in?" Suzume was still quiet, and there wasn't anything pushy in her question. I was surprised enough to finally pull my eyes away from the gray front door and look over at her. She looked back at me, waiting.

"That's a real question, isn't it?" I asked, almost won-deringly. "You don't already know what you want, and are just pushing me in that direction. You'll stay if I ask, or go with me if that's what I want." I paused, and turned it over in my mind. "Why?"

Suzume tapped her index finger against the tip of her nose. "This is different, Fort. Coming here is . . . hurting you."

"You can smell that?"

She nodded, and then waited.

I looked back at the door. I hadn't been alone with Prudence since the day that she'd killed my foster par-ents. No one had ever mentioned it, but looking back I realized that there'd always been someone else around on every other occasion we'd come into contact. Chiv-alry or Madeline, always one of them in the background of every encounter, every unpleasant run-in or holiday duty. I hadn't felt Prudence's undiluted presence in al-most two decades, or spoken to her alone.

I wanted Suzume with me. I wanted it very badly. I could imagine her strolling into the house beside me, snapping off sassy comments at Prudence and making her boil, negotiating the situation with that mix of savoir faire, provocation, and lethal understanding that had made her so effective at Dr. Lulu's. It was very easy to picture her taking over the situation so that all I had to do was sit in a corner and nod at what she said, to use her as a shield against the memories my older sister al-ways incited. It was very, very tempting.

I asked her to stay in the car, and she nodded, making a show of settling herself and closing her eyes for a nap in the sunshine.

I walked up the plain gray flagstone path to the door with all the speed of molasses in winter. With every step I wanted to turn around and go back to the car, give all of this up. Spend the rest of the afternoon on the sofa watching movies, and get up early for my scheduled work shift tomorrow. I knew that if I did that, no one would think any worse of me. A few people might actually think better of me. And I wouldn't have to face the horror that had ended my childhood in a night of blood and terror.

It wasn't any kind of courage that got me to her door. It wasn't any greater sign of adulthood that made me ring her doorbell, or keep standing there when I heard the sound of her footsteps inside. If I could've avoided facing her alone for the rest of my very, very long life, I would have.

It was Amy who kept me there as the door began to open. Because I was the only hope she had, and wasn't that completely unfair? She deserved a hero, and all she had was me. Poor little girl. But I'd let Maria down, and I wasn't going to do the same with Amy.

Prudence stood in the doorway, her lip curling ever so slightly. "Fortitude," she said coldly. "What an unwelcome surprise." Her critical gaze swept downward, taking in my T-shirt, my pajama bottoms, and the orange blotches that were visible on my face and arms. "I see you have decided to give me another example of your so-called age-appropriate attire."

I gritted my teeth and forced myself to be pleasant. "I'm so glad you're home, Prudence," I said. "Can I come in?"

Prudence was dressed down for a day at home, or at

least as dressed down as she ever got. I guess that when you grew up in the times of lace-up dresses, tri-corn hats, and stomachers, there's really only a certain level of casual-wear that you're going to be able to handle. For Prudence, a casual day at home meant beige linen slacks, low matching heels, and a short-sleeved white sweater. A string of pearls around her neck completed her Stepford wife look. Her clothes went with the house—or from the snowy white carpet, the white walls, and the very modern beige furniture, at least as much of the house that I could see. The first floor was just the garage and a small stairwell that led up to her living room. Through an open doorway I could see a formal dining room, and the closed door probably led to her kitchen. Another staircase led up again, I assumed to the bedrooms, but I hadn't come for a tour and Prudence didn't offer one. The only point of color anywhere was Prudence's fire-engine-red hair.

Ever the gracious and welcoming hostess, Prudence got a towel out of the downstairs bathroom for me to sit on, rather than risking the possibility that I would get her sofa dirty if my clothing was allowed unimpeded contact. Since I was here to try and ask a favor, I bit my tongue and didn't comment, just spreading the towel out as directed and sitting down on it gingerly. I waited in the living room while Prudence went into the kitchen and returned with a warm Diet Coke, which she handed me.

"Don't spill this," she said. Oh, the manners of a more civilized era. She settled herself down in a small upholstered chair across from me. Beige on beige. I set the Coke down, unopened, on the coffee table.

There was a small scuttling sound from the kitchen.

"Did you get a cat?" I asked politely. Maybe some ice-breaking conversation would soften her up.

"I acquired a pet recently," Prudence said.

I waited. She didn't say anything else. Oh-kay.

"So, how is business going?" I tried. Prudence works in finance, dipping her fingers in a lot of stocks and investment banking, and so far has been extremely successful at having other people go to jail for her. Madeline's political contacts always manage to give her a heads-up when people in suits are about to start asking questions about certain unsavory and borderline illegal business practices, and so Prudence is able to take her retirement package and liquidate her stock right before FBI agents storm the building with warrants.

"Fine."

Another pause. A few blinks. Some more scuffling sounds from the kitchen, then nothing but long and uncomfortable silence.

Finally Prudence leaned forward and said, "I don't like you."

I nodded. That hadn't exactly been the family secret.

"You hate me," she continued. Again, very true, and I nodded again. "Yet today you have arrived on my doorstep. I don't want to exchange pleasantries. I don't want to feign an interest in your opinions or life. I want you to tell me what you want so that I can say no and get you out of my house."

No one can be blunt like my sister, but I nodded. "Okay," I said. And then I told her.

I told her everything, starting from when we parted ways after Madeline's hospitality ceremony for Luca. Maria's body, the Grann girls' abduction, killing Phillip finding Jessica's body, realizing that Amy was still alive. I laid it all out, and she listened, not saying a word. She sat perfectly straight in her chair, her ankles precisely crossed, watching me intently. There wasn't a single flicker of emotion in her dark blue eyes at any point, but for once I had her full attention.

I finished, and waited. Prudence leaned back slowly, and steepled her hands, tapping her index fingers together with a slow, thoughtful precision as she considered.

"You have suddenly become very interesting, little brother," she finally said.

My heart leaped, and I struggled to contain my hope as I asked, "So will you help me?"

"I could." The tapping of those two fingers was the only movement in her body, and it stayed slow and steady. "Mother cannot command my obedience as easily now, and she has not asked me to stay out of this. And I may well be stronger than Luca, for all that he wanders free of his blood parent and I do not. And it would be sweet indeed to kill him." Her expression changed for the first time, her eyelids dropping slightly, and an almost sexual anticipation crossing her face when she considered killing Luca.

My heart was beating faster, and I had to clench my fists. The thought of being around Prudence when she killed was enough to make my stomach roil, but if that was how I could get her to help me, I would take it. I didn't care what her motives were, just what her actions resulted in. "Will you help me?" I repeated. "Will you save Amy?"

Prudence's eyes opened completely when I mentioned

Amy's name, and then she gave a short, high laugh tha grated on my nerves. "You really are foolish," she said that familiar sneer returning to her face. "Mother ha not commanded me because she does not need to. Why should I care about a child I have never met? Why should I care whether her death is quick or messy? Bu you care very much. How interesting."

I fought down my temper hard. "You don't have to care," I said, forcing out each word. "You wouldn't do i for her. You'd do it for you." She lifted one eyebrow cu riously, and I rushed on. "To prove that you're stronger than Luca." I could only hope that ego would work as ar appeal. Prudence had plenty of that. "He made a host even though he's younger than you. You haven't done that, so people would think he's stronger than you. I you beat him, and take his toy away, no one will think that anymore."

Something flickered in Prudence's blue eyes, some thing dangerous and feral, but it was gone in an instant and her mouth widened in a cold, thin smile. "Is tha what you think?" she asked. Then she called, "Desiree Come here!"

The shuffling sound from the kitchen got louder, and I turned and looked as a thin woman in her early thirtie crawled into the room. She had long dark hair and a face that probably used to be very pretty, and she was clear and presentable, her clothing a near match to Pru dence's. But there was nothing sane in the dark brown eyes that passed over me as if I were another piece o furniture. There were no marks of any kind on her, ex cept where she'd bitten into her own lip so many time that it was just raw meat, but she flinched when Pru dence looked at her, and cringed backward, whimpering, like a beaten dog.

"Desiree, come here," Prudence repeated sharply, and the woman crawled to her. There was something wrong in the way she moved. Muscles spasmed, making her shake constantly, and when she pulled herself forward on her arms her elbows wiggled bonelessly, empty sausages of flesh that moved against the joints.

There was no way to look away. There was something rotten in the way she smelled that had nothing to do with dirt, because she was immaculately scrubbed. Finally she was at Prudence's feet, and pressed her face against Prudence's knee. Prudence leaned down and patted the top of her head absently, as if rewarding a half-senile dog. Then my sister looked back up to me, and smiled at the revulsion that I had been incapable of hiding.

"Yes," she said. "You see now. Why should I care what Luca does?"

"You've made a host?" My voice was barely above a whisper, and my throat still rasped against it.

"Not a very good one, I'm afraid," Prudence said with another negligent pat to Desiree. We might as well have been talking about a poorly cooked casserole for all the emotion Prudence showed. "I've only had her a month, and she's failing fast. I'm a long way from brooding yet. But Desiree is a sign of something better—that my days at Mother's skirts are drawing to a close."

I knew without asking that it was definitely something that Prudence had been doing behind Madeline's back. But if she'd kept it secret from Madeline, and was now showing me . . . I stiffened. "You're showing me this because you plan to kill me?" I asked. I didn't quite achieve that James Bond level of careless inquiry that I was aiming for. My voice was tight and tense, but I was at least able to say it. I didn't look away from Prudence, whose smile widened at my question, showing me that her fangs had partially extended, razor-sharp needles in her mouth. She could kill me well before I could make it to the door, and I'd left my bodyguard behind. I kicked myself mentally at my stupidity—my family members were probably the very people I needed the most protection from.

Prudence let the tense moment drag on; then she laughed again, high and cruel. "No, stupid boy. Mother would know in an instant if I spilled your blood, and I won't move yet. But Luca will be quite capable of killing you, and you're going to be so thoughtful as to give him the chance." Prudence's eyes brightened, the pupil expanding to cover her bright blue irises with gleaming black until looking at her was like looking into the eyes of a great white shark.

"Don't you think I'd tell Mother about your activities?" I asked, struggling to find some kind of hook, some element of blackmail. Anything to force Prudence to do what I needed her to. "I could call her on a cell phone. I could text her right now." Well, I could've if my phone was still working, but Prudence didn't need to know about that.

Prudence made a sharp, impatient gesture. "Stop these empty threats. You won't even dare contact her because you won't risk her stopping you from trying to get that little girl away from Luca. Because you're the last hope that child has, even though it's as false as fool's gold."

Prudence moved the hand that had still been patting Desiree's head down to caress the back of her neck. Desiree's whimpering became louder, but she never flinched or moved her eyes away from Prudence's face. Another stroke, and then Prudence's hand tightened, and there was a movement too fast for my eyes to follow, a cracking sound that filled the room, and Desiree slumped to the floor, her head flopping on a neck that could no longer support it. Her mad eyes emptied, and her mouth dropped open in a silent O of surprise. Prudence nudged the body with one expensive shoe and sniffed. I stayed where I was, frozen.

"Mother is old and powerful," Prudence said, "and perhaps even wise. But she made a mistake when she made you the way she did, Fortitude. A mistake she continues even now." Her vampire black eyes were blazing as she stared at me, and none of her hatred was hidden now in that virulent glow. "No vampire should care like you do. Mother refuses to see the implications of her actions, and Chivalry has always been too weak and loves you too much to ever move against you, but I see. I am glad indeed that Luca will correct Mother's mistake." Her voice dropped, and she hissed, "I envy him the opportunity."

"What do you mean?" I demanded. "What was different about the way she made me?"

Prudence reached down and squeezed the dead girl's neck, crushing the remaining bones beneath her deceptively delicate hand. "Run away, little brother," she whispered. "Run away and die."

There were no answers here, and no help at all. I left, walking fast, but forcing myself not to run even when I had to turn my back on her as she sat there in that bland living room, grinding up Desiree's body in her hands and staring at me with deathly malevolence. I was shivering when I got back to the car, despite the hot afternoon sun, and Suzume took one look at my face and didn't have to ask me what Prudence had said.

Back to the apartment, where I changed clothes in the bathroom. An old pair of broken-in hiking boots, jeans, and a long-sleeved shirt. That was about as vampire-hunter-y as my wardrobe could supply. It would've been nice to top it off with a cool leather jacket, but the best I owned was a cheap windbreaker that had my alma mater stamped on the back. Besides, it was June and temperate. I'd put an undershirt on under my long-sleeved shirt and was already uncomfortably warm in the un-air-conditioned apartment, but I had to keep in mind that I might find myself having to clothe Suzume again, so I'd made it a point to have two layers on top.

I scrubbed my face in the sink, getting off a little bit of the orange stain, enough that at least at first glance I looked unremarkable again. I looked at myself in the mirror and took a few deep breaths. Prudence had been the monster in my nightmares since I was nine years old. It should've been at least marginally therapeutic to face her alone and on her own turf. I thought of Desiree, changed into something no longer human and then thrown aside because she hadn't been what the monster had wanted. Just like Jessica Grann, who'd been stolen, broken, then killed because she wasn't the kind of toy that Luca wanted. They were both monsters, Luca and Prudence. The only difference was in who held their leashes.

My hands were shaking a little as I dried them. Finding Phillip yesterday had been a shock, and the violence that had followed had been completely unexpected. Now I knew that I might be facing blood and bodily injury, and that Suzume was capable of tracking Luca to his lair. I wished that the thought of those two things didn't scare me, but they did. Maybe my sense of self-preservation was stronger than my desire to engage in heroics. I rested my hands on the edge of the sink and squeezed the cool porcelain for a minute. Okay, I clearly wasn't Batman, or even Antman, but I was all that Amy had. And wasn't that just a shame?

Clearly I needed to work on my personal pep talks.

I combed some gel into my hair and tried to crunch some of the dark brown tangle into spikes. The result was semisuccessful, but it did look marginally more badass, and that helped cheer me up. Now all I needed was black leather pants, combat boots, and a black T-shirt to look like an extra from *Underworld*. It turned out that I actually could laugh in the face of danger, so I called that a win and left the bathroom.

I went out into the living room, where Suzume was seated on the futon, flipping channels on the television. She'd put her hair up in a ponytail, and on impulse I reached out to tug at the silky black rope. She tilted her head slightly, but didn't object, as I kept my hand around it, stroking it a little with my thumb, before letting it go again. It made me feel better, and when I rested my hand on the arm of the futon, it finally wasn't shaking anymore.

"Are you still going to try to find Amy?" she asked, her voice so quiet that I barely heard her over the droning of the television.

"Yes." There was something in her voice that worried me, but I answered quickly, a little annoyed with her. She should've known this.

Suzume flipped channels faster, hitting the buttons on the remote with restless, aggressive motions. "And what are you planning to do once we find her?"

"I'll ask Luca to give her to me."

Suzume didn't look at me. "And when he doesn't?"

The question hung between us. I breathed in deeply, and let it out again. If this came down to a fight between me and Luca, I was beyond screwed, and she knew it. I had hopes for the best and no defense against the worst, but it was all that I had.

"Suze," I said, desperation in my voice. "I have to find her."

She kept flipping channels.

"We can make this happen," I insisted. "I can lie to him, tell him that Madeline got pissed about the publicity, tell him that she sent me to get Amy."

"And if he calls your mother to verify that?"

"Chivalry will lie for me if he answers the phone." That wasn't the answer she was looking for, but I reached out and squeezed her shoulder, willing to her to believe in this, to trust that this could happen. "He will." I knew that repeating it was the wrong decision, but I needed the reassurance as well.

She turned off the television and set the remote down on the arm of the futon with exquisite care. Then she turned to look at me, and I could finally see how angry she was.

"Fort," she said. "You aren't responsible for any of this."

"I know."

"Not for Maria." Her voice was rising as she continued. "Not for Mr. and Mrs. Grann. Not for Jessica. Not for Amy. *None* of it." She was shouting in my face now, but I didn't object, or try to stop her or quiet her down.

She pressed a hand to either side of my face and pulled us close, until all I could see were her dark, beautiful, angry eyes. Her voice dropped, became soft and gentle. "You are not going to be able to save Amy."

"I can," I said. "*We* can."

"Those are lottery odds, Fort." Her voice was like a warm blanket, urging me to roll up in it, to just accept that truth. "Everything has to go right. You don't have a fallback, you don't have some ace in the hole to pull out if it goes bad. And even if you try, it still won't bring any of them back. Do you understand me, Fort? None of them."

I'd never told her about Brian and Jill, but I realized in that moment that Suzume knew about them, and had known about them this whole time.

"I have to find her," I told her, needing her to understand. "It's not about guilt or wanting to be some kind of hero." I reached up to press my hands over hers, to feel the warmth of those long fingers that seemed so capable of trickery and violence. She was the reason that Phillip was dead, the whip that had driven me to go to Prudence's house when I thought that nothing could ever have made me go there. I knew all too well how much I needed her to understand why this was so important, and why I needed her so badly. I thought about Amy from the newspaper photo, in the baseball uniform, with blond ponytail, freckles, and coaxed smile. "She's only nine, Suze," I said, trying to put it into words. "I was nine when Prudence killed my parents . . . it was like she'd destroyed my whole world. And that's what is happening to Amy right now. I can't just turn my back on her. Not when I can try to do something. If I don't do anything, then it's like I helped kill her. Do you understand?"

I pressed harder at her hands, knowing it was too tight, but pushing anyway. I wanted to leave her handprints on my face. Her eyes were so beautiful, dark and perfect, and looking into them I finally said what had been gnawing at me. "What if I hadn't let go of Maria?" I asked. Suzume's face immediately turned stormy, and she tried to free her hands, but I held on, pushing it. "What if I'd just held on to her arm? What if I hadn't given up on her?"

"Nothing would've changed, Fort," Suzume said fiercely. "It all would've ended the same damn way."

"But you don't know that. *I* don't know that. If I'd forced it, pushed it, thrown a goddamn tantrum like a two-year-old, *maybe* he would've given in. Maybe she'd be alive. You can't say that it was impossible. I could've tried harder. I could've saved her."

Suzume pushed harder, forcing down my hands. I could feel the loss the moment her palms no longer touched my face. She pulled back, away from me. I reached out, tried to touch her, but she got up too quickly, and was out of my reach.

"Suze," I said. "I need you. Please. I need your help."

There was a small moment of hesitation, but I knew when she'd made her decision, because her face hardened, became certain. She reached down behind the futon and picked up her duffel, which she must've put behind there when I was in the bathroom. It was full again, stuffed nearly to overflowing. She'd packed up.

"Please, Suzume." I got off the couch, following her as she walked to the door. My voice raised, and I yelled at her as her hand touched the doorknob, "Goddamnit, Suze, don't leave me!"

She paused again, then turned to look at me, and her face was a stranger's. I'd already extended a hand to grab her shoulder, but now I pulled back, not touching her. "Despite what my cultural heritage might suggest," she said coldly, "I'm not a fan of kamikaze missions. Do what you think you have to, Fort, but you'll do it alone."

I felt a sharp pain in my chest. A loss, a betrayal.

She walked out, and I watched from the doorway. When she'd reached the end of the hallway and had taken the first step down the stairs, I called to her, "What does *nogitsune* mean, Suzume? What did your grandmother try to warn me about?"

I could see that my last barb had hit by the way her spine stiffened, and the sudden tension in her shoulders and arms. She froze for a second, then replied without turning around. Her voice was flat, but I could hear her suppressed anger. "It means field fox, Fort. It means to be without kindness, to just be a trickster, a nuisance, a danger. It means not caring about consequences. It means to have to live outside the human cities." She paused, and I could see her take a deep breath. "But it also means to value your own survival. And Amy Grann is not worth risking my life for."

I watched her walk down the stairs. Then I went back into the apartment and looked out the window.

Suzume exited through the front of the building.

There was a cab already waiting at the curb, and she got into the backseat. That made it hurt even more—that she'd known even before she started talking to me that she was leaving, that she'd already called her cab. She'd been that sure that nothing I said could possibly have changed her mind, that there was no reason in the world worth staying with me. I watched as the cab pulled away, merging into traffic and disappearing around the corner.

She never looked back. Not once.

I still waited. I waited for five minutes, for ten minutes. I waited because I still hoped that this was a joke, a prank. That she would slink her way in through the door and laugh in my face, mock me for my lack of faith in her. And so I clung to my belief that she would be back.

Ten minutes turned to fifteen, and the truth began to sink in. At half an hour, I accepted it. She wasn't going to be coming back.

I was on my own.

Chapter 10

Suzume was gone.

I was on my own.

Those two thoughts chased each other around in my head. I sat on the futon, still reeling at the realization that Suzume had really left me, that it had really just happened. She'd just packed her bag and walked out. I had to reconsider everything that had happened today after I realized that Amy was alive. All those moments that I thought had been Suzume beginning to respect me more, to treat me more as an equal and less like the village idiot—those long quiet drives, her insistence that I talk to Prudence—they'd really been about her cutting her ties to me, deciding that the money Madeline was paying her wasn't worth the bother and risk of sticking around with me.

I'd only met her two nights ago. She'd barely been in my life forty-eight hours. She'd been so annoying that on many occasions I'd wished I'd had more money so that I could pay her to leave me alone. But seeing her ride away in that cab had hurt more than when I'd walked in on Beth having sex with Larry.

I pressed my hands over my eyes and told myself that

I had to get a grip. She was a fox and a trickster who delighted in screwing with other people—all the moments I'd thought that we were starting to form a weird little friendship had been just as fake as the times when she'd come onto me just to play with my head. The money she'd taken was the only reason she'd been staying with me. Her own poor attention span was the only reason that she'd been helping me hunt down the Grann sisters at all. But when entertainment and money hadn't been enough to offset risk, I'd been dropped. Her own grandmother had warned me, but I hadn't listened. I'd believed that no one who'd seen Jessica Grann's body lying on the ground could walk away.

More than that, I'd trusted Suzume. And she'd walked.

She'd been the one who'd found Phillip, the one who'd finally killed him. I'd been relying on her to find Luca for me. I didn't have a fox's nose; I couldn't hunt him down by a smell.

I'd been scared before of what it meant to challenge Luca when Suzume was with me. Now I was beyond scared at what that meant. Now what I really wanted to do was hide under my bed. Or drive down to the mansion and hide under *Chivalry's* bed.

I forced myself to get up off the futon, then walk back into my bedroom. There was a piece of paper sitting on my laptop, and I picked it up. It was filled with looping, girlish handwriting dotted with little hearts, and I knew immediately that it had to be Suzume's. I might've considered not reading it, just crumpling it up manfully and throwing it away, but I was already reading it before I realized that I should've done something else.

It took me a second to realize what it was. It was a list

of all the passwords that Suzume had changed. Facebook, bank account, e-mail log-ins, everything. They were all there. It hurt again, because this meant that she was even done with tormenting me, but I gritted my teeth, pushed that down, and dropped the password sheet back onto my desk. I briefly thought better of that and tucked it into the bottom of my underwear drawer, but that, I promised myself, would be the last time I'd think about Suzume. Unless she'd done something like short-sheet my bed on her way out, which seemed like a distinct possibility.

But that was for a later discovery, and I almost forcibly restrained myself from checking the sheets. I opened my closet and started digging though it. I'm not the stereotypical single-guy pig in terms of cleanliness, but I also don't do too much to keep my bedroom in order. I keep dirty clothes and random stuff off the floor, but I mostly manage that by tossing items like that onto my closet floor, where they're less visible to unexpected female company, but still available in a nice little heap whenever laundry day has passed me by again and I need a shirt that only needs to pass a very lax sniff test.

Now I dug through that pile, and the piles behind it that consisted of old school textbooks, a few DVDs that I preferred not to display out in the living room (not because of salacious content, but more because I felt slightly embarrassed to own copies of *Clue* and *The Princess Bride*), a box of stuff from my last apartment that I had still never gotten around to unpacking, and finally reached my goal.

It was a plain metal footlocker, about the size of a normal shoe box, with a combination lock. It had sat in the back of the closet since the day I'd moved in, and hadn't been opened for years before that. I used a sock from my dirty laundry pile to wipe away the dust that had accumulated on it.

The combination was simple, and I spun it from memory. Brian had believed that if he hadn't told me the combination, one day the mystery would be too much for me and I'd take loppers to it. That thought probably spoke more of Brian's childhood antics than mine, but I can still remember sitting at our kitchen table while Brian spun the dial and told me the combination. Twenty-four, seven, twelve. His day of birth, Jill's day of birth, then my day of birth.

The box opened, releasing a whiff of stale air. I reached in slowly, and withdrew Brian's 1911 Colt .45 automatic. He'd bought it about two months before he and Jill were murdered, for reasons that I never knew. He'd kept it locked in a back closet, out of sight. His .38 had been his police-issued sidearm, and the gun he'd taught me to shoot on, but this one had been different. I'd never shot the .45, and he'd never taken it with us when we went to the range, even for him to fire. He'd promised to teach me how to use it eventually, but he'd told me that even with his help, it was too big for a nine-year-old to fire.

After the murder, most of Jill and Brian's belongings were sold or given to distant family members. Chivalry and Madeline didn't interfere, or try to save anything for me, saying later that they'd had their hands too full with me to think about my foster parents. The few things I still have of them, the old photo albums, a few of their records, and this, had all been saved for me by Brian's partner, Matt. He'd given them to me when I was eighteen and in college.

The .45 was heavy in my hands, much more solid than the .38. There was ammunition in the box, and I loaded it into the clip carefully, and then the gun, checking to make sure nothing was sticking. When a gun hasn't been fired in a long time, it's usually a good idea to take it down to the range for a safe test to make sure that when it's necessary, it fires without a problem, but I didn't have that time today. I hadn't even opened the box in all the time I'd had it, but Brian had obviously stored it carefully, and it wouldn't have surprised me if Matt had oiled it regularly when it had been in his care.

There was a holster in the box as well, and I looped it onto my belt, wiggling it around until it was positioned at my back. I had no intention of sticking another gun in the back of my jeans, but with my shirt untucked, the gun would be hidden from any glances. I had a license to own this gun, but not a permit for concealed carry, and getting arrested wasn't on my list of things to accomplish today.

I sat at my desk and considered. I was now armed, and officially a danger to myself and others, but I still didn't know where to go to track Luca down. I started up my computer and spent an hour scanning over news sites. While I was working I heard the apartment door open. For one heart-stopping second I thought that Suzume had reconsidered, and I was out of my chair and at my doorway so fast that if I'd been in a cartoon, there would've been one of those little smoke outlines left at my desk. But it was just Larry. I stood for a moment, the disappointment almost choking me, and stared at him.

He'd brought in the mail, and was sorting it in his usual considerate fashion—namely, his mail was separated out, and most of mine was flicked in the direction of the trash can. I'd spent a lot of time since he moved in rooting through the trash for my telephone bills.

I trudged back to the desk and dropped back into the chair. For a long second I stared blankly at the computer screen. That moment of hope had been incredibly cruel, and it was hard to get over the lump of discouragement that seemed lodged in my chest. Finally I gripped the edge of my desk until it cut into my hands and reminded myself that Suzume was as gone as she'd been a minute ago, but now I really had to accept it. I really didn't want to, but at last I was able to turn my attention back to the news sites I'd been reading. All of the Providence papers were full of the murders, and the topic had even managed to migrate over to some of the Boston outlets, which was pretty unusual, since the Boston area looked at Rhode Island as its mentally slow country cousin. The calls were still out for information about Maria's identity, but most of the attention was firmly fixated on the Grann case. Amy's grandparents were holding press conferences, begging the killer to let Amy come home, and there were hotline numbers being advertised, but nothing that would help me find her.

I cursed Suzume again. How I was supposed to track down a vampire when I couldn't smell him—

Wait. I paused and reconsidered. I might not have a fox's nose to track down vampires, but I had always been able to feel my family members. I'd used that to track Chivalry down just yesterday, practically without thinking about it, just following the tug in my head until it took me to him. And I'd been around Luca, so I knew what he felt like—not the clear certainty of my family, but that low-level, almost annoying buzzing that seemed stripped of that bright bugling of identity, obnoxious enough that I could almost understand why most vampires only associated with direct family members.

Maybe if I'd been trying to track Luca down in a group of strange vampires, that might've been a problem, but right now he was the only vampire in the state who felt like that. If I could get close enough to him, I could find him.

Of course, that meant getting myself close enough.

Suzume had left behind her map of Providence, and now I spread it out on the floor of my bedroom. There were some papers folded up with it, and I flipped through them quickly—the commissioner had e-mailed her the police report, and she'd printed them out early this morning. We hadn't looked at them yet, but I folded them back up, just in case I needed them later, and refocused on the map. She'd marked the spot where Maria's body was found, and now I took a marker and drew an X on the spot where we'd found Jessica. They were fairly far apart, but maybe Luca was staying somewhere in the middle of those two points. It seemed as good a place as any to start looking.

That, of course, led me to the intimidating thought of what exactly I was going to do to Luca if I actually found him. The orange witch paste had cleared up the worst of what Phillip had done to me last night, but there were still plenty of aches to remind me that if it hadn't been for Suzume, I would've had my ass pounded into the pavement. Well, more so. And that was just Phillip. I was on my own, and massively overmatched in any direct confrontation with Luca.

Of course, Samuel Colt had made all men equal.

I pulled the .45 out of its holster and considered it. My best odds of getting Amy were probably to try and bluff, hoping that my powers of deception were stronger in this situation than during a poker game. But if that didn't work, everything was going to rest on the gun.

Last night had been the first time in my life that I'd shot at anything other than a paper target or the occasional bottle on a fence, but I'd done it, and I'd even hit what I'd aimed at. But a bullet in the shoulder hadn't put Phillip on the ground like it should have, which was making me wonder what kind of result I'd get going against Luca.

I pulled out the ammunition clip and checked it, my stomach sinking at what I saw. This was my foster father's gun, and the clip was the last ammunition he'd ever put into it. Standard round-nose bullets, perfect for poking a small hole in a burglar as a deterrent. Probably less perfect for a stopping shot against a vampire. And given Luca's age, if I didn't get him down with one shot, I probably wouldn't get the opportunity for a second. Shit.

I needed better ammunition, and for that I needed money. I mentally scratched my head. Even emptying my bank account and adding it to the last few dollars in my wallet would leave me far short of what good ammunition was going to cost. Grimly, I realized that I might've finally reached a line that I'd never come to before—the pawnshop. In all the time that I'd lived on my own, I'd been broke a few times, but I hadn't reached the point of needing to selling treasured belongings to get by. The really sad part was how few things I owned that would actually bring in cash—only my computer, my TV, and my DVD player, and none of those were new or had even been exactly top-of-the-line when I'd bought them.

A thump and a loud curse from the living room brought my mind momentarily back to the apartment. From the sound of it, Larry had just tripped over one of the drums that were scattered around the futon. I smiled a little, appreciating the justice that whatever bruise he was sporting had, however indirectly, come from Beth's actions. Then my smile faded as I reflected on how much money Larry owed me. Much, much more than I needed to buy the ammo.

I'd tried many times to get that money out of him, but Suzume's advice from earlier whispered in my ear. I'd asked him reasonably, I'd appealed to fairness, to decency, to his duties as a roommate. But I'd never tried threatening him.

Well, really, I'd never threatened anyone in my life.

I'd never bullied, never pushed, never even been in a fight (okay, I'd been in fights, but only the kind where I was beaten up). As a parent, Jill had been a big proponent of books like *William's Doll* and cartoons voiced by Alan Alda that emphasized talking through conflict. Under normal circumstances, that probably wouldn't have had a lifelong effect, but from the moment Jill and Brian were killed I'd been horribly reminded of how vulnerable people were to vampires, and I'd spent all of middle and high school avoiding direct confrontations or contact sports.

But I'd also avoided ever asking Prudence for anything, but today I'd done that. I'd certainly avoided doing anything that reminded me that I wasn't human, but just last night I'd gone hunting for a vampire through alleyways. And I'd certainly never risked my life before, but I was sure planning on doing that.

Put in that context, I could certainly grit my teeth and go threaten the shit out of Larry.

As soon as I decided to do it, it was easy to walk across the apartment and pound on Larry's door.

"Jesus, Fort," he said as he opened the door and glared at me. "What's your problem?"

I'd lived with Larry for months, but I don't think I'd ever really looked at him before. He was handsome, with blond hair and very Germanic good looks. He also affected a kind of preppy-meets-hipster personal style that, combined with self-deprecating but pointed remarks about doing graduate-level research into Kant, had proven to have a catniplike affect on women.

But standing in front of him now, feeling almost excessively righteous in my course of action, I processed that I had a good four inches of height on him and that while I might be no one's idea of a fighter, the only exercise Larry did was a little light cardio to keep the ladies flocking in. I'd been in a fight last night that would've made cage-match professionals cringe, and today, I was feeling goddamn *scrappy*.

I looked straight into Larry's eyes and didn't even bother with faking pleasantries. "You owe me four months of rent," I said, my voice so cold that I actually sounded related to Prudence. "I want it by the end of the week, and I also want fifty dollars right now. Cash."

Larry blinked in surprise, but recovered fast. His tone was dripping with all the heavy insincerity that had practically been my third roommate for months. "Listen, Fortitude, you know that I'll get you the money as soon as I can, but I just don't have it right now."

"No, I don't believe a word of that," I said. "Open your wallet."

"Excuse me?" Now I'd clearly shocked him. Hell, I was shocking myself. I never would've guessed that I had an inner Dirty Harry.

"You heard me. Get your wallet and open it up."

"I don't believe this," Larry said, and laughed. The look of shock on his face disappeared, and that old look of smug superiority slid right back on. "I don't know where this caveman routine is coming from, but I can tell you that it is not going to be effective. Have you ever considered that your inability to hold a real conversation is something that bothered Beth? Oh yeah, she and I used to talk about that a lot. You see, we live in a time of modern discourse—"

I punched him in the stomach. It knocked all the air out of him in a big whoomph, and he went completely down on the floor.

I shouldn't have been proud of myself, and there were a lot more important things going on right now, but I took a good mental snapshot of the sight of Larry rolling on the floor, clutching his belly and gasping like a landed fish.

"Holy shit," he squeaked out as soon as he could hold on to some oxygen. "Oh my God, holy shit."

I barely resisted the urge to make some nasty comment about the usefulness of modern discourse, but I reminded myself that this was a beating in the name of justice, not vengeance, and just said, "Money, now."

That smug look was long gone, and Larry was still clutching his stomach, but now he looked plenty pissed. He yelled, "That is assault and battery, you asshole, and I am going to call the cops, and then you're going to see me in court."

I couldn't help it—I laughed. Really hard. On the scale of minor annoyances, my family considered arranging a murder cover-up to be less of a hassle than getting the Historical Society to sign off on changes to the front door facade. And Larry was threatening to call the cops? Making an assault and battery charge disappear wouldn't even merit having whatever local politician who managed it over for dinner—my mother would probably just send an Edible Arrangement over to his office. As for lawyers, good grief, my mother didn't just have one lawyer on retainer—she had an entire firm.

Not that any of that was even worth mentioning. I gave one last snort before getting serious again. "Call whoever you want. Cops, lawyers, the Ghostbusters. Because right now there's no one here except me"—and I grabbed Larry by his shirt collar and gave him a hard shake—"and the guy who owes me four months of rent." I let myself smile at him, just enough to be really creepy, once again channeling my older sister. "And you're not making any calls until I let you."

Larry glared at me, but he was pale under his perfect tan, and this time he kept his mouth shut.

"I want the rent by the end of the week," I said. "And I want fifty dollars. Now."

It was slow, and very reluctant, but as I kept a hold of

his shirt, Larry reached into the back pocket of his pants and pulled out his wallet. Opening it up, he revealed a billfold packed full of cash.

"All I have are twenties," he said with a shadow of his old self, peeling two out of his wad.

I didn't say anything, just looked at him. After a long second, he silently pulled out a third and handed it over.

I took the money, then let him go and stood up. "Thank you," I said. I wasn't sure what the appropriate action after extorting funds was, but that felt right. I turned and walked out.

There were no sounds as I collected what I needed out of my room and headed out. But just as I was closing the front door behind me, Larry's generally dickish nature finally reasserted itself enough for him to yell after me, "I'm deducting that from the rent!"

I let the door slam shut.

The Fiesta felt lonely without Suzume there to chatter, and with my radio gone there was nothing to listen to except the sounds of traffic and the steady crinkling of wind whipping the plastic taped over the remains of my back window.

I pulled into the parking lot of Kravec Firearms. After the financial downward slide of the last couple of months, to say nothing of the depredations of the last few days, my wallet felt unusually fat in my back pocket. I also couldn't deny that there'd been something incredibly satisfying about seeing Larry so begrudgingly fork over that money. No matter which way I looked at it, I couldn't help admitting that Larry had more than had that coming.

The last time I'd been in a gun shop had been with my

foster father. The store had also doubled as a bait shop, a coin collector's shop, and as a must-see for anyone who was on the hunt for a 1766 Charleville musket or other examples of antique firearms. The owner had been our local Cubmaster, and my memories of going there were fond, particularly since it was next door to a frozen yogurt shop.

This trip required an element of speed that would simply not be attainable if I went to that particular shop. With my luck, I would end up cornered by old Mr. Dunkerly and spend two hours looking at pictures of his grandchildren and hearing about the entire career paths of every other boy in my old Cub Scout troop. That had led me to Kravec Firearms, whose sole recommendation had been that it was, according to the Yellow Pages, close.

Inside, it was very different from the gun shop of my childhood. Instead of a jumbled assortment of fly-fishing rods, antique muskets, coin displays, dusty ammo boxes, and stacks of white foam containers with their wormy contents documented on the side in Sharpie marker, Kravec Firearms consisted of several very long display cases filled with handguns, and a few racks of shotguns. Everything displayed was sleekly modern, and security cameras were mounted in every corner. Behind the counter sat a balding, middle-aged man built roughly on the scale of a rhinoceros, flipping through a magazine whose cover was displaying the assets of a young lady who must've made her home in a very tropical environment, judging by her choice of attire. Or lack thereof. From the clerk's look of complete disinterest, either this was an old magazine or the contents were failing to meet his standards.

There's always a certain awkwardness when addressing a clerk holding a porno magazine, but after years spent scouring the most bargain-basement car parts stores to maintain the Fiesta, I'd figured out that the only way to proceed was to pretend that the magazine did not exist. As I walked up to the counter, the man glanced up and pinned me with a flat "do not fucking waste my time" glare that only reinforced my earlier rhino comparison.

"I'd like to buy some bullets for a .45 automatic," I said. In a certain kind of store, it's often best to lead with the fact that you plan to be a paying customer, rather than a pain-in-the-ass window shopper. Given the miniscule brightening of the clerk's face (going from completely grim to slightly less grim), that was clearly the right opener.

"Standard round?" he asked. His name tag might've read YURI, but this man had clearly spent his entire life in the Boston area.

"Actually, I need something a little heavier duty than that." I said it as coolly as I could, but Yuri's bushy eyebrows rose in the same shenanigans-calling arc that liquor store clerks used when faced with the blatantly underaged.

"Got a particular reason in mind for that?" And now we were back to the rhino impression.

Shit, he was calling me on this. Whatever sense of being a badass that I'd carried over after the successful shaking-down of Larry left me, and my voice squeaked unfortunately upward as I said, "Just exercising my Second Amendment right to shoot stuff, sir." Oh yeah. That was smooth.

Yuri stared at me blankly for a long second, then burst out in a deep, belly-clutching laugh. I smiled and laughed as well, grateful that he had chosen to be amused rather than stomp me into the floor. "Good one, good one," he said once he'd finished, wiping a hand over his eyes. Then he leaned forward, and it was clear that I'd managed to break the ice, and we were back to business. "No, seriously. You have to match the bullet to the job, and if a regular full-metal-jacket round-nose in a .45 isn't doing it for you, we've got to find the right one."

"Well," I said cautiously, "I'd been thinking of hollow-points . . ."

"Oh, those make a nice big impression, no doubt." And we exchanged laughs again, his a knowing chuckle and mine just trying to keep up. One of his giant hands dipped under the counter, and without even looking, he came up with a box of .45 hollow-point bullets.

"Yeah, yeah . . . because I'm dealing with . . ." Here my mind raced frantically, trying to come up with some legitimate and totally nonillegal reason why I was trying to purchase this. After a long pause, I finished, lamely, " . . . bears."

Yuri paused, and that lie-detecting eyebrow started inching back up. "Bears?"

Well, I was committed now. I pushed forward, forcing confidence into my voice as I spun lies as fast as my brain could supply them. "Yes. My girlfriend has been seeing this black bear in her backyard lately, and she's starting to get worried."

"Oh, out by the state forest area?" Yuri's eyebrow lowered to resume its bushy post beside the other, and he relaxed a little as he helpfully filled out my mistruth.

"Yes," I responded. Because that clearly made a lot more sense than bears in the middle of Providence. "Yes, right around there."

"Bet she put out one of those damn bird-feeders, right?" Yuri was now nodding knowingly with that universally acknowledged Those Silly Darn Women expression.

"Yeah, yeah, that was absolutely the start of the problem." I was right there with this now, returning that expression and raising it a What Will You Possibly Do With Them? head shake.

Yuri shook his colossal rhino head in commiseration. "Might as well call those things *bear*-feeders. Nothing better to start a problem."

Now that the backstory was completely agreed upon, I tried to shift the conversation back to business. "So, the hollow-points . . ."

Yuri actually guffawed. "Oh, *definitely* not the hollow-points, son. Not for a bear." With another of those quick movements that belied his sheer size, he swept the box off the counter.

"Really?" I asked, startled.

"Really. Hollow-points are great for thin-skinned critters like us. Absolutely great. They just peel open and cause incredible damage. Fantastic on a human." I nodded encouragingly to him while he entertained these happy, reminiscent thoughts. "Problem is"—and his sharp eyes fixed on me from under those massive eyebrows as he raised one thick finger to emphasize his point—"on something with a good fat layer or a tougher bone density, like your black bear, it just causes a little surface abrasion and pisses the damn thing off. Which if you or your girlfriend are in an area with a bear is really

not what you should be going for. What you need"—
again, without even looking, he reached under the
counter—"is stopping power."

He smacked two boxes of ammo down on the counter. "So I'm recommending either full or semiwad cutters."

"Huh," I said, looking down at the boxes. Sure
enough, both were marked for a .45. This was clearly a
guy who believed in organization.

"Yep. And since you've got an automatic, I'm going
to lean you toward the semi. Better ballistics on them.
The great thing on these bullets is that because of these
flat-edge areas a lot of energy gets transferred, and the
bullet just mushrooms out and *punches* a hole. If you're
close enough to your target, this won't just penetrate—
this will come out the other side and leave one hell of a
hole." He gave me a wide smile that promised awful
things for whatever my gun was aiming at.

I considered what he'd said. Bone density is one of
those things that makes vampires different from humans. Basically, once we mature, ours is way the hell better. And it might not have looked it, but I knew that
Chivalry had tougher skin than I did, because he seemed
endlessly flummoxed by my ability to get paper cuts.
And even if I was wrong, really, if it got to the point
where I had to shoot at Luca, a bigger hole was probably
a better hole. I nodded at Yuri and said, "I think you've
got yourself a sale." We shared a manly handshake (perhaps too manly on his end—he had hands like Bigfoot),
I handed over the cash, and then I was the proud owner
of two boxes of bullets. As my foster father used to say,
you don't want to need a spare clip and not have it. Better to be prepared.

As I was heading out the door, Yuri called, "Oh, and, kid?"

"Yeah?" I asked.

"Head or throat. You do not want to be aiming for a shoulder when you're dealing with a bear. You put a round in its shoulder and it'll just keep coming and absolutely mangle you." Yuri gave me a grim look that suggested that he'd been hunting a few times, and for something a bit more aggressive than deer.

"I will remember that," I promised, for the first time telling him the honest truth.

Following my marked-up map of Providence, I found a parking spot as close to the true midpoint between the Maria and Jessica locations as I could, and sat for a moment in the car, not quite certain what to do. This far away, I couldn't even feel Chivalry and Prudence. I tugged at Madeline, and felt the faint echo of her, fifty miles away in Newport. It wasn't much, but I knew what direction she was in. Letting go of Madeline, I reoriented myself, trying to keep that slightly skewed mindset that I'd fallen into to locate her, and then just started walking. I circled the block completely, feeling around for any whispers of Luca.

Three hours later and I was sitting in a hole-in-the-wall pizza joint, gulping down water and eating a reheated slice of cheese pizza, feeling frustrated and dispirited. There hadn't been anything, no tugs, no whispers, no tickles in my brain for the entire time that I'd combed around the area, working in a grid pattern to try to cover all the middle ground between the two sites.

I pulled out my map again. I'd crossed off all the streets that I'd eliminated in my search, but it was a pitifully small area, and I might have just wasted three hours. Luca could've been sending Phillip from any point from the sides of the dump sites, or he could've gone farther the first night that he dumped Maria, and not as far the night he dumped Jessica, meaning that Luca could be hiding out somewhere beyond the Jessica point. Or it was the wrong direction entirely, and he was somewhere beyond the *Maria* point. . . .

My hands tightened, crushing the sides of the map. There were too many possibilities, and I wasn't capable of covering nearly enough ground in my search. Suzume's nose led her on a straight line, point A to point B, but here I was, fucking around with geometry, when two points weren't enough. I needed a third point, but Luca had only provided me with two.

I paused and considered, looking at the map again. Each of those points was someone that Luca had killed. But he'd killed more than two people since he arrived in Providence—he'd also killed Jessica and Amy's parents. And he'd done that the same night that he'd gotten rid of Maria, within two hours at the most, in fact. Possibly even closer, since it had taken so long for each to be discovered.

I pulled out the police report and tried to read it. Suzume had apparently been conserving paper, because she'd sized it down to the smallest font she could find, single spaced, and double-sided it. I had to squint to read, but the information I wanted was at the top of the page. Looking again at my map, I carefully wrote in a new X at the location of the Grann house, then sat back and considered it.

The Granns had lived on the edge of a residential area. A block down the hill from them, the area turned to businesses and industrial. Three blocks farther it became the revitalized strip of clubs and bars that Suzume and I had walked through on our way to where Maria had been found.

Luca hadn't been in the city long at all, I reminded myself. He'd had to present himself to Madeline the same night he arrived. That wouldn't have given him much time to find the Granns, that family with its beautiful young daughters who seemed so tailor-made to appeal to him.

I doodled a little on a napkin, making notes as I thought through the timeline. He'd killed Maria after he learned that she was useless to him, then gone to the Granns. Given when he'd left Madeline's mansion that first night, the earliest he could possibly have made it back to Providence would've been midnight, since I'd left barely ten minutes after him, made good time, and pulled into my parking lot at twelve thirty. According to the original news article, the police had placed the murders of the Grann parents at just after two in the morning. That gave Luca about two hours to locate his newest victims, but the times weren't matching up. A family like the Granns would've been safely tucked away in their beds between midnight and two, safely out of view of a child-molesting vampire on the hunt. He must've seen them earlier.

He was older than Chivalry, not as old as Prudence. If their preferences held true for him, then he'd avoid the worst of the afternoon sun and come out in the early evening or morning. It had happened on Wednesday, so when would he have seen Jessica and Amy together, that perfect pair of golden girls? I closed my eyes and tried to think. We'd been nailed by snow this last winter, and school was just finally coming to an end with all those snow days to make up, so maybe he'd seen them waiting for the bus together, or getting off the bus at the end of the day. But that was a little chancy—it meant arriving early enough to see them and at just the right time, which seemed a little unlikely for a guy just coming in from Italy. And school let out around three—a very uncomfortable time for a vampire his age to be out strolling.

Something tugged at me, and I thought back to that dinner at the mansion. He'd said something when Madeline asked him how long he'd be in the area . . . something about . . . it sprang into my mind—he'd wanted to "see the sights." Now, if I were a pedophile in a new city, what places would be at the top of my list of sightseeing?

I looked back at the map. There was a little park two blocks away from the Grann house. The kind of park that parents might take a pair of active girls after they finished work for the day, or maybe even the kind of park where softball games were played. The kind of park in the city that was filled with all the neighborhood kids on hot summer evenings, just the time that an out-of-town vampire would be getting up and looking around his area. For a pedophile, it would've been catnip, and the first place he headed. If the girls caught his eye there, it would've been easy enough to shadow them home, since they were so close that they would've walked there. So he would've known exactly where they'd be later that night, after he'd killed Maria and been feeling sulky because all his "sacrifices" in keeping her around after he didn't want her anymore had been for nothing.

I drew a circle around the park and the Grann address, keeping its edge at where Maria's body had been found. He would've been in a hurry that night, eager to get to his new toys, and Maria would have been dumped quickly. The next night, getting rid of Jessica, he would've been more cautious, more like vampires were told to be, and instructed Phillip to take her farther away, to draw the eyes of police to the wrong area of the city.

I played with that thought for another second—the wrong area of the city. Maria and Jessica had been in dirty alleys, near bars and clubs and businesses. Luca had planned this trip. A predator trying to avoid attention might be interested in abandoned warehouses and neighbors who wouldn't be around at night, but Luca had seemed to fit right in with my family, who tended to be pretty picky about their personal surroundings. I couldn't quite picture him walking around on old concrete floors and sitting on boxes. Chivalry had come to visit my first off-campus apartment once, and when he'd learned that I was sleeping on a bare mattress on the floor that I'd bought off the previous tenant for twenty dollars (which smelled only mildly of cat urine), he'd been so acutely horrified that he'd gotten right on the phone and paid double to have a new mattress delivered within an hour, and I'd found myself marched straight over to a furniture store for a new bed frame.

Prudence or Chivalry would probably have stayed in ritzy hotels if they were traveling, but they weren't in the habits of raping young girls, so anything with that kind of oversight and security was probably right out the window. Apartments have shared walls that are usually the same thickness as paper, and somehow I didn't think Luca was interested in having neighbors who might overhear any suspicious noises.

I tapped the map again, but I couldn't think of anything to narrow my search circle down any further. Maybe a town house like Prudence preferred, maybe a rented house, but I needed to hurry up and find him. Older vampires aren't exactly sleeping in coffins when the sun is out, but it can make them a little logier and sluggish. I'd take any sliver of an edge that would give me.

I ran all the way back to the Fiesta.

Parking wasn't exactly plentiful, so I finally parallel-parked in a residential-sticker-only area and hoped that I'd be gone again before some irritated local called the cops or the traffic officer rolled through. It was easier to focus on little things like that than consider the really stupid thing I was about to do.

I went straight over to the park, the city kind with one baseball diamond and a small playground area. There were a lot of kids running around, but also plenty of anxious adults keeping watch, and I got more than a few nervous looks as I passed by. The police might not have realized how important this park was, but the parents were very aware that it was a local girl who was missing.

I walked over to some swings and crouched down under the pretext of tying my shoe. People were really jumpy, and I didn't want to risk having some mother dial 911 to report a suspicious single man if I sat on a park bench, not when I was carrying a concealed gun filled with bear-killing bullets, so I let my hands fiddle around with my shoelace on autopilot while I reached back to that quiet place in my head and felt for vampires.

For the first time all day, something responded to me. There was that buzzing I'd been looking for—so faint that I almost couldn't pick it up, but when I gave that little line a tug, it tugged back and gave me a direction. I got up and followed it.

It led me out of the park and down the street, past tidy little houses. If there were kids playing in yards, parents were always out with them. There were a lot of fliers posted, some with Jessica's and Amy's photos on them, but most with just Amy's. I concentrated on that tugging, feeling it grow just a little stronger with every step I took. Just like back at the mansion, feeling for Luca was different than trying to locate my family. If I stopped concentrating and specifically looking for it, it dropped away immediately and I had to fumble to find it again. Which was lucky, since unless Luca was looking for me in the same way, he wouldn't feel me approach.

It pulled me down a one-way street, where the distance between the properties widened and the houses got more expensive. These lawns weren't tended with old push mowers from the garage; these were the product of professional care. The sidewalks here weren't concrete anymore; they were the older brick kind, the kind that cities hate maintaining and replace whenever they have the chance. The tug led me to a small Tudor house, set back from the street and partially obscured by a large and well-pruned hedge. The low-level buzz was like a bee rattling around in the back of my skull when I concentrated on it, and I knew that Luca was inside. I just hoped that Amy was still with him.

I circled around the property, hunching down slightly to stay below the old-fashioned gabled windows. I really hoped that no one in the neighborhood was keeping an eye on me, because everything about my actions was screaming *prowler*. All of the windows had modern turn blinds, all of which were, obviously, turned. I made my way around to the back of the house. There was a tall wooden privacy fence, and the gate was locked, but a landscaper had left a wheelbarrow and a few bags of lime next to it. Maybe he'd gotten called away in the middle of a job, or maybe the new renter hadn't liked having service personnel around and had told him to drop everything and get off the property until he was told to come back. Either way, I wasn't going to waste this stroke of luck. By turning over the wheelbarrow and stacking up the lime bags, I gave myself just barely enough added height that I could hop up and snag the top of the fence, then haul myself over. My landing on the other side wasn't very graceful, but I'd spent enough time trying to run away from Madeline's mansion that it was quiet, and I managed not to break any limbs on the way down.

With so much space between the house and the street, there wasn't much room in the back. Most of it was a large stone patio, but Luca had let the tall fence lull him, and the glass patio doors were open to let in the afternoon breezes, leaving the closed screen doors with thick privacy mesh as the only barrier to the outside. I crept up the patio as quietly as I could, then peeked inside. It was hard to see through the dark mesh, but after a second for my eyes to adjust I could see that at some point an owner had decided that their Tudor house needed an open floor plan—probably the reason it was now rented out to roaming European assholes. From the door I could see a kitchen nook, a lot of recently waxed hardwood floors, the kind of generic furniture that you see decorating time-shares, and one of those spiral staircases that invite death going up to a dark loft area.

I didn't see Luca, which was a good thing, but I also couldn't see Amy. The odds of having her waiting next to the door for me had been pretty low, but I had been hoping that for once Fortune would have smiled on me.

I wiggled the screen door push knob. It was one of those with the little latch on the inside that is marketed as a lock, and that owners seem to place a great deal of trust in, but Jill and Brian had had one on the back door of their house that was about the same age as this one, and I remembered from the many times that I'd accidentally been locked in the backyard that to open it you just had to try hard. It would stay locked against a normal attempt to open it, but the manufacturers clearly hadn't intended to keep out young boys who had no appreciation for how much their foster parents had just spent on a new screen door.

I pushed the handle in, and the lock engaged right where it was supposed to. This was the part where the wicked intruder was clearly intended to give up and go burgle elsewhere, but I kept applying steady pressure to the handle, increasing it slowly. The locking mechanism was just a tiny stick of metal that held against the door frame, and the more pressure I put, the more it bent. I could feel it starting to wiggle, and then with one last push, it gave way with a soft but startling bang. I waited, holding my breath, but I couldn't hear anyone moving, and I slowly opened the door just enough for me to sneak inside.

My eyes adjusted fast to the dim afternoon light that seeped around the edges of the blinds and gave everything a twilight look. There was nothing in this main open area, but I could see a partially open door along one wall that I hadn't been able to see from the patio. I could just barely make out the corner of a bed inside it. The spiral stairs led to one of those half-loft areas popular among people who have no children or any need for privacy. I knew that Luca was in the house, and given the time of day and that he hadn't come to investigate the sound of the lock breaking, he was probably sleeping. There were two possibilities in front of me.

I looked from one to the other. I could see a few skylights in the ceiling above the half loft, but they'd all been blacked out, probably with towels and masking tape. The bedroom on the main floor probably just had closed blinds, because it had the same low level of light seepage as where I was standing. It was brighter than the loft, which was shrouded in inky shadows, so I crossed my fingers and made my way over to it. I crept along the wall, mincing along and shuddering at every scuffing sound my boots made against the floor and silently cursing whatever deranged owner had decided on wooden floors instead of carpet. At the door, I took two deep breaths to try to slow my racing heart, then peeked inside.

The bed took up almost all of the room—a huge, frothy concoction with white sheets, fluffy pillows, and even a kind of open-lace canopy that was stretched between tall honey-colored wooden posters. Unlit candles covered every surface, tall white tapers and shorter, squatter red ones, and red and pink rose petals had been scattered across the sheets.

I'd thought that I'd discovered a new benchmark of disgusting when Suzume had ordered me to stamp on Phillip's severed heart, but clearly I'd been very wrong. Luca's lair of pedophilic romance was going to haunt my dreams for a long time—assuming I got out of here again.

That's when I heard breathing, high and fast, from somewhere farther in the room. I followed the sound, and when I rounded the far side of that high bed, I found Amy Grann.

She'd been locked in one of those portable metal wire dog crates, the kind for Labradors and poodles, and the ceiling was low enough that she had to stay seated. She was dressed in a blue teacup dress, with a snowy white apron and white tights. I knew from the photos that her hair was always in a ponytail, but now it was brushed out and fell down her back, and there was a shiny black ribbon tied in a bow right where most little girls wore a headband. If it was Halloween, every door she knocked on would know at a glance that she was Alice in Wonderland. My stomach churned, but I knelt down to put myself on her level. I couldn't see any marks on her, none of the awful bite marks that had disfigured Maria and her sister, but Amy's blue eyes were wide and glassy, and it didn't look like anyone was home.

"Amy," I whispered as I got closer to the cage. The cage was locked from the outside, but just with a little chain and a pin. It was easy to undo, so easy that she could've done it from inside, and I hated to think about why she hadn't. She hadn't responded to my whisper, and I tried again. "Amy Grann," I repeated, and something flickered in those dull, dull eyes. I eased the door open, wincing at each squeak of the metal. Now the door was completely open, but she was sitting at the back of the cage and not making any moves.

"Amy," I tried again. "My name is Fort. I've come to take you home."

She blinked, then shook her head slowly. "Can't go home," she said, that little voice hoarse and barely audible, so low that I had to strain to hear her. "The monster killed Mommy and Daddy."

"I know," I said, creeping closer, trying to see if I could fit my shoulders into the opening of the cage. I couldn't risk the time it would take to coax this broken little girl out on her own, but if I startled her and she screamed . . . I whispered to her again. "Amy, I'll take you away from the monster."

She shook her head again, and her lower lip trembled. "Can't go," she said. "The monster will hurt Jessie if I don't stay here. I have to stay here."

My throat tightened. No wonder she hadn't tried to open her cage—she thought that her sister's safety depended on her. She didn't know that Jessica was already dead. I could've lied to her then, and I thought about doing just that, saying that Jessica was already safe, and that I was going to bring her to see her, but I couldn't bring myself to do it.

"Amy." I reached my arm into the cage but stopped just short of touching her. I couldn't imagine how this little girl would react to being touched. "Amy, the monster lied to you. Jessica is dead." The words were like acid, but I forced them out. I couldn't let her believe that lie.

I could see the shock go through her, and that eerie stillness started to break as she shook. Her mouth opened, but nothing came out.

"Amy, please," I whispered urgently. "I need to take you away from the monster."

She gave a jerky nod, then leaned forward onto her knees to start crawling out. Relief flooded through me, and I scooted back to give her room. But just before the cage door, she froze again.

"It's okay, Amy," I said, my hands itching to just reach in and grab her and then run like hell. "I'll keep you safe. Come out."

She wasn't looking at me anymore, though. Her eyes were fixed at the door, and a high, terrified noise came out of her throat, the sound a trapped rabbit would make. A cold knowledge slithered up my spine, and I slowly turned to look.

Luca was leaning against the door frame. He must have just gotten out of bed, because his feet were bare and he was wearing a pair of loose black satin pants, like a genie from a shitty 'sixties movie, with a red silk shirt tossed on but left completely unbuttoned. Euro-trash pajamas.

"Why, Fortitude," he said. "What an unexpected visit."

Chapter 11

Luca was not pleased to find that I had broken into his house at such an inconvenient time, and was not hesitating to let me know about it. Under normal circumstances I might've found something inherently amusing in having a man dressed in such ridiculous clothing launch into a scolding lecture that would've been better suited to a high school principal, but with Amy frozen in place and my bladder under only very questionable control, there wasn't anything funny to be found in the situation.

Plan A—grab girl and run—had failed miserably. I now had to fall back on plan B—bluff Luca into giving up girl.

"I am really shocked at your behavior, Fortitude," Luca was saying. "I can only imagine that it was some incredible failure on the part of your mother and older siblings that gave you the idea that it was somehow acceptable to interfere with another vampire's hunt. Perhaps they have been lenient enough to let you take prey that you have not hunted yourself, but I am no mother cat to drag an injured mouse home for a kitten."

I'd practiced this argument a few times in the car, trying to draw back on the lessons I learned during those halcyon days as the second alternate on the high school debate team. The most important lesson that had been emphasized over and over to us was the importance of knowing the audience we were addressing. That had put anything that relied on appeals to inherent decency and moral behavior entirely in the trash can. What I'd ended up relying on was the one thing he did seem to value: manners. Well, vampire manners. I don't think that Miss Manners had any sections on the proper etiquette for kidnapping.

"Amy Grann is part of my mother's territory," I said, trying to push down my revulsion and pretend that I was talking about a head of cabbage. Here was a moment to regret joining the Film Club rather than the Drama Club. "Removing her would be poaching, and my family will not allow you to do that." In for a penny, in for a pound. I only hoped that if he decided to verify my story, Chivalry was the one who would answer the phone. My brother has stretched the truth to the breaking point for me before.

Luca had been pacing by the doorway, but now he stopped. His eyes narrowed. "I was granted hospitality," he said. "Hospitality grants me the right to hunt, the same right that you and your siblings enjoy."

"You have made excessive use of that right," I said, feeling like I was heading down the right track. "You've been in my mother's territory since Wednesday, and you've already killed three people." No indignation, no outrage, I reminded myself over and over. I was discussing cabbages and a rude guest; that was how I had to force myself to look at this. "That's more than my sister kills in a year." Well, I couldn't be sure about that, but I could certainly hope so. And to my direct knowledge, so far this year she'd only killed Desiree. That was just one person. Cabbages, cabbages, cabbages. Luca was looking unconvinced, and I reached into my back pocket and pulled out a thick rolled stack of printed-out articles and newspaper clippings that I'd prepared beforehand. I threw it down on the bed, where it lay in bizarre contrast to the rose petals. "Do you have any understanding of how utterly sloppy you've been?" I pressed. "This is just a tiny sampling of the kind of coverage that your activities are receiving. The local press is hysterical, and you've left behind a mess that we will be dealing with for a long time. Hospitality might give you the same rights as we enjoy, but it also demands the same restrictions, and my mother is very displeased with your actions." I really hoped that that last part was true.

Luca looked a little less certain now. "These matters are handled somewhat differently in Italy," he admitted. He frowned a little. "I had assumed that your mother had more control over the police, and that she would've directed them to some kind of arrest by now."

"My mother's control over the police is entirely sufficient in normal, restrained circumstances," I said, making my voice as cold and disapproving as possible. "But an unidentified dumped body, followed by a bloody home invasion coupled with two abductions and a subsequent murder? People are talking about a serial murderer, and there are calls for the FBI to get involved. Your actions have been utterly unacceptable."

Luca looked outright nervous now. "I had not considered it that way."

"A mistake any traveler could make," I assured him. "Now I'll just retrieve the girl and be on my way, and I'll make sure that my mother knows that you were doing your best to act in good faith."

His eyes narrowed at the reference to Amy, and he gave me a very sharp look. I kicked myself for bringing her up too soon. "It is unnecessary to concern yourself with my bit of baggage," he said smoothly. "What is out of sight will soon be out of mind, and it would be easiest for me to simply take her with me to where no one will ever recognize her. I am of course deeply apologetic for the difficulty that my actions have caused for your family, but I would never expect your mother to have to take the trouble to dispose of my little Amy herself."

"A missing child will bring in too much attention," I countered desperately. I could feel plan B circling the toilet, and I knew that I was grasping at straws now to save it. "And you have no chance of getting her out of the country. They put out an AMBER Alert this morning—there are people in every airport looking for her."

Luca gave a superior little chuckle, and all signs of concern were erased from his face. "If that is your mother's concern, then assure her that it is nothing. I have already acquired the paperwork that will say that she is my daughter, along with the drugs to keep her quiet and cooperative while I am traveling. And if I am questioned, well, *my* father has the police well under control in Naples. One phone call will confirm that all is well, and your mother's problem will be swept under the rug. This one has no family left, and soon enough attention will turn to other tragedies, and my little pet will be utterly forgotten."

He was certain now, confident, and began to walk closer to me. I stepped back, automatically putting myself between him and Amy. I couldn't think of any other lies that could save her; all I could do was blurt out, "No."

Luca arched one debonair eyebrow. "No?"

"No," I repeated. There was no going back from this, and I took a deep breath. "You can't take her."

Luca's expression was past suspicious. "Why has your mother sent the least among her children to creep into my home like a thief?" he asked slowly, his eyes never leaving my face. There was a pause, one that I didn't dare fill; then he nodded, certain now. "Your mother does not know you are here, does she?"

"You aren't taking Amy anywhere," I said, not moving.

"This is ridiculous and I do not have time for your playacting," he said impatiently. "I have a number of activities planned for this evening, and if you continue to interfere in my business I will not hesitate to administer the discipline that your mother has obviously neglected."

I drew my gun and pointed it right at his head. "I'm very serious," I said. "You aren't going to take Amy."

Luca was completely shocked. His mouth dropped open and he gaped at me for a long moment; then he began to laugh hysterically, gesturing at me, miming me drawing the gun, as if this was the funniest thing he had ever seen. I didn't say anything, just adjusted my stance and held the gun in a solid two-handed grip, careful never to lose my target, which was right between his eyes. I'd learned my lesson with Phillip—a stopping shot in this situation needed to be a kill shot.

"My little American cousin," Luca finally said, still

gasping for breath between the last trickles of laughter, "I believe that you have been watching too many John Wayne movies." He smiled. I didn't. "Put the gun down," he said.

I cocked it, the sound loud in the suddenly quiet room.

The smile slowly oozed off Luca's face, and now there was something very dangerous looking back at me. He meant business now. "Put it down."

My fear was gone. It was if I'd finally overloaded myself on it, and now it didn't even exist at all. There was no shaking in my hands, no confusion. The gray areas of morality that had forced me to sit and eat dinner at the same table as the woman who had killed my foster parents had no place here. Good was behind me, evil was in front of me, and now I had the means to do something about it. "This is your last warning," I said, and I meant it.

"You appear to misunderstand the situation." Luca's voice was vicious and velvet soft. "This is *your* last warning."

I sighted down and shot, my arms barely able to absorb the kick from the .45, which was significantly more than I'd ever experienced with the .38, but the bullet went right where I'd aimed it. But Luca was already moving, and the bullet hit the wall that had just moments before been where his head had been. I reacted, too slow, turning the gun to fire again, but Luca was already at my side, and he slammed one hand down hard on my wrists, loosening my grip enough that he could pull the gun out of my hands. With speed I couldn't even dream of matching, he brought the gun whistling back across my face, bludgeoning me with a force that sent a bright shock of pain through my cheek; then his other hand was wrapped around the front of my shirt and with one flex of his arm I was flying through the air, thrown out the open doorway and into the living room. I fell hard, my hip slamming into an end table and sending a lamp to the floor in a shower of porcelain pieces. For a moment my body was a single throb of confused pain, but then I blinked and it was all in my back and hip, and I struggled to draw a breath into my shocked lungs, which had had all the wind knocked out of them.

Luca walked out of the bedroom, now moving at a human-paced stroll. He held the gun in one hand loosely, like some filthy object you might find on your car after you leave it parked overnight in a bad area, staring at it with utter distaste. I rolled, struggling, forcing my body to move, and managed to haul myself up to my hands and knees.

"That a vampire would even imagine to carry a human weapon like this is utterly incomprehensible," he said, still looking at the gun. In my first year of college I'd lived in a coed dorm, and one day there had been a whole group of boys gathered around a trash can, staring at a used tampon with just that expression of revolted fascination. Then he shifted that look over to me. "You're still an infant," Luca said, and now I was clearly the tampon. "Barely more than a human. Look at you, crawling and mewling. I could crush you right now. It's only as a favor to your mother, despite her useless advice, that I'll let you walk away at all. But perhaps"— and now his eyes narrowed and his voice became coldly thoughtful—"a lesson might be in order."

I was struggling to get to my feet when Luca slammed

one hand into my lower back, smashing me down to the floor again. I tried to roll away, but not fast enough to escape it when he kicked me in the side with enough force that I fell back. What followed was a horribly systematic beating, utterly unlike my earlier experiences with my muggers or even with Phillip. Luca hit me with his open hands, not fists, and he wasn't wearing shoes, but he knew just how much force to put behind each strike so that it hurt, and I stayed down. He toyed with me, so that when I managed to slap away a hit coming down to my face, it would turn out to be a feint, and that the real strike was a kick to my kidneys. If I pulled away from a kick, it put me directly in line for a slap to my throat. Even as I struggled, and flailed, I knew that I had no way of stopping this, and that if I just rolled up and went limp it would probably end a lot sooner, but I couldn't make myself do that. Not with Amy in another room.

Then one moment came when he leaned in just a little too close, and by more luck than design one of my fists caught him across that perfect nose. He pulled back with an outraged snarl, and before I had any chance to feel a sense of pride at my Pyrrhic victory, he'd shot out a hand to grip my right forearm and lift me completely off the floor.

He squeezed, just tightly enough that I could actually feel the bone begin to bend under the pressure, and he held it there, just a hairbreadth from the point where it would have to break.

"Stupid child," he spat in my face. "What were you imagining, coming here and threatening my property? What could something as weak as you *possibly* hope to do to me?"

There was a roaring in my head when he called Amy his property, when he reduced her to something without value or spirit or worth, and for a moment all I could think of was Prudence and the way that she had treated my foster parents' death as a particularly monotonous chore, with no sense of remorse or even awareness of their humanity. Or the way that Maria had looked when she walked out the door of my mother's mansion, walking to her death and not even caring anymore after God only knows how many years of being treated like nothing more than an object to bite or abuse, with that last little spasm of hope she'd shown when I'd grabbed her so completely crushed, about to be thrown away now that she wasn't useful anymore. And it didn't matter what had just happened to my body; I *needed* to hurt Luca somehow. To make him lose something. And fortunately enough, I had a way.

Blood from my nose had run into my mouth, but I spat it out and asked, in the most taunting voice I could muster, "Where's Phillip today, Luca?" Luca froze, and I laughed, even while more blood ran down my face. "Ooh, big bad vampire doesn't know where his pet is," I heckled. "Someone went out last night and never came home, didn't he?"

Luca was pissed. In an instant his eyes were completely black, cold, and lethal. He threw me back against the wall, and I knew on impact that this time he hadn't been holding back. A lot of drywall dust came with me as I slid down, and from the lightning pain running up my back I knew that I wasn't getting up after this. "And what do *you* know about my creature?" Luca demanded, stalking forward.

My voice was high and singsong when I said, "Should've put tags on your pet. According to the Humane Society, only five percent of lost cats ever make it back home."

Luca's hand flashed down and wrapped around my shirtfront again, shaking me with a force that rattled my brains. "Idiot!" he yelled, and when he spoke again I could see that those needle fangs were now fully extended. "I felt Phillip die last night. What did your family do?"

I smiled up at him. "Not them. Me. I killed Phillip."

Luca screamed, a sound of pure, unadulterated rage. The hand dropped from my shirt, and he slammed his fists into the wall above my head, sending down a rain of dust and chunks of drywall. "Twenty years!" He drove his fists in over and over, all control gone. "Twenty years to craft! Twenty years of feeding my own blood into those wretches, of watching them twitch and die and *waste my blood*! Twenty years of feeding from my father like an infant so that the experiments could continue! All to make *one creature*!" He screamed one last time, and then just stood, all action stopped, his breath heaving in and out, spittle gleaming whitely from his lips.

"Back to square one, asshole," I said.

And then I meowed like a cat.

His hand was around my throat before I even saw him move, and he began to squeeze very slowly, like a constrictor. I ripped and yanked with my hands, but nothing made his grip even flinch. His eyes were wide and unblinking. "This I won't forgive," he crooned. "This will be worth the price paid for killing you." My vision began to gray out at the edges, and my lungs were screaming for air. Blackness starting creeping in, but I held on to the fact that this had cost him, that I'd made him pay in some way for what he was doing. Then I couldn't hold on to it, and all I could think about was that I needed air, and all I could see was the smile stretched across Luca's face.

There was a scrabbling of claws against hardwood, and a black shape slammed into Luca, knocking him back. The hand finally lost its grip, and I gasped in the breath I needed, rushing through starved lungs and clearing my brain. I slid sideways onto the floor, still gasping and gagging in air through a throat that felt like a partially clogged straw, but I was able to look and see what was happening.

A black fox was ripping and tearing into Luca's face like a mad thing, teeth embedded just above one eye while those feet with their wickedly sharp claws, so strong and suited for digging, raked huge furrows into his flesh.

It was Suzume.

Luca screamed and slapped her with his hands, the force finally breaking her hold on his face, though even as she was thrown backward I could see her jaw snap shut, the gout of blood, and knew that she'd taken flesh with her. She tumbled in the air and, with the same freakish twist that a cat would use, landed on her paws, sinking down as those four furry legs acted like shock absorbers for her hard landing. In one motion she was bouncing forward again, those white fangs snapping wildly, and Luca stumbled back and out of range. She bounced forward again, and the same reaction. But then Luca shook his head, blood still streaming out of his face to leave droplets spattering across the walls, and he seemed to shrug off his horrendous injury. With the shock of Suzume's sneak attack lost, I could see him evaluating her, and I could see the moment that he decided that she wasn't something to be afraid of.

Now he was the one lunging forward, those strong hands reaching for Suzume, and she leaped backward, barely evading them. Another grab, another jump and near miss. Grab, jump, grab, jump. Each time, Luca's hand came within millimeters of that dark fur.

I'd gotten myself up onto my elbows. I couldn't seem to push myself up, and I started to crawl forward. With each jump Suzume was drawing Luca farther away from me, and across the room I met her brilliant black eyes. She yipped at me, a high, demanding sound, and suddenly I realized that she was doing all of this on purpose, that she was distracting Luca so that I could run.

I looked around frantically. A dark spot caught my eye, and I focused on it. There was the gun, halfway under the sofa, where it must've been thrown out of Luca's hand when Suzume slammed into him. I started crawling toward it.

Then Suzume jumped back too slowly, and Luca had her. She made one agonized yelp as his hand closed on her back leg and squeezed, and then his other hand was around her throat and he was holding her off the floor. Her back left leg dangled, and I could see the white flash of bone sticking through her skin.

I screamed her name.

"Idiot vermin," Luca said, and I could see his hand flex against her fur, knew that he was about to crush her throat.

Suzume bared her teeth, snarling defiance.

The gun was too far away; I was never going to reach it in time, but I pushed myself to crawl forward and then—

There was a snapping feeling inside me, like a rubber band I'd never realized was holding things in place had suddenly broken. Everything around me slowed to a crawl—I looked at Luca's hand and could see each muscle engaging to choke the life from Suzume, but they were all so slow. I could see beads of saliva forming in Suzume's open mouth, but I knew that it would take them forever to form a single droplet.

But if everything around me was slow, I was fast. I could hear my heartbeat in my ears, but the beats were too close together for me to differentiate—it was a thunderous, deafening drumming. Everything was clearer to me now—the room that a moment before had been barely lit by the few tendrils of sunlight that could creep around the closed blinds now seemed as brightly lit as if I were outside under a noonday sun. There was the taste of blood in my mouth, but this had nothing to do with what had been running out of my nose and from a few cuts. This was hot, rich, and thick, a mouthful that I swallowed eagerly and that replenished itself instantly, so that I was drinking it down, and I could feel it spread throughout my body, brilliant and exciting. This blood wasn't mine, wasn't like anything I'd ever tasted before, and I felt a pang of sadness when I swallowed the last of it.

Luca's hand still moved on its inexorable move to squeeze; Suzume's growl was a long series of individual motes of sound.

I could still feel all the pain in my battered body, but it didn't seem to matter anymore, and I could ignore it enough to do what I needed. The gun was still there, waiting under the sofa for my hand to wrap around it.

For the first time in my life, I moved like a vampire.

The gun was in my hand, and then I was beside Luca. I pressed the muzzle of the gun against Luca's head, just above his ear. I didn't say anything—there were no warnings. I pulled the trigger, and I saw each nanosecond of Luca's head tearing apart as the impact mushroomed through his skull and his brains splattered on the wall. Somewhere in my brain I noted that Yuri had been absolutely right about what this bullet could do.

Then time was moving again. Luca was on the floor, Suzume was as well, rolling back to her feet from where the spasm of Luca's hand had dropped her. A big chunk of Luca's head was missing, but I stood over him and squeezed off two more shots until his head above his jaw was simply gone, just a pile of meat on the floor. Luca's arms and legs were lashing out, kicking and flopping violently, and I stepped back, horrified, wondering if this was like the decapitated running chicken phenomena that I'd read about in so many Gary Larson comics, but then Suzume was moving forward on her three good legs, hopping with amazing ease, and with her front two feet she began to dig frantically at Luca's chest, his skin flying away like pieces of dirt in a garden, and I remembered what she'd once told me about what it took to kill a vampire.

The movements of his limbs took on a new horror, and I pushed Suzume back from his chest. I pressed the gun point-blank against the spot she'd been digging and unloaded the rest of the clip into him, feeling the body heave as each bullet slammed into him and blood spattered upward and onto me. Four more shots and my gun clicked empty, and I slid backward onto my ass. Luca's movements stopped, and for a moment we both just stared at him.

I turned to look at Suzume. Her silky black fur was matted with blood, and her back leg was dragging grotesquely. I reached out and brushed my fingertips against her jaw, not daring to touch any more in case it hurt her, and I whispered, "Suze. You came."

She gave a little throaty gurgle, her pink tongue sneaking out to give my fingers a quick lick; then she let out a loud, bossy yip and pointed that long muzzle decisively toward the bedroom.

I scrambled back to my feet while she scampered off on three paws in the other direction. I staggered as I moved, reeling almost drunkenly. The pain was harder to ignore, like a loud knocking on the back door of my brain, but what I had to do next was too important for distractions. I heard a loud scuffling and breaking sounds from the kitchen, but I even ignored whatever the hell Suzume was doing, and focused on getting back into that bedroom.

Amy Grann was exactly where I'd left her, sitting inside her cage, the door still swinging open. Her body was fixed and frozen, and she'd covered her eyes with her hands, not daring to see who was coming back to get her.

I'd been her age when Brian and Jill were murdered. I remember what it felt like when Prudence forced me to look at their bodies, forced me to put my hand in the blood that was still warm while she told me that this was all my fault, that if it wasn't for my actions they would have been alive and well. That she was the train that hit them, but I was the one who tied them to the tracks. I remember the nights of sitting alone in my room, the fear so bad that I couldn't even move far enough to flip the light switch. I remember those dreams that have never gone away.

I couldn't stop any of that for Amy. Her world had been torn away as well, with blood and violence, and she'd have all of those moments, along with the horrible crippling guilt of being the one who lived. I couldn't help her with any of it.

But I could do one thing for her. Something that I'd never had.

I crouched down and called to her. "The monster is dead, Amy," I said. "He can never hurt you. Not ever again." Slowly she took her hands down, and she looked at me with her eyes that would never be nine years old again. She didn't say anything, but she didn't pull back when I reached inside the cage and took her out. She didn't resist when I picked her up and cradled her against my chest, my hands smearing blood all over the clothes that he'd dressed her in.

I carried her out of the bedroom, but I didn't cover her eyes or hurry her out of the house. Instead I carried her right over to the body and put her down. She didn't flinch back; she just stared.

"He's really dead, Amy," I told her, giving her something that she'd always be able to cling to on those long nights of fear. "He is never going to touch you again."

Amy got down on her knees and leaned over him. Every movement she made was slow and absolutely precise. Someday she might be spontaneous again, but not now, and she'd never move with a child's scattered motions ever again. Carefully, never touching Luca's skin, she tugged at those hideous satin harem pants of his, tugging the waistband down about an inch to reveal a large brown birthmark. She looked at it for a long minute, then looked back up to me and met my eyes.

"That's really him," she said flatly. "He's really dead."

My throat tightened, and I nodded.

"Okay," she whispered. There was no crying, no tears, but something behind her eyes changed just a little, and those small shoulders relaxed just a fraction.

There was another loud crash from the kitchen, followed by an awful scraping, and I finally looked over. All of the lower cabinet doors had been opened and (literally) pawed through, and the floor was now covered with half-open containers of Windex, baking soda, a bag of rice, and any number of little scrubbing pads. Suzume was dragging a tall glass bottle across the floor, her teeth slipping as she fought for purchase against the tall mouth of it. I stared as she leaned it against my arm and sat, panting shallowly and looking extremely proud of herself.

I was less impressed. "Bacardi 107?" I asked incredulously. "You want me to get drunk? Right now?"

She gave an impatient little foxy huff and scampered off to the bedroom, long tail swishing behind her, and returned a moment later with two long white candle tapers clenched in her teeth. She spat them out onto the floor and looked at me expectantly.

I looked from the tapers, to the alcohol, to what was left of the body. I looked at all three again, then back to Suzume, who wagged her inky black tail.

"You're kidding," I said.

She gave a loud bark and glared.

"We seriously have to *burn* him?"

She eyed the corpse closely, then looked back at me. Her tail flipped once, as if asking if I wanted to risk *not* burning him.

Fair enough, I supposed.

I poured out the entire bottle, making sure that the whole corpse was saturated with it. Suzume made one last trip to the bedroom and returned with a box of matches in her mouth. I lit one taper, then considered it for a second.

Amy was surprised when I wrapped her small hand around it, and Suzume gave a slightly uncertain chuff, but I thought again about what Luca had taken from her, and knew that this was right.

"He can *never* hurt you again, Amy," I told the little girl. "You're going to make sure of that. And this is for your family too."

She hesitated, then nodded firmly. As she stretched out the candle, she whispered their names.

"Daddy. Mommy. Jessie."

The Bacardi did its job, and the fire caught immediately, spreading quickly over the body.

"Daddy. Mommy. Jessie." Amy repeated her mantra as the body began burning, never looking away from it.

The fire was spreading, already jumping onto the sofa. Hopefully it would take the entire house, with all the evidence it contained, with it. There weren't any fire alarms wailing as I scooped Amy up and we all went out the back door. If Luca had been in a habit of lighting all those candles in that bedroom, he would've had to take the batteries out of his smoke detectors to avoid having the fire department on his doorstep.

Amy looked over my shoulder as I carried her, and I could hear that small whisper in my ear as we left. "Daddy. Mommy. Jessie."

The sun hit me like a sledgehammer the moment I stepped outside, and the last of whatever had been holding all my pain back broke, and it rushed through me in a wave. I went down, barely managing to turn so that I took all the impact and Amy stayed safe and unharmed in my arms. I could feel every place I'd been hit, but more than that, it felt like every muscle in my body from my smallest toe to the top of my ears had been overextended in one full-body scream of pain. It was too much to hold out against, and the last thing I saw was Suzume's dark muzzle changing into her human face.

Then there was nothing.

Chapter 12

I woke up in a series of stages, each one bringing with it another snippet of sensory information. At first I was just aware of how much my body ached, and that I was covered in bandages, with a hard cast on my right arm. Then I realized that I was in a bed, with clean, cool sheets. There was a breeze that carried the smell of the ocean, and I could hear the distant sounds of birds chirping, while closer to me there was the quiet, occasional sound of book pages being turned. My eyes were almost sealed shut, but I slowly managed to force them open, blinking a few times against the blurriness until my vision finally sharpened.

I was in my bedroom at Madeline's mansion, tucked into my old bed and propped partially up with a few pillows. Light was streaming in through the open windows, illuminating the movie posters that I'd covered my old walls with. *Jurassic Park*, *Independence Day*, *The Matrix* . . . my taste in movies had been pretty typical for a teenager. It wasn't until a freshman film class that I realized that the value of a movie wasn't entirely conditional on the number of explosions it contained. I hadn't been up here in a few years, and I would've expected the posters to have been cleared out, but they were all still up, and still attached with strips of masking tape.

Bhumika was beside the bed, reading quietly in her wheelchair. Today she was wearing a bright yellow sundress topped off with an oversize white T-shirt that was decorated with googly-eyed cartoon lobsters. She was about halfway through *Guns, Germs, and Steel*. Her taste usually ran more toward Charlaine Harris and Jodi Picoult, but every now and then I'd seen her pick up something from Chivalry's pile of books and read through it. I watched her for a long minute, seeing the way she occasionally frowned at whatever she was reading, the way that she'd unconsciously lick one finger before turning each page. The book was a large hardcover, and she held it partially propped against the arm of her wheelchair, as if it was too heavy for her to hold upright.

Eventually she glanced up at me, and saw that I was awake. "Fortitude!" she said, a wide smile creasing across her face. She dropped the book down onto her lap, not bothering to mark her place, and reached out to take my hand. "How are you feeling?"

I tried to talk, but at first nothing came out of my throat, which felt like it had been thoroughly buffed with sandpaper. I coughed, trying to clear it, and when Bhumika passed me a cup of water with a straw in it I sipped at it gratefully. I tried to talk again, barely rasping out a single word, and Bhumika squeezed my hand gently.

"Don't try so hard, honey," she said. "You've been out for three days."

I looked around, taking in a little more of my surroundings. In addition to the plaster cast on my right forearm, there was an IV taped to my left wrist. It led to a bag of what looked like regular saline just behind the head of the bed. Among my many bruises and aches, there was a particular throb coming from my groin, and Bhumika seemed to understand the nervous glance I tried to sneak under the sheet, because she patted my hand and said, "The catheter just came out this morning."

There weren't too many happy thoughts about that one, and whatever look I gave her made her smile a little. "Don't worry, everything is okay. You've got a few broken ribs, but the arm bone isn't broken, just stressed enough that the doctor thought that the cast was a good idea to help it heal so that you wouldn't risk it ending up weak. Your left knee was partially dislocated, but as long as you keep it wrapped up and go easy on it for a while, it will be okay. Lots of cuts and bruises, but everything is looking a lot better after three days of sleep."

"Why was I out so long?" I finally managed to croak. I felt like a herd of cows had run across me, but nothing she was describing should've put me out for so long.

"Your mother asked the doctor to keep you asleep. She says that you pushed yourself too far, and needed to rest."

There was a hard, icy fear at that, and I wondered if there was another reason that Madeline had wanted me unconscious for a while. I forced myself to ask the question. "Amy Grann?"

Bhumika pulled a folded newspaper out from where she'd stuffed it between her hip and the side of her wheelchair, and handed it to me without a word. I opened it slowly and read.

Amy's homecoming had been front-page news, and was being hailed as a miracle. A fire had broken out in the house where she'd been held captive, and the man who'd murdered the rest of her family hadn't gotten out. Some remains the fire marshal found inside what was left of the house were presumed to be his. Amy had been sitting in the backyard when the fire department arrived, and was with her grandparents, and the police had declared the case closed.

"Will she be okay?" I asked Bhumika. She'd lived in this house a long time, and she didn't pretend to misunderstand me.

"Chivalry talked with your mother," Bhumika said quietly. "She agreed that even if the little girl talks, all the events were so traumatizing that the police and all the people around her will think that it was just a broken child making up rationalizations for what she'd been through. No one will listen if she says the word *vampire*, and by the time she's old enough that anyone might listen, she'll have been through at least a decade of intense therapy, and probably will think that what she remembers is just a child's fantasy."

"So she's safe." Relief bubbled through me. I'd been terrified that after everything she'd gone through, Amy's life might've been ended to cover up the last of Luca's crimes.

Bhumika nodded. "Safe for her whole life," she said, squeezing my hand again. I squeezed back, and relaxed against the pillows.

We were both quiet, just sitting there and listening to the sounds of the birds chattering outside, and beyond that the steady crashing of the ocean waves. I was tired, but not quite ready to go back to sleep, and in that odd little moment I asked Bhumika the question that I'd always wondered but never really dared to ask.

"Why are you with Chivalry?" I asked. She stiffened, and I knew she didn't want me to ask this, but I pushed ahead anyway. "When did you know that it would kill you?"

Bhumika dropped my hand and leaned back in her wheelchair. She looked away from me, staring out the window. "I always knew," she said.

I gaped at her, shocked, as she continued. "I met Chivalry when he was still married to Linda, when she was at the end of her life. I saw how he was with her, how much she was the center of his whole world, even at the end, even when things were at their worst. And I fell in love with him then."

"You—you mean, the two of you...," I sputtered.

"Of course not," she snapped, more harshly than I'd ever heard her talk before. "He *loved* Linda. I was just a friend to him. But . . ." She paused a long time, thinking, probably imagining the person she'd been before. "Everyone could see that Linda was dying. I became friends with her, would come over to visit, would take her out on days when she was feeling well enough." Bhumika bit her lip, and I could see the guilt in her eyes.

"Did she know?" I asked.

"I didn't think so then. I was sure she didn't. I was so smug, thinking about what a nice person I was being, how selfless. But now . . . I know that she knew. She knew that I was in love with her husband and was just waiting for her to die and be out of the way so that I could have him."

"What happened?"

"Linda died, of course. Chivalry mourned her. And I made so sure that I was the one who was comforting him, who kept him company, who was available at the drop of a hat every time he called." A tear streaked down Bhumika's cheek, but she didn't wipe it away, didn't even seem aware of it as she looked back at the past. "She'd been dead three weeks when we slept together the first time, and that was the night that he showed me what he was." A hard, self-mocking smile twisted her mouth. "I was so in love with him. I thought it was *romantic* when he fed from me the first time, when he promised that he'd be true to me for the rest of my life, never feed from anyone else, never *love* anyone else."

"He didn't tell you that it would kill you?"

"Of course he did!" Bhumika gave a strangled laugh. "Don't you know your own brother? He never hid anything, never lied, never blunted the truth. But it felt so good to be with him, and the first few times he drank from me and then gave me a drop of his own blood, I felt stronger and healthier than I ever had in my life. He warned me that it was only temporary, but I didn't want to believe him." Her voice dropped, and the tears stopped. "I told myself that Linda had been weak, and that I was stronger. That it wouldn't affect me the way that it had affected her. And for the first few years, everything was perfect. When I felt the start of it, the disease that he'd warned me was coming, I lied to myself and said it was just a summer cold. And when I finally couldn't lie to myself anymore, I was already creeping toward the end." She was quiet; then her face slowly cleared, the bitterness sweeping away as if it had never even been there, and a little contented smile formed. "But Chivalry is still with me. He loves me. And he'll love me every day of my life."

"Would you still do it?" I asked. "If you knew then what you do now, would you still do it?"

She sighed and leaned forward in her chair, giving me an almost pitying look as one thin, wasted hand stroked over my forehead. "Silly Fort, haven't you been listening? I'd watched Linda die day by day, and Chivalry had told me to my face that the same thing would happen to me. I wanted him so much that I ignored every warning, every truth, because I thought that my love would somehow overcome everything. Nothing would have stopped me." She kept stroking my forehead and whispered, "Now go to sleep."

And I did.

I napped on and off for the rest of the afternoon. Bhumika kept me company for most of it, but when she got tired I told her that I was perfectly capable of sleeping without an audience, and her nurse took her back to her own room. As soon as the door closed behind her, I pulled out the IV needle and started making my way to the bathroom. Sitting up almost made me pass out again, but after one bad moment my brain apparently remembered that this was something we used to do all the time, and I was okay. The clothes I'd been wearing the day of the fight were gone, and if my memory of their final condition was accurate, Madeline had probably had them burned. Someone had dressed me in an old-fashioned nightshirt, possibly a confluence of its similarity to a modern hospital gown and Chivalry's habit of storing all his old clothes in the vain wish that someday white lawn suits and bowler hats would come back into style, and I felt like I was on the run from a company performance of *Peter Pan*. My left knee wobbled a lot, and crossing the room involved a lot of hobbling and a bit of cursing, but I finally made it to the bathroom attached to my bedroom and was able to empty my bladder.

That had been a better idea before I'd realized what it would feel like to pee after having been very recently catheterized, and I cursed a blue streak.

Finished and feeling a bit worse for it, I made my way back to the bed, collapsed on top of it, and was just trying to figure out what I should do next when I conked out again, my still-tender brain apparently deciding that having accomplished the task of peeing, it deserved another nap.

It was dark the next time I woke up, and the breezes coming in from the window were very cool. I felt a lot better than last time, better enough that my stomach was working to make its presence known. I sat up cautiously, but had no problems at all.

There was a brisk rap at the door, and it opened before I could say anything. Chivalry stood in the doorway frowning at me, some plastic bags and one brown paper sack of takeout in his hands.

"You're supposed to let doctors decide when to take those things out," he said, nodding at the IV drip that still hung behind my bed.

I shrugged a little. "I felt better."

"I figured you'd do that," he said, sighing as he reached into the takeout bag and withdrew a tall drink container, striped with red and white, and handed it to me.

I laughed when I took it from him and saw what was written on it. "You got me an Awful Awful?" I asked, delighted. Awful Awfuls were milkshakes made at the Newport Creamery, a small local chain of greasy spoon diners. Awful Awfuls were made with iced milk instead of ice cream, and were marketed as being "Awful Big, Awful Good," which was probably one of the only times in marketing history that all statements about a product were true. I took a big sip and felt the chocolaty concoction soothe the last of my sore throat. "Thank you," I said.

Chivalry shrugged it off. "If you're feeling better, Mother wants you downstairs for dinner. I figured that might take the edge off. Here." And he handed me the plastic bags. "I got you some clothes. We trashed the ones you were wearing, and none of the clothes you still have here would fit you anymore. And I'm guessing you're not interested in wearing a nightshirt downstairs."

I opened the bags cautiously. From the names on them, Chivalry had been shopping at his kind of store, and I knew from experience that Chivalry's ideas of what I should wear tended to diverge pretty dramatically from my own. But to my surprise I pulled out a pair of jeans and a gray T-shirt. Just the kind of thing I would've wanted, though given where Chivalry had shopped he'd probably paid five times what he could have at a mall. Eyes wide, I stared up at Chivalry.

"Sneakers are in there too," he said. For a guy who usually carried himself with impeccable grace, there was almost a look of discomfort on his face. "I was able to save the boots you were wearing, but they were pretty worn out and I dropped them off at the cobbler. And when I saw your other sneakers last week, they looked ready for the trash, so I figured that you could use another pair. Hope you like them."

Chivalry was actually babbling. I stared up at him. "You didn't have to do this," I said.

He looked at me, and there was an intensity in his face that surprised me. He dropped one hand onto my shoulder and gave it a brief squeeze, then looked away. "Yes, I did." He paused, then took a deep breath. "I'm very proud of you, little brother."

"For saving Amy Grann?" I asked, confused. "But I thought . . ."

"For doing what you thought was right," Chivalry said. He looked back at me, his dark eyes sad. "I wouldn't have gone after that girl. I tried to take Maria from Luca because you wanted me to and she was in front of me, but I wouldn't have hunted that other girl down like you did. I can't feel like you do, but I am very proud of you, and I'm sorry that you weren't able to ask me for help."

My throat tightened at his sincerity, and I nodded, wishing I had the words to tell him what that meant to me. He squeezed my shoulder one last time, then let his hand fall back to his side. My eyes drifted from him to the glowing numbers of my clock. It was after nine. I looked around the room. It was dark, with heavy clouds that covered up the moon. I shouldn't have been able to see his expressions so clearly, yet I did.

"Chivalry," I said tentatively. "Something happened when I was fighting Luca. Something about me is different."

"I know." His face closed up. "Mother will talk to you about it after dinner."

There was one last thing to ask, and he was the only one I trusted to show this new weakness to. "Chiv, how did I get here? The last thing I remember was getting out of Luca's house."

"The kitsune brought you to us," Chivalry answered.

I hesitated, then pushed forward. "Was Suzume Hollis there?"

Chivalry frowned a little. "Which one is that? I always have trouble telling any of Atsuko's offspring apart."

"She was the one hired to be my bodyguard. Dark hair, dark eyes, very pretty." I wasn't ringing any bells, so I played the odds and added, "Kind of a pain in the ass?"

"Oh, that one," Chivalry said immediately, with the kind of glower that he usually reserved for me when I was being my most little-brother bratty. "Yes, she was definitely there. She had the nerve to send Mother an itemized bill for additional services rendered. Somehow she came up with a dollar amount for what following you to certain death was worth."

I couldn't help smiling at that. It was very her. "Did she look okay? When they brought me here, I mean."

Chivalry shrugged. "I had my hands full with getting you upstairs and then getting a hold of a doctor who would treat you and keep his mouth shut." He must've seen something in my face, because his voice gentled and he added, "I haven't seen her since then, and she hasn't tried to contact us since Mother sent them the check." A pause, then, "I'm sorry."

Dinner was a shockingly normal affair. Chivalry quietly ate his stew, Prudence glowered at me over her soup, I ate around my steak, and Madeline was doing her best dotty grandmother act, gossiping contentedly about the cook's cousin's niece (aka "our Jenny"), who apparently was periodically brought in to help out with the spring cleaning, and had just returned from adopting a baby girl in China.

"And would you believe it?" Madeline burbled contentedly. "No sooner had she gotten home with the baby than she realized that all that nausea *hadn't* been that ungodly food they were serving over there, but that she was actually pregnant!"

"How incredible," Prudence snarled, stabbing her spoon into her soup with decidedly vicious motions.

"Eight years of trying!" Madeline sighed. "And then to have it happen when they'd completely given up. Well, I can assure you that our Jenny is just over-the-moon. All that time spent trying for one, and now she'll have a set of Irish twins! Well," she corrected herself, "Chinese-Irish twins."

"We should have one of those baby shops put together a basket for her," Chivalry suggested politely.

"I believe we sent one over just before she left for China," Madeline said, tapping her wineglass thoughtfully. "But women never seem to have enough baby clothes."

"*Mother!*" Prudence shrieked, having clearly blown through whatever restraint had been holding her together.

"And, of course, there is always the chance that this one could be a boy," Madeline continued as if Prudence hadn't said a word. "She'll want a few things that aren't pink in that case." After a long drink of wine, she then turned a gimlet eye on Prudence and asked, "And now, darling, do tell me what has been gnawing away at your mind."

"I would think that the issue of Fortitude completely ignoring your orders would be a bit more important than some servant's pregnancy, however long in the making," Prudence said in icy tones.

"Really, darling, how old-fashioned of you. I don't think I've been able to refer to any of my employees as servants in at least forty years, after I nearly gave my poor lawyer a heart attack at the thought of lawsuits." Madeline dabbed her mouth daintily with a napkin and then raised an eyebrow at Prudence while I sat on pins and needles, having been suffering through the entire meal waiting for the sword to fall. "And I cannot recall a single order of mine that Fortitude has recently ignored," she finished blandly.

My mouth fell open nearly as far as Prudence's, who sputtered like a wet hen. "Have you gone completely *senile*, Mother? Fortitude *killed* Luca!"

"Oh yes, that." Madeline turned and gave me a smile as sweet as cotton candy. "Good work, my darling."

Now even Chivalry looked shocked. "Mother?" he asked cautiously.

"Really, my pets," Madeline said, "I'm a bit surprised at you all. A vampire I have no true blood tie to, coming into my territory with a full-fledged host in tow? Very suspicious. There are only three other vampires in the entire country, and I've made sure that they stay well away from even our boundaries. I have all of you to consider, someday when I've passed off to my reward and there are two of you thinking of striking out and setting up your own nests. No, I didn't like the thought one bit of Luca going back to Europe and spreading stories of just how much good land there is out here. Most of the vampires out there only have a single heir, but there are a few left who have produced two, and a few more who have poor territory who might be interested in a move. Luca's death serves my purpose quite well."

"But," I stuttered, completely confused. "The hospitality . . . thing . . ."

"Yes, Mother you *swore*." Chivalry's tone was horrified.

"Of course I did. And when Dominic made an international phone call, *very* irate at feeling his son's death, I was able to quite honestly tell him that I had no idea what he was talking about, and had not laid eyes on the boy since he left this house after I granted hospitality."

"But, Mother, your orders—" Chivalry began, and Madeline cut him off with a few little tutting sounds.

"Dominic knows that you are my closest child, the one who works often in my name, the one who would never disobey me. If you moved against Luca, it might as well have been me. But Prudence and Fortitude"—she encompassed both of us in a glance—"are known to live apart from me. Hospitality bound me alone, and action from the two of you would be far less suspect."

"You wanted me to kill Luca?" I asked.

"Well . . ." Madeline gave a rather feral smile. "It was certainly convenient." She focused on Prudence, her brilliant blue eyes narrowing. "I had hoped that your sister would have . . . assisted."

"That is not in my nature," Prudence bit out.

"Perhaps not, my child," Madeline conceded. "But I did hope." She glanced over to me, and there was definitely a rebuke in her tone. "Though, admittedly, I did assume that Fort would've been a bit wiser in his course of action, and chosen discretion over bravery when it became obvious how overmatched he was."

Chivalry and Prudence both snorted a little at that one, though Chivalry's was fairly gentle, while Prudence gave me a glare that told me exactly how unhappy she was that Luca hadn't killed me.

Madeline turned back to my sister. "And how, daughter," she asked pleasantly, "go your experiments? How long did your last host survive?"

Prudence hid her surprise quickly, but not quickly enough. It was obvious from his face that Chivalry hadn't known about what she'd been doing, and he looked at her nervously. Prudence regained her composure enough to answer Madeline coolly, with just the slightest tremor in her voice. "Longer than I had thought, but less than I'd hoped." There was some rebellion in the way that she emphasized the last word, and Madeline dipped her head slightly in acknowledgment.

"Thank you for coming to dinner this evening, daughter. I do value your company so highly. And, Chivalry, I'm sure that Bhumika is missing you." Effectively dismissed, both got up and left. Chivalry with a small pat on my shoulder, and Prudence refusing to look at me at all.

"Alone at last, my darling," Madeline said when the door closed behind them. "Now that I believe you've been both sufficiently scolded and praised for your actions, I believe that you have a question for me."

"I was an experiment, wasn't I?" I blurted out the question that had been circling the back of my mind since I'd visited Prudence's house.

Madeline raised an eyebrow. "An interesting turn of phrase, my darling. All children are experiments. Even human ones. Will this child look like me, or like my lover? Will he be like his siblings, or different? A child is a gift whose unwrapping will last a lifetime."

I shook my head, frustrated. "But I'm different than Prudence and Chivalry. You *made* me differently."

"Yes, I certainly did." Madeline gave a Cheshire Cat smile.

"Why?"

"All in its own time, dear. And I am quite curious where this line of questioning has sprung from, but that is not what I intended to discuss with you." Her voice dropped, became businesslike. "You've been moving differently this evening. Better balanced, more certain. I've been speaking with your doctor, and he was quite surprised at how quickly you've been healing. A number of days ahead of schedule, he told me."

"Something happened," I said. "During the fight."

"Yes." She nodded. "Transition has begun."

I'd known it, but I hadn't wanted to admit it, and I felt the hurt deep inside. "Why now?" I asked, bitter even knowing that it had almost certainly saved my life, not to mention Suzume and Amy. "Why did it start now?"

Madeline steepled her fingers, and seemed to consider something. Coming to a decision, she fussed briefly with her wineglass and said, "Grace died three days ago."

"What?" I asked, stunned.

"Her keepers had become complacent," Madeline said. "Grace was always so very intelligent. Part of the reason I chose her, of course. Apparently she'd begun sharpening the base of her toothbrush. Quite clever, really. She'd honed it to a knife's edge. I shudder on behalf of Albert for what she was planning to do with it, but she turned it on herself instead. Stabbed herself quite madly. Hosts are tough creatures, but she put that knife into her chest twelve different times—absolutely shredded her heart. Dead before anyone could even reach her."

The pieces came together horribly in my mind. "When it happened," I said, my voice harsh, "I tasted blood. It wasn't mine."

"Yes, darling, now you begin to see." Madeline was pleased. "Your host parents bind you while they live, tie you to those shreds of human DNA that rattle around in you like a vestigial tail. Henry and Grace held back the beginning of transition. Quite fascinating, actually. I only regret that vampires have never maintained any sort of university press or scientific journal traditions. This incident would've been well worth a write-up."

"So I'm more vampire than I was before Grace died," I said slowly.

"Much more." Her blue eyes gleamed.

"And when Henry dies?" I asked, dreading the answer but having to ask.

"Well, it's quite obvious, my darling." Madeline's smile was very wide. "Transition will be complete. And now that you have begun traveling down that path . . . your responsibilities will increase. Time for you to stop acting like a child and begin assisting your brother with the task of guarding our territory. But there's time to speak of that later." She took a long sip of wine.

I stared at her, a thousand thoughts chasing each other through my brain. With a little harrumph, Madeline reached out and gave my arm a small pat. "Now," she said comfortably. "You have a birthday coming up, and Chivalry told me that you were in need of a certain something." She fumbled around in the purse hung on the corner of a chair and pulled out a new cell phone, putting it onto the table in front of me. When I remained speechless, she gave me a coaxing smile. "Chivalry picked it out. Apparently he was even able to have the technicians connect it to your own number. Isn't that clever?"

I visited Henry before I left the mansion.

It was strange to see him, sitting in his usual spot in his plastic cage, with the enclosure beside him empty. I'd never seen him without Grace, and he seemed oddly smaller, older and more fragile.

His eyes were closed when I sat down, opening slowly when I greeted him to reveal those twin pools of madness, barely leashed. I thought briefly about the way that Phillip had crouched over Jessica's body, remembered his gibbering ranting, and felt relieved that Henry was separated from me by thick walls and locks.

"Hello, Fortitude," Henry said in that soft, deceptively gentle voice. "You've come to ask me why your mother did it."

"Yes." I forced my body to stay relaxed in the chair, to try to prolong this interlude of sanity.

"Because you needed it," he said, voice calm and unemotional.

"What?"

"I have heard your heartbeat since you first stirred in Grace's belly." Henry leaned forward, placing one hand against the plastic barrier, and began tapping his fingers in the exact beat of my heart. "We both knew when you needed to be more than you were." His tapping sped up and I tried to take deeper breaths, slow them down, but he kept diabolical rhythm. "It simply happened to be Grace who had the means at hand."

He said it so calmly, so coldly, when he would've had a front-row seat for her grisly suicide. Looking at Henry, still horrified at the proof of how linked I was to him, I felt a surge of pity fill me.

"Do you miss Grace?" I asked. "You spent so many years together."

Henry shook his head slowly, his mad eyes never moving from my face. "You don't understand me, son. I don't think you ever could. Grace and I spent many, many years together. But if I'd had the chance, I would have torn her throat out with my teeth, and she would've done the same. You do not understand what it is to live with whispers in your mind, to feel foreign blood inside you that twists and claws. The only way to quiet it is to offer it other blood, and it has been a very long time since I have been able to kill." It was only at the end that emotion filled his voice, and then I heard his deep, terrible longing for blood and death. His hand was drumming almost without stopping, and now he rose out of his seat to begin the familiar pacing, and I knew that there was nothing more to say.

"Thank you, Henry," I said. Then, helplessly, "I'm sorry for your loss."

I turned and left, and behind me I could still hear him tapping, and hear his soft, beseeching whispers as lucidity passed into mania.

The Fiesta was waiting for me, parked outside the mansion. Chivalry had told me earlier that he'd rescued it from the Providence impound lot, but my new, keener eyesight could pick out in the dark that it had obviously had a small detour to a mechanic's garage along the way. The broken window had been replaced, along with the bumper. There'd been a lot of body putty work, topped off with a completely new paint job. After so many years of fighting so hard for my independence, I probably should've been annoyed, but I was still completely broke, and it felt good to see the Fiesta patched up again after all that it had suffered while I'd been hunting down first Phillip, then Luca. And didn't every hero in a Western need a faithful steed?

When I got in I saw that the radio had been not only replaced but upgraded. But the Fiesta still didn't start on the first try, and I smiled a little. It was good to see that some things stayed the same.

It was late enough that not many people were on the road, so on the drive home I used my new phone to go through all the voice mails that had accumulated since the Bruins fans had destroyed my phone six days and half a lifetime ago. There were a lot of messages from Beth, who had been increasingly irate at my failure to be true to form and immediately call her back, and I listened to each one carefully before deleting it. Jeanine had called two days ago to tell me that I was fired, so that meant that I'd be spending the foreseeable future scrambling for a job. Then one last message from Beth, left just two hours ago, in such a completely different tone of voice that I wondered if she'd had a concussion or maybe a round of hypnotism.

"Fort, baby," she cooed. "I'm so sorry that I missed you. I know you must be crazy busy, but it's been forever since we saw each other, and you know how much I hate being without my boyfriend." That was certainly news to me. "So call me when you get the chance, and let's do dinner and have some fun." There was no doubt about what she meant with that last part, and then she ended with some kissy sounds and a few more admonitions to call her.

That one was pretty damn weird, and I shook my head a little when I deleted it.

But there weren't any messages at all from Suzume, and I couldn't help feeling hurt after I'd cleared out the last of my voice mail.

I pulled into my old parking spot just after midnight. Matt McMahon's battered and nigh-indestructible Buick was beside me, and as I got out I could see him stretched out in the driver's-side seat, a messy pile of used Coke cans, empty sandwich wrappers, and completed crossword puzzles covering the seat next to him, the usual debris from a stakeout. Seeing me, he got out as well.

I waved as I greeted him, pleased to see him as always, but a little confused. "Matt, were we supposed to do dinner or something?" I asked. It wasn't completely unusual for him to come by my apartment to say hi if he was in the neighborhood, but it was pretty late for a social call.

"No, no, buddy, just swinging by," he said with a hearty jocularity that was pretty much at odds with how he usually talked.

"Are you staking me out, Matt?" I teased him. What I was really wondering was if there were a few beer bottles mixed in with his junk pile. He didn't look drunk, but he didn't look like my usual Matt either.

"Just a bit," he said calmly, as if he staked me out every day. "Hadn't seen the Fiesta in your parking spot lately. Had a friend run the plate, found out that your brother had it pulled out of a lot. Figured I'd just wait around tonight and see if I needed to go looking for you. Glad to hear I don't."

"I'm sorry, Matt. I should've called." I immediately felt like shit. After three unconscious days, I'd never considered that Matt might've realized I was missing, and I hated that I'd worried him.

"No harm done, Fort," he assured me with a wide, and very phony, smile that I'd never seen him direct at me before. "Funny thing, though," he continued in that hearty tone that was now raising the hair on the back of my neck. "The car was towed out of a residential street in the same area of town that the Grann family killer torched himself in."

"Really?" I asked, staring at him. I'd known him my whole life, yet now there was a weird opacity about his eyes. Those were his cop eyes, I realized suddenly.

"Yeah. Have you been following that case?" He was so friendly, so casual, but suddenly this conversation was filled with knives. I forced myself to paste on a bright, fake smile, to match that easy, just-boys-talking style of speech.

"Just what I've seen in the papers."

"Odd case. That body was completely toasted, and the official report says that he fell asleep with a lit cigarette, but I talked to a forensics guy who says that the body was missing a few pieces, and not the kind that burn off. Talked to a first responder who says that the little girl was covered in blood that wasn't hers. Bloody handprints all over her dress, like someone had picked her up and carried her somewhere. Good prints too. Too bad they couldn't run them through the system. There was a funny little mix-up in the evidence locker, and the clothes were thrown out by accident. And then the brass came down really hard on this one, hushed everyone up and made sure that they stuck with the party line. Haven't seen something like that since . . . well, not since your parents."

"Pretty weird," I said. I knew right then that secret agent was never a career option for me, because I was sweating so hard that my new T-shirt was sticking to me.

"Yep, it is that. Everyone shut up real quick. If I hadn't already been asking questions when it first happened, I never would've gotten a peep."

"Why were you looking into it?" I asked. I didn't really want to know, but I had to ask.

"The way the Grann parents were killed was familiar. And when the body of the older girl turned up, it had a lot of similarities to the mystery girl who was found the same night as the original murders. Funny thing is, no one seems interested in connecting the two cases."

"I don't know what to tell you, Matt." That much, at least, was the honest truth. I couldn't see a single way out of this conversation that wouldn't end in Prudence on Matt's doorstep, and because of that it was everything I could do to keep that big, dumb smile on my face.

"I know, buddy." Matt paused, then dropped his own fake smile to give me a narrow, assessing look that seemed to go right through my clothes and measure every bruise on my body. "You know, that little girl said that a man rescued her."

"Oh, really?" Oh, shit. My guts clenched even further,

because now it wasn't just Matt in danger, now it was Amy as well.

"Yep. You won't find it in the official report. She was also talking about a fox that turned into a lady, and the higher-ups said that it was just a lot of nonsense from the smoke inhalation and the trauma, and they had it taken out. But I had a talk with her grandfather yesterday, and he says that she says a dark-haired man came and took her away from the monster. Says that she knows his name, but that the fox told her that it was important to keep it a secret. But she was a little worried, because he'd gotten hurt, and she hoped that he was okay."

"What an amazing story," I choked out. I couldn't hold that fake smile any longer, and I was almost shaking when I looked at Matt.

"That it is." He gave me a hard look. "Did you have a little trouble lately there, Fort? Got a nice cast on that arm."

"Oh, you know me. Clumsy, clumsy."

"All right, then, buddy. I'll be seeing you soon." He got back in his car and started the engine.

"Can't be soon enough," I told him through his open window, waving as he pulled out, and watched as he drove out of the lot. He knew that I'd been the one to rescue Amy, and now he was also suspecting what he'd never even dreamed of before, that I knew more about Brian and Jill's murder than I'd told him. He'd followed that case relentlessly for almost twenty years, let it control his career, wreck all chances at a family, consume his thoughts. He wouldn't, couldn't, stop now.

The taillights of his car disappeared into the darkness

and I knew that everything had just changed between us. I was no longer his partner's kid to protect—I was a possible lead. That's why he'd come to talk with me to-night.

Matt was the kind of threat that Madeline wouldn't hesitate to eliminate. I didn't know what I could do to stop him, to halt that headlong sprint toward death, but I'd have to do something. Brian and Jill had died because I hadn't kept the truth from them—I wouldn't let the same thing happen with Matt.

I thought about it as I walked up the stairs to my apartment. Now I had two big things on my to-do list—get a new job, keep Matt from getting killed.

The lights were off and the apartment was quiet, meaning that for once Larry was having sex at someone else's place. But as I flipped on the lights and walked in, I stopped suddenly, and looked around. Something was different. Something was . . . missing.

Specifically, the microwave.

Shit, I thought, looking at the spot where it usually rested. We must've been robbed. But I'd had to unlock the door when I came in. I looked around again. The TV was still in place, all my DVDs were still there. Even the drums were still present, meaning that the Brown University drum circle was still using my apartment as free storage. Something was definitely missing.

I stared, and then it occurred to me—for the first time since he'd moved in, Larry's clothes and stuff were no longer coating the floor of the living room. Seeing the bare floor again was a huge shock. I walked to his bedroom and gave the partially open door a nudge. It swung open easily to show a room that had been completely stripped. No bed, no piles of junk, no random floozies. Herpes germs probably still coated the entire room, so I'd probably have to wipe everything down with bleach, but even so . . . Larry had moved out.

Well, moved out after stiffing me for months of rent, minus sixty very-well-spent dollars, but still.

I walked back into the living room. It looked like he'd left all my stuff untouched, when I wouldn't have put a little on-the-way-out roommate robbery and petty pay-back past him.

"Well, that's interesting," I said out loud. It was nice to hear only my own voice. Too bad I couldn't just live alone.

Which added a nice big third item to my list. Get a new job, keep Matt from getting killed, get a new room-mate who hopefully isn't a shithead this time.

There was a pile of mail on the kitchen counter, and I flipped through it. Bill I couldn't pay, bill I couldn't pay, credit card offer that was probably a bad idea, oooh, Netflix, and one plain envelope that had my name writ-ten across the front in Larry's crabbed, almost indeci-pherable handwriting. It was pretty bulky, and, curious, I opened it up.

"Well, *fuck*," I blurted out to the empty room. Inside was his apartment key, plus all the rent money he'd owed me. In cash.

"Shit," I said reverently. Now I wouldn't get kicked out of the apartment while I scrambled to find another job and a new roommate. I would actually be able to buy food for myself—a wholly unexpected luxury. I thumbed through the wad of bills reverently.

I still didn't doubt the validity of the life lessons that

my foster mother had taught me, but I had to acknowledge that she'd fudged the truth on one of them. Sometimes violence *did* solve problems.

I considered the pile of money again. It hadn't just been about threatening Larry, though that had certainly been great. It had been about finally refusing to let him keep dodging the issue. And with that particular lesson in mind, I headed toward my computer.

It was time to reply to Beth's sixteen-page relationship manifesto.

A small scuffling sound at my window woke me up at just past three in the morning. I pried my eyes open and smiled at the sight of Suzume propped up on her elbows at the foot of my bed, wearing nothing except one of my T-shirts. It covered just barely enough to keep her from being arrested for indecent exposure, but that foxy smile on her face should've been enough for any judge to recommend incarceration.

"How did you get in?" I asked. It didn't bother me how she got in; I just cared that she was here at all, but I knew that she'd love the chance to show how clever she was.

"You have a loose window screen and a really nice maple tree that is a few years overdue for a pruning. I'm surprised that you don't have colonies of squirrels camping out under your bed." She was pleased, and her eyes sparkled even in the darkness.

"You said something to Beth, or did something," I said. It wasn't even a question. I knew that had to be her, I just had to know how.

She was smug, almost wiggling. She always was happiest with an audience. "I might've convinced my cousin Noriko to make a few salacious posts on your Facebook page, photos included. A few of them ended up getting censored, but I think Beth got an eyeful before they were pulled."

"Why would that make her call me for a date?"

Suzume laughed at me. "A girl like Beth only wants what other people have. A few pictures, some graphic posts, and suddenly you're a challenge, and she must have you again." She waggled her eyebrows.

"Assuming I still want her," I pointed out.

She tilted her head. "Don't you?"

"No." I'd surprised her, and it filled my chest with warmth. "Before I went to bed, I let her know that we were over. That she should get her drums out of my living room and go cheat on some other guy."

Suzume lifted her eyebrows. "Must've been a fun conversation."

I shook my head. "I didn't bother calling her."

"Oh?" Suzume looked intrigued.

I smiled. "Facebook post." I'd timed it for when I knew she would've logged off for the night, and there'd already been quite a few comments by the time I turned in myself. Apparently I hadn't been the only guy she'd pulled that "open relationship" crap on, and now that I'd actually said something, it had opened the floodgates. She'd be in for quite an eyeful tomorrow morning, but the best part was that I really didn't care. It was over, and I was better off for it.

"That's cold," Suzume said. "I like it." Then she burst out laughing, delighted.

I watched her laugh for a moment. "I didn't think

you'd come for me, Suzume," I admitted. "At Luca's. You said that Amy Grann wasn't worth risking your life."

She crawled up the bed in a sinuous, almost catlike motion until her dark hair fell around my face like a cloud, and it was only because of my new, keener eyes that I could see that wicked smile on her face as she leaned down, so that our mouths were just a breath apart, and I could feel as well as hear the next words she said in little puffs of air, and the sweet smell of her filled my head.

"You're an idiot," she whispered lovingly.

I blinked. She smiled.

"And I didn't risk my life for Amy," she said.

And then a fox was on my chest instead of a woman, wiggling agilely out of my T-shirt and scampering off the bed and onto my windowsill.

She paused there for a moment, and a break in the clouds let out a small shaft of moonlight that allowed me to see what even my sharper eyes had missed in the darkness, the new, perfect snow white tip of her coal black tail.

She yipped once, high and amused, and with one last swish of her tail she was gone.

ABOUT THE AUTHOR

M. L. Brennan cut her baby bibliophile teeth on her older brother's collection of Isaac Asimov and Frank Herbert, but it was a chance encounter with Emma Bull's *War for the Oaks* as a teenager that led to genre true love. Today, she'll read everything from Mary Roach's nonfiction to Brandon Sanderson's epic fantasies, but she'll drop everything for vampires and werewolves in the big city. After spending years writing and publishing short works in other genres, she decided to branch out and write the kind of book that she loved to read, resulting in *Generation V*, her first full-length work of urban fantasy. Brennan lives in Connecticut with her husband and three cats. Holding a master's degree in fiction, she teaches basic composition to college students. Her house is over a hundred years old, and is insulated mainly by overstuffed bookshelves. She is currently working on the second Fortitude Scott book.

CONNECT ONLINE
www.mlbrennan.com.